BROTHERS
ON THE
RUN

BASED ON A TRUE STORY

PAT LORRAINE SIMONS

ISBN: 1479299081
ISBN 13: 9781479299089
Library of Congress Control Number: 2012916985
CreateSpace Independent Publishing Platform
North Charleston, SC

For Jordan, Ella, Skyler, and Sierra

"In life, you know, there are three
or four fundamental choices.
The rest is a matter of luck."

—Raymond Aubrac, French resistance hero
(1916–2012)

CONTENTS

PREFACE

When I was six years old, my German father sometimes tried to teach me piano duets. That was when I first realized my father's right hand was paralyzed and had only four fingers. When I asked him what had happened to his pinky finger, he told me a little bird bit it off. When I asked why he couldn't move the rest of his fingers, he gave me all sorts of answers. All I knew was his condition had something to do with a fish bone and an airplane.

It wasn't until I was fifty years old that my father, Gottfried, finally told me the truth. Dad was eighty-one years old by then, and I was recording his life story as well as that of his seventy-nine year-old brother, Rudolf, who had just been diagnosed with end-stage cancer. I'd been thinking of recording their astonishing story for years, but it took my uncle's tragic diagnosis to make me do it.

Gottfried and Rudolf were the youngest of six children born to middle-class Jewish parents, a traveling salesman and a cook. Before the boys started school, neither of them knew their father, who was off fighting in France. When World War I finally ended, their father came home with a medal for bravery and a bad case of shell-shock, which rendered him delusional and unable to help support his family. As hyperinflation set in and postwar Germany sank into turmoil, all but the oldest boy had to quit school to find work.

By 1930, the three oldest children had moved to the United States. By 1933, when Hitler came to power, only the three youngest boys—Gottfried (nineteen), Rudolf (seventeen), and their intellectually disabled brother, Martin (twenty)—were still living in Giessen with their parents.

Like most German Jews, the Kahns were patriotic Germans, who participated in all aspects of German life. They, like most German Jews, believed the fanatically antisemitic Nazi Party would not last, but they were tragically mistaken. When the Nazis took over Germany at the beginning of 1933, Gottfried and Rudolf were among their earliest victims.

The events in this book closely track the true story of two spirited young brothers who fled from Germany and fought to survive—first as unwanted refugees, and then as soldiers in the Spanish Civil War. While I made no changes to historical facts, I added dialogue and some events to fill in gaps in their narratives. In so doing, however, I sought to remain true to the brothers—to their unique personalities and perspectives, to their tenacity and intelligence, and to their extraordinary luck in escaping Europe before the Nazis started World War II.

—*Pat Lorraine Simons*

Gottfried
1933 Giessen, Germany

I

GOTTFRIED

We're only thirty minutes away from Giessen when Rudolf's bicycle chain breaks, and he crashes into a pile of rocks. Naturally, he doesn't see them sitting on top of the road, even though they're right in front of him.

"For crying out loud! Didn't you hear me? I yelled at you to watch out!"

"Huh?" He grins a little sheepishly, then picks himself up.

"We needed this like a hole in the head," I grumble. We drag our bicycles off the road and back into the forest. The pine and spruce trees are dense here, so I'm hoping it's hard to see us from the road. I open up my rucksack and take out a couple of tools.

Then he says, "I guess I cut my leg. You got a bandage, Gott-fried?"

He looks a little pitiful with that crooked grin of his and that windblown brown hair. I rummage in my rucksack, take out the iodine and bandages, and toss them to him. He fixes up his cut, then goes and stands behind a tree to watch the road. He keeps quiet. He knows good and well I'm furious.

It's early May in Hesse, so of course it starts to rain. Not heavy, but enough to make my hands keep slipping. "Goddamn it," I hiss. "How can I fix this thing? It's wet and cold, and I can't see anything!"

"Take it easy, Gottfried," he says. "You can fix that piece of junk without looking."

He's right about that. Matter of fact, one time he bet a guy I could fix a broken chain with my eyes closed, and I did. But right now, I can't concentrate. What if Werner and his Nazi buddies are already at our house? What are they doing to Mama and Papa?

"Look, it's raining," he says. "Nobody's coming after us. Any-how, they don't know which way we went."

"Damn you, Rudolf. If they catch us, it's all your fault!"

"Okay," he says. Naturally, this makes me even madder.

I don't know how, but somehow or other, we get lucky. I man-age to fix the damn chain, and they don't come. But now we're riding in the rain, which makes our trip go very slow.

It takes us the rest of the night to get down to Frankfurt. It should have taken us a couple of hours at the most. We should have been back on the road by now, instead of being here—close enough to Giessen for them to catch up with us. But I guess I should have expected my little brother to do something stupid. He's always been a klutz with his head in the clouds. Doesn't pay attention when he should. That's why he's always breaking something or other. Matter of fact, the first thing he broke was me.

We were little kids playing doctor, and he decided to give me an operation. We were pretending, so I lay down to be his patient. He picked up a knife from the counter in Mama's shoe shop and waved it around my head. But then he accidentally cut me on the temple. It didn't hurt much, but it bled like the dickens. When we saw the blood, we both started screaming, so naturally Mama and my older sister rushed in. Clare picked up Rudolf, and Mama pressed some wet cloths on my head. Then Mama gave Clare a good bawling out for not being in the room with us. Clare made up some excuse, like she always did, and the minute Mama left the room, Clare started yelling at me.

"Gottfried, you little dope! Why did you give him that knife?"

Do what? *I* was the one who ended up with stitches, but she blamed me anyhow. Clare was the oldest, so she was in charge of the rest of us, and she liked to put me in charge of Rudolf. That way, if anything bad happened to him, it was my fault.

Oh well, I'm used to it. It's always been my job to watch over Rudolf, to take care of him. Somebody had to. See, all six of us came very close together. Mama and Papa had us bam-bam-bam after they got married. First Clare and then five boys—Siegfried, Hubert, Martin, me, and Rudolf. On top of all this, my brother Martin was a blue baby—very simple-minded. Didn't learn how to talk until he was almost seven years old. So Mama and Clare had a lot of work to do just to take care of him.

Clare was a bossy girl, but I guess she had to be. She had to grow up fast. She was only eight years old when Rudolf came along in October 1914. And two months later, Papa was gone. He went off to war and left Mama with six mouths to feed and very little money.

Rear: Ernestine Kahn (Mama) holding Rudolf
Left to right: Martin, Hubert, Gottfried, Clare, Siegfried
1914 Giessen, Germany

But Mama was smart. She heard German war prisoners had to work for us—on farms, in the mines, and so on. She also heard there was a big shortage of shoes in Giessen. So she put two and two together, picked herself up, and marched over to the POW camp in Giessen. She said she needed a few prisoners of war who knew how to make shoes. What did she know about making shoes? Nothing.

But she cleared a small room in our old house and bought some wood, some leather, and some knives, and presto! She had French POWs making shoes for her. They weren't exactly regular shoes—more like sandals. A piece of wood with a leather strap. Mama sold the shoes, but there were plenty of times she didn't have enough money to feed us. So she was very happy when the war finally ended, so Papa could come home and start working again.

But it turned out Papa couldn't help us or anyone else. See, he had been fighting in the fire trenches. And when big shells flew and he heard the constant blasts, he couldn't take it. He got very nervous, sick in the head. Shell shock, they called it. The army used electric currents on him, but it didn't help. Then they put him to work on a farm, but he was no farmer. Finally, they gave up and sent him home.

Rudolf and I didn't remember Papa before the war. We were too young when he left. But when he first came home, his looks scared us. He was very thin, and his hair was so short we could see his scalp. His eyes darted back and forth, back and forth. And for a long time, he acted afraid of everything—even of us. Any little noise would make him shake or scream.

Times were hard, and poor Mama couldn't help Papa or feed us kids, so she went a little crazy herself. Bertha, one of her sisters from New York, came to Giessen to help out. She took Hubert back to New York with her, because Mama couldn't control him, and because without him, she would have one less mouth to feed. Bertha also gave Mama some money, so Siegfried could take her to Bad Nauheim to get a good rest.

When Mama and Siegfried left, Clare told Martin, Rudolf, and me that *she* was Mama now, and we better listen to her, or we would go to bed without supper. We didn't know what she was talking about, but we did know Mama was leaving, and we were hungry. All of us started bawling. So Clare took Rudolf on her lap, and she pulled Martin and me close to her, and she sang to us. I remember she sang an old song about the sky crying and angels watching over Mama and Siegfried. She told us not to worry—they would have a good trip and come home safe.

They did come home safe, and Mama seemed to feel better, but not much changed with Papa. In time, though, we got used to him. And now and then, he acted almost all right. I remember the first time he told us to come closer to him. We were still a little afraid, but he smiled at us, so we went. He wanted to show us his war medal, which he was polishing with a big rag.

"This is the Iron Cross," he said, "for bravery. A German soldier must always be brave."

Papa called us his "little soldiers" and told us to address him as Adolf. It's very strange that of all the names in the world, Papa picked out that name. Still, it's the truth.

"Adolf is a good German name," he said.

Mama laughed out loud at that. "Papa's name is Abraham," she said. "A good Jewish name.

After this, Papa sometimes let us sit on the floor near him, and later on, he taught Rudolf and me a card game called skat. So then, we started to play cards with him when he felt like it. But mostly, he sat on a chair and peeked outside through a hole in the drape. If he saw somebody, he would get frantic.

"Get down! Get down, or they'll shoot!"

We knew he was imagining things, but it was also true that we had enemies out there. Sometimes we didn't even know who they were. Like after the war when we needed a suitcase full of money to buy a loaf of bread. There was an enemy out there, but who was it? Who was the enemy?

Losing the war was hard on everybody. But for us—for Jews—it was even worse. What happened was some big shots said Germany lost the war because Jewish soldiers and civilians had stabbed the army in the back. Was a big lie, of course, but so what? It wasn't the first big lie or the only one. See, according to the communists and a lot of other crazy people, everything bad was all our fault.

After a few years, things seemed a little better. New businesses opened up again, and more people were working. There was more to eat too. But then things started to get bad again, and when the American stock market crashed in 1929, things went from bad to worse—not just for us, but for all Germans. That was also the time when the Nazi Party started catching on.

Before 1929, everybody knew about Hitler's party, but most people didn't take them seriously. Matter of fact, Siegfried was working in Munich, where Hitler was nesting, and he went to hear Hitler talk. This was in 1928, a few years after they let him out of jail. See, he was in jail for high treason, but for some reason or other, they let him go after a few months.

"*Momzers*, bastards." Siegfried told us. "All these Nazis. And that Adolf Hitler? He's nothing but a degenerate house painter. Looks like Charlie Chaplin. Puny. A nothing. Not even a German, for God's sake. Screams and shouts like a madman. And the SA? The idiot Stormtroopers he keeps around him? My God! What a bunch of shady characters. Hoodlums, all of them. Give them an ugly brown shirt and a pair of boots, and they're suddenly *machers*—big shots."

Well, we all laughed—everybody did. But the Nazi Party was getting plenty of money from somewhere. They had uniforms, and they paraded all over Germany. They drove big, fancy cars like new, black Mercedes. People said the big banks and the *junkers*—the rich industrialists—were giving them plenty of money. So by 1929, when everybody started losing their jobs again, the Nazis were getting much more powerful.

Seated, left to right: Ernestine and Abraham (Adolf) Kahn
Standing, left to right: Gottfried, Martin, Clare, Siegfried, Rudolf
1929 Giessen, Germany

This was around the time when Siegfried got a job in New York and decided to leave Germany. Then a year later, Mama's sister came to see us again. This time, she took Clare to New York too.

So by the time the Nazis got into power in 1933, only Mama, Papa, Martin, Rudolf, and I were living in Giessen. But we weren't planning to move. Mama had taught Martin to bake, and the two of them brought in a little money. Rudolf and I had jobs and people who needed us. And we had our friends. So why should we leave? Giessen was our home.

But in the meantime, the Nazi Party kept growing. All of a sudden, boys we had known since we were little kids completely stopped talking to us. Boys in our rowing club, in our soccer club—old buddies of ours. Some of them started whispering when they saw us on the streets. Some of them stopped coming to games when we were supposed to play in them. For Rudolf and me, this was something completely new. We didn't understand. Other kids never acted like this before. Everybody liked us, and we got along with everybody. Why not? Who cared if you were Jewish or some other religion? We didn't care. And before this, nobody else cared. Matter of fact, most of the boys in our sports clubs weren't Jewish, and most of our friends weren't Jewish either. See, Jewish people were the same as everybody else. We lived everywhere and did everything. There were actually very few Jews in our hometown and very few Jews in all of Germany. Rudolf and I, we knew only a few Jewish boys. They were from our *shul*—our synagogue—and from a Zionist club. We used to go skiing with the Zionist boys sometimes, but that was it. Why? They thought we should move to Palestine. We didn't think so. Why should we move to some faraway desert? We were Germans. Germany was our home.

Rudolf and Gottfried
1932 Giessen, Germany

Most of our friends, most people we knew, they didn't talk about politics much. But if they did, they said the Nazis were crackpots, which was what we thought too. Even when the Nazi Party got strong in Giessen—which happened by 1930—it was just another party to us. Temporary. All kinds of crazy parties had been coming and going since the end of the war. Seemed like new parties every day. Fatalists, anarchists, communists, this one, that one, another one. It was the communists who seemed to be growing the most. They hated Jews too, and I think the Jews in town probably worried more about the crazy communists than about the crazy Nazis.

But we were completely wrong. It turned out the Nazi Party was strong enough to stick around. Hitler traveled everywhere to speak. He even came to Giessen twice—in 1931 and again in 1932. People were cheering at Nazi parades and hanging Nazi banners from their windows. Some of the boys in our rowing club got very excited when Hitler came to speak, and they went to hear him.

Still, nobody thought he would take over the country. See, we had a very popular president by the name of Paul von Hindenburg—an old army man, a hero in the war. He didn't like Hitler and his Nazi Party. Matter of fact, neither did the communists and the socialists, and they were the majority of the politicians.

But to our surprise, at the end of January 1933, President von Hindenburg turned around and named Hitler as his chancellor. The next month, somebody set fire to the parliament building in Berlin, and Hitler's Stormtroopers—the SA—started running around arresting people and beating them up. Then all of a sudden—just like that!—there were no more freedoms. Anybody said anything against the Nazis? That was the end of them. The Nazis threw the anti-Nazis into prisons and made them do hard labor. Matter of fact, Clare's old boyfriend got thrown into one of the first prisons, a place by the name of Dachau. We never found out what happened to him.

It was when Hitler took over as chancellor that big trouble started for Rudolf and me. And not just for us, but for Jewish people all over Germany. The Nazis started grabbing people on the streets and beating them up—even killing them. Mama used to tell us about these things happening in Poland and Russia—but that was far away. Not here. Not in Germany where Jews were doctors and lawyers and judges and everything else. Now, though, it was happening here, and Mama worried about us. She started talking to us like we were little kids, telling us to be careful every time we left the house.

We didn't do anything different though. We went to work, went out with our friends, came home, kept our noses clean. But it didn't matter what we did or didn't do, because problems started anyway.

One day, when we were at work, two Nazi SA men came to our house and demanded money. They said Papa owed them money on a loan they had given him. What a joke! Papa never borrowed money. He never even left the house. Who would lend him money anyway? Not Nazis! But of course, Mama gave them some money, so they would leave. And luckily, they did.

Then the problems started with the *Hitlerjugend*, the Hitler Youth. We knew a lot of these boys. All of us were little kids together. They were our friends, the boys in our school and in our sports clubs. We were exactly like them, so naturally, we belonged to the same clubs like soccer, biking, rowing, track, skiing, group calisthenics, and so on.

But now all of a sudden, our buddies were walking around in uniforms and boots. It was "Heil Hitler" this and "Heil Hitler" that. They were joining up with the Hitlerjugend. Some of them said they had to, but some of them really wanted to. I guess it made them feel important, getting uniforms like their older brothers and their fathers and uncles.

Then one day in March, some Hitlerjugend went marching down Steinstrasse, which is a street near the Orthodox synagogue. They stopped and spat at old Jewish men—the ones dressed like Polacks. They knocked them down, cut off their beards, and jumped on them while they lay on the street. A big crowd gathered in the street, but nobody did anything. People just watched. Nobody stopped what was happening. People in buildings along the street leaned out their windows and watched too. The Hitlerjugend were marching and singing, "We won't stop until Jewish blood spurts from every knife."

Soon after this, when we went to a meeting at our soccer club, a guy by the name of Werner stopped us at the door. He was a big guy, Werner, like a tank. Liked to lift weights. The other guys crowded around him, backing him up.

Left to right: Gottfried, Rudolf, other players
1932 Giessen, Germany
Soccer (football) club

Werner said, "Get out. We don't want you filthy sons of whores here."

He pointed to a new sign on the front door in big block letters: *Kleine Juden Laupt.* No Jews Allowed. It was for us, see. We were the only Jewish boys who happened to belong to this soccer club.

Now, when Werner insulted us like this, Rudolf got very red in his face, and I could see he was ready to fight. So I grabbed him by the arm and twisted. He knew what that meant—it meant no. See, if somebody insulted us, Rudolf always wanted to fight with them. But to fight right now made no sense. There was a good reason to fight, but not good enough. There were ten of them to two of us. So I twisted his arm, and we turned around and left.

But as we were turning to go, we saw this guy by the name of Ernst Bloch, who sort of hung back from the rest of them. Ernst was one of the boys we went to school with. Came over to our house many times. We invited him over, for instance, on holidays like Passover. We even exchanged Easter eggs and matzos with him. And ever since we quit school, Rudolf had been working with him at a leather shop. They were good friends. They liked to go to the *stammtisch*, where the men and older boys played cards and had a beer after work. So on that day at the soccer club, Ernst hung back, but he didn't dare say anything, and naturally, we didn't blame him.

A few weeks later, Rudolf and I decided to go skiing in the Taunus Mountains near Frankfurt. It was late in the season, but there was fresh powder, and the Zionist boys were going, so we decided to go along. Plenty of Hitlerjugend went up there to ski too, but if we saw them on the mountain, we tried to ignore them. This was a big mountain, but sometimes there were fights anyway. Not this time though. The snow was fresh, the weather was good, and the skiing was good. Our boys stuck together, and their boys stuck together. Well, by this time there was no choice anyhow. The Nazi Party required all sports clubs to kick out Jews. Everybody was a Nazi. Even the new mayor of Giessen was a Nazi.

On Sunday afternoon, we finished skiing, and we took the bus home from Frankfurt. By bus, it's a short ride to Giessen, and it was getting dark when we left the Giessen bus station and started walking home. We were close to our street, Wilsonstrasse, minding our own business, when we suddenly heard a racket behind us. We turned and saw three Hitlerjugend boys coming up fast behind us, all of them shouting and cussing at us. I didn't know what the hell was happening. Then one of them backed me up against a picket fence and bashed my head with a rock.

Next thing I knew, Rudolf was trying to help me stand up. I could feel a bloody bump on my head, and I had a hell of a headache. But the Hitlerjugend were gone.

I rubbed my head. "What the hell happened?"

Rudolf shrugged. "Guess they gave up and went home."

He was standing there grinning, holding a broken picket from a fence behind us.

"I tore this loose board out of that fence. Had a nice big nail in it. Busted one of them in the jaw with it. Got him good! Man, oh man!" he laughed. "You should have seen them, Gottfried! You should have seen the cowards run! Guess they didn't expect a Jew boy to fight back, huh?"

"Who were they?"

"Don't know," he said. "Too dark. Only got a good look at one of them—that schmuck, Werner. Wasn't him who I busted though. Too goddamn bad."

"You're a regular Max Schmelling," I said, and I clapped him on the back. Max Schmelling, he was a famous German boxer. One of our heroes.

For a few weeks after this, we didn't hear anything about the fight. The bump on my head went away, so we put it out of our minds. But that fight changed our lives.

We were having supper at our house—my parents, Rudolf, my brother Martin, and me—when the phone rang. Rudolf picked up, listened a couple of minutes. Said, "Thanks, Ernst," and hung up.

It was Ernst Bloch, our old buddy who had hung back when we got kicked out of the soccer club. He told Rudolf that the Hitlerjugend guy, the one Rudolf hit, was dying. The nail in the picket—

the one Rudolf hit him with—put a hole in his jaw. So now this guy had yellow jaundice, and his jaws were completely locked.

Rudolf and I didn't know this guy. He wasn't somebody from any of our sports clubs. But Werner was part of the fight, and Ernst overheard him talking about teaching the Jews a lesson. Ernst listened carefully, and then he called Rudolf and said a bunch of Hitlerjugend would be coming to our house in a couple of hours to kill us.

I remember Mama's exact words. "Not my boys, they won't."

She took over right away. First thing she did, she made Papa get dressed in his army uniform, and she pinned on his Iron Cross. Everybody knew what this medal meant, even Hitlerjugend. Mama felt sure if Papa was in his war uniform and wearing his medal, the Hitlerjugend wouldn't dare hurt Papa or her.

The next thing Mama did, she packed a bag for Martin with a note for some Jewish friends who lived nearby on Liebigstrasse: "Family emergency. Please keep Martin with you tonight."

It was very hard for poor Martin to go someplace at night by himself. But this was a familiar place, and he seemed to understand he had to do what she told him.

After Martin left, Mama helped us pack our rucksacks. We took some water, my bicycle tools, and a few things in case of emergencies. Mama got a couple of slices of bread and wrapped them up in paper, and she stuck them inside. She thought of everything. I only thought to pack my *Mitgliedsbuch*, which was nothing but a booklet from our bicycle club. I don't know why I took it along. I guess I thought it looked like something official in case we got stopped.

So now what? Where do we go? Rudolf and I had never gone anywhere outside Giessen, except to ski near Frankfurt or to visit our relatives, like our Uncle Josef in Zwesten. We had no idea where to go, but Mama did.

"First," she said, "you'll go to Jacob Gessner in Frankfurt."

"Mama," I told her, "we hardly know them."

"Doesn't matter," she said. "He's family. He has to help you." She gave us Gessner's address, then said, "Jacob Gessner will tell you how to go to Lindau. I want you to go there and cross the border."

Lindau was a town on Lake Constance, which is a big lake on the border with Austria and Switzerland. Mama had friends in Lindau, Justus and Amala Nordlinger.

"You don't know them," she said. "But Amala was my friend as a girl. She and her husband will know how to help you go to Switzerland, where you'll be safe. You should go to Basel and stay there with Selma and David Haas."

We knew the Haas family. They were cousins of Mama's and friends of our Uncle Josef's. Some of them had moved to Switzerland from Zwesten a few years earlier. Mama wrote everything down, and I stuck the papers in my rucksack.

Me, I was scared and nervous. I admit it. To go away like this and leave our parents alone. I begged them to leave the house, lock it up, go with Martin, and stay with the neighbors. But Mama said no.

"Look," she said, "the Hitlerjugend are only boys like you. When they see Papa's Iron Cross, they won't hurt us. Papa is a war hero, and they will respect him."

I argued with her and Rudolf did too, but it was no use. Mama was a very stubborn woman. When she made her mind up—right or wrong—that was that. You couldn't change her.

Mama took me aside. "Take care of your little brother," she said.

We took our rucksacks, and we went outside. It was 1:00 a.m. by the time we got on our bicycles. We went out on Wilsonstrasse and started to ride off, but we had to stop right away, because we could hear Papa chanting—more like shouting—in Hebrew. There was a street lamp, and we could see him standing outside there in the street in his *pickelhaube*—his spiked army helmet—and his army uniform. He stretched his arms out like wings and spread his fingers apart in the shape of a *V*—the sign of the high priests, the *kohanim*. Then he started chanting, praying, giving us a blessing.

"May God bless you and protect you! May he cause his light to shine on you and be gracious unto you."

The whole goddamn world could hear him! So Rudolf and I stopped our bicycles and turned back. We got off and walked Papa back inside the house.

"We'll be back soon," Rudolf told him. "We're going to a party."

Mama didn't even know Papa had walked outside to watch us leave. When we came back inside with Papa, she was lying on the bed in the bedroom, crying. It was very hard for us to see this, because Mama almost never cried. We told her what had happened, and she got up and washed her face.

This time, she came outside with us. We grinned at her and acted like we really were going to a party. We got back on our bicycles and waved at her. We acted excited. Well, to tell the truth, we *were* excited. I mean, it *was* exciting—an adventure. We were young. Stupid too.

Mama stayed outside and watch us ride away. This time, though, we didn't look back.

I was riding in front, and Rudolf was following me. We didn't talk while we were riding out of town. I guess we both had our own thoughts. But after we were riding for about an hour, Rudolf yelled up to me, "By the way, Gottfried, happy birthday!"

It wasn't until that minute when I realized it was already the next day—May 6, 1933. It was my birthday. I was twenty years old.

Rudolf
1933 Giessen, Germany

II

RUDOLF

You have to know my sister, Clare. Amazing girl. Little mother-sister. Mama's right hand. Helped Mama all through the war when Papa was gone. Sewed our clothes too, all of them. Smart, pretty, nice figure, nice legs. And talented too. She could really sing. I remember her singing me to sleep, especially since I'm the baby and all this. "Guten abend, guten nacht, mit rosen bedacht, mit näglein bedeck..." Means something like, "Good evening, good night, with roses and meadows around you..."

But one thing my sister couldn't do. Couldn't keep away from boys. The first ones might have been the French boys, the prisoners of war. I was little, so I don't really remember them. But

Gottfried said Clare got very friendly with those French boys, sitting on their laps, giving them kisses. She claimed she was learning French from them. They would give her chocolates, and she would give them to us, so we would keep quiet and do the chores she didn't like.

Clare always liked boys, but she fell for the wrong one when she got older. His name was Albert Roper. A journalist. Nice guy too, but not Jewish. Clare met him at a bicycle club, and they fell in love, plain and simple. The two of them started sneaking around together, because Clare knew Mama wouldn't like it. And Gottfried and I found out, but we didn't tell. Of course not. But when Mama found out, Aunt Bertha came from New York and took Clare away like she had taken Hubert before that. Next thing we knew, Aunt Bertha married Clare off to some fisherman. But he was a Jewish fisherman, so Mama was happy. Clare? I don't know if Clare was happy. But right now, I'm plenty happy. Why? Because Clare's husband has relatives here in Frankfurt, and they are helping us out.

When we get to their house after riding all night in the rain, they help us clean up, and they give us breakfast. After this, Clare's brother-in-law, Jacob Gessner, gets us a couple of uniforms from somebody in the uniforms business. This makes us look official, right? Like a couple of Hitlerjugend on holiday.

Rudolf and Gottfried
May 1933 Frankfurt, Germany
In new uniforms

We had a long night riding to Frankfurt.

So I tell my brother, "Let's stick around a little while, rest up, visit a few of our friends here."

But Gottfried has to be Gottfried. Always has to call the shots. Plus he can't sit still. Has ants in his pants. Says he wants us to leave now. *Right now.* Now, I love him and all this. He's my big brother. We're close. But some days, he drives me completely nuts.

One thing about Gottfried is, he can't relax. Doesn't know how. Always in a hurry. Busy busy busy. Stubborn too. When he makes up his mind, you better go along, or else he gets mad. Or he mopes. Mopes or gets mad, gets mad or mopes. It's one or the other. Sensitive too. Gets his feelings hurt real fast.

So he's going on and on, saying we better ride down to the border right away. I know it's partly that he's scared to stay this close to Giessen. But there's another reason too. Gessner told him the *Graf Zeppelin* is landing in Friedrichshafen, which is very near Lindau. It's coming from South America, and Gottfried doesn't want to miss seeing it.

Now this Graf Zeppelin is nothing but a flying balloon, but Gottfried gets himself all worked up. Why? Because there's almost nothing my brother likes better than machines. He likes bicycles and cars—fixing them, driving them, watching them race. But machines that fly? He doesn't *like* them, he *loves* them. Loves them almost as much as he loves girls, and that's a lot.

After the war, Gottfried started going to garages to learn about cars and to the airstrip to learn about airplanes. He drove me crazy talking about Deutsche Luft Hansa and all the different models of airplanes. Then one day, he stopped going to the airstrip.

"I'm not going back there again," he said.

"Why?"

"A guy over there keeps bothering me."

"Who?" I asked.

"A pilot. He took me up in his plane. Said he would teach me to fly."

"So did he?"

"Yah, but that's not all he did."

"No?"

"No. He took me up for a ride and slobbered all over me. Wanted me to hug and kiss him. Made me sick to my stomach."

"Yah," I laughed. "But was he good-looking?"

Gottfried tried to throw a punch at me, but I ducked and ran off. Naturally, he was mad at me, but I couldn't help it. He's so easy to kid.

Siegfried liked to kid him too. After he had moved to Munich to work, he came home to visit us. Gottfried told him about this pilot, and Siegfried said—with a completely straight face—"Yah, there are some guys like that. Stay away from them. If you let them touch you, your balls will fall off."

Gottfried was so dumb he believed it.

Cars. Airplanes. Bicycles. Gottfried likes them all. Likes watching them, running them, figuring out how they work. Likes breaking things, fixing them, breaking them. Go figure. Some fun, huh?

Now, I don't care about the Graf Zeppelin, but Gottfried nags me so much, it's not worth arguing with him.

He says, "You know, Rudolf, down there at Lake Constance, they've got bands, great beer, tourists, girls. It's a big resort down there."

Okay, okay. Enough already. Let him think I don't know his real reason for hurrying up to leave. I tell him, "Yeah, okay, fine."

I make like I'm convinced. Happy to go on account of the girls and the parties. Why? One, I would rather leave tomorrow, but it's not that important. With my brother, I have to pick and choose my battles. And two, if there are girls and parties down there, which I figure is true, that's good. I'm a friendly guy, no?

So after lunch, Gessner gives us a few marks, and we take off again on our bicycles. Rotten old bicycles. Used to belong to Siegfried and Clare. They said Hubert found them in an alley. Oh, sure. More like he stole them. He would take anything from anybody. He even stole stuff from the French war prisoners during the war. To tell the truth, Hubert scared us. After the war, he shot a neighbor boy with a stolen pellet gun. Didn't do much damage, but Mama couldn't take it anymore. She wrote to her sister, and Aunt Bertha came over and took him to New York with her.

But right now, I'm glad Hubert was a thief, because Gottfried and I have these bicycles. They still work, more or less, and when they don't, I've got a brother who likes to mess with them, fix them up. It can take us quite a while to get someplace though.

So we ride our bicycles out of Frankfurt. We're riding along, following the Main River, all dressed up in our new uniforms. It's not too bad out, a little rain, a little sun. I'm enjoying the ride. We stop in Offenbach and buy ourselves a couple of hats.

"Six marks, eighty pfennigs," Gottfried says. He's writing down every little thing we spend.

Gottfried, he's a worrywart. Somebody's after us, it's going to rain, we're running out of money. The money thing is his biggest worry. Comes to money, he's tight as a duck's ass, and that's watertight. Keeps track of every mark, every pfennig. Not me. I say, "Let it come, let it go." But mostly, I let him take care of the money, all the other details too. Where we go, where we eat, sleep—all that kind of junk. Why? One, he thinks he has to take care of me. Makes him happy. He's happy, I'm happy. And two, I've got no head for details. Especially when it comes to money. I have holes in my pockets.

Nights, he says, we can sleep in a cheap place, or if it's not bad out, we can stay in a park. Save money. Mornings, he says, we can go from shop to shop, asking for work. He's got it all figured out, how we're going to get by.

We get to Darmstadt, buy some bread, some raw eggs. We punch a hole in the eggs and then drink the insides out. We always like this. Mama says it's healthy. Later on, we pedal into Heidelberg. We're on a big sandstone bridge, which is up on top of the Neckar River. Looks golden-red in the light. It's got famous towers on both ends of it. Gottfried says they look like Papa's pickelhaube, which I admit, they do.

"Beautiful place here," Gottfried says. "Much prettier than Giessen."

He's got eyes for artsy stuff. Not me. I never cared one way or the other about what Giessen looked like. It's home, that's all. But I have to agree this place is a whole lot prettier looking. Hilly, lots of red tile roofs, a big old castle sitting up there above the Konisgstühl River.

"So how about we get some beers?" I say. "I'm thirsty."

Gottfried likes this idea, but he says, "Let's ride over to see the university first, and we can get some beers over there." Gottfried says he's got to see the university. Says there are famous writers connected to it. Like the poet Goethe. I don't say this, but what I'm thinking is, Big deal. Some dead poet. Who cares? But anyhow, I don't argue. I'm thirsty, but it's not that bad yet.

So we ride around a little while, and when we come to the university, we get off our bikes, walk around. Gottfried gets all worked up. Says, "Wish I could finish school. Wish I could come to a university like this one here."

"Yah, yah. The important thing right now is, we need to drink something."

He makes a face. "Always thinking of your stomach, aren't you, Rudolf?"

"Always wanting what you can't have, aren't you, Gottfried?"

I guess I'm not that patient. Why should he be moping about school now? We quit a long time ago, and what choice did we have? Poor Mama, who managed to feed us all through the war, she couldn't do it afterward. Everything cost too much. They kept printing more money, but it wasn't worth anything. Matter of fact, Siegfried brought home boxes full of paper money one day, and he used it as wallpaper for his room. So naturally, all of us—except for Siegfried, who was almost finished—had to quit school and find work. That was in about 1925.

Left to right: Martin, Gottfried, Clare, Siegfried, Hubert, Rudolf
1925 Giessen, Germany

I hated school, so I didn't care about quitting. Hubert didn't care about quitting either. Matter of fact, Hubert said he had already quit to go to the School of Life, which was all anybody needed. Our brother Martin, he didn't know the difference. He couldn't learn anyway. But quitting school upset Gottfried, and it still does. It upset Clare too. She was a year ahead of Siegfried in school, and she was very good at her schooling; but Mama said girls didn't need to graduate the way boys did.

Well, that was then, and this is now. And now, I'm thirsty.

"You can't drink a book," I tell Gottfried. "Let's get some beer."

I spot a bunch of Tyroleans going into a rathskeller. Three guys and a girl. The guys, all of them in costumes—white shirts with colored suspenders in the shape of the letter *H* and wearing lederhosen. The broad who is with them, she's in a big dirndl with a big white apron. One of the guys, he's lugging an accordion, which I like. Uncle Josef used to play one. Was good at it too. Another guy, he's dragging a bass. Looks too big for him, but he's grinning anyhow. Well, this place looks like fun, so I go in, follow the entertainers, and sit down at a table. Gottfried, he follows me inside and sits down next to me. We look over the menu. He perks up when he sees they have *Köstritzer Shwarzbier.*

"This is the black beer Goethe drank."

"Yippee," I say. "You've got the money. So go and get us some."

I wouldn't care if the pope drinks it. Anyhow, he goes off to get us a couple of beers. So I'm sitting and relaxing, watching the people, having fun. Pretty soon, the music starts. I'm feeling good, feeling happy.

Now, sitting at the next table, I see two boys our age in Hitler-jugend uniforms. I nod at them, and right away, they start talking to me. Brothers by the names of Willie and Fritz Bremen. Biking down to Lake Constance. Stopping on the way to see an uncle in Stuttgart. I start thinking. I get an idea.

I say, "My brother and I, we're going to the Lake too."

All very friendly. So they move over to our table, and we're talking. Blah-blah-blah. Well, mostly they're the ones talking. They both have some beer in them. They tell me how rich they are, how they've been riding around, seeing all the sights, having fun with the fräuleins. They say they've got some free time now before they start working in Munich, which is where they come from.

They're both the bragging kind. Don't look like much to brag over, though. Chubby, both of them. Faces like pancakes. How I can tell one from the other one is that Willie's got long, thick, dirty-blond hair. Keeps jerking his head to get it out of his eyes. Makes him look like he's got a bad nervous tic. Fritz's hair is shorter.

Fritz says, "Our Uncle Heinz knows Hitler personally."

"You don't say," I answer. I'm impressed, right?

"Yah," Willie says. "He's in very tight with Hermann Göring."

"Yah," Fritz echoes. "Uncle Heinz, he's right up there with Goebbels and those guys. Big in the new Reich."

"Heil Hitler," I say. I salute. They salute back.

So I'm sitting at the table with these two jokers across from me, and we're kidding around, laughing at this and that. And here comes Gottfried with our beers. He sees my face, he sees these two guys with me—the backs of their heads anyhow. And right away, he scowls. I can tell he's getting mad at me. So what I do is, I stand up and give his arm a good squeeze. He gets my point.

"Meet my brother, Gottfried," I say to the boys. "Gottfried, meet Fritz and Willie Bremen. Brothers from Munich."

The boys stand up, shake Gottfried's hand. Gottfried, he shakes theirs, but he gives them a quick, nervous look, puts down our beers, and sits himself down. He doesn't smile. He's not having fun.

"Try this black beer," I say, sliding the two steins across the table to the Bremen boys. "Gottfried says it's real good."

I turn to my brother. "Gottfried, be a pal. Get us some more?" I can see he's upset, but he stands up and walks off. Which is good. Gives him some time to cool off and think.

"Yah, this is good," Fritz says, licking his lips.

"Gottfried says Goethe drank it."

"Hmmm..." Willie says. "Smart guy, your brother."

"Not really," I say. "Just likes drinking smart guys' beer."

We all laugh. A few girls pass by, wiggling and laughing. We whistle at them. Try to get them to sit on our laps. They pretend to be offended and wiggle away. Some more Tyroleans stroll in, sit down, and right away, they start singing along with the band. We all watch. We drink, clap, sing along. Fritz says, "Watch this!" He sticks two fingers in his mouth. Comes out with the loudest goddamn whistle I ever heard.

"Say," Willie says. "I have a great idea! How about you guys ride down to Stuttgart with us? Meet our uncle. He'll be good for a nice lunch."

"Sure," I say. "Why not? Sounds great."

Gottfried comes back with our beers. Sits down, starts drinking.

"Hey," I say, "guess what, Gottfried? We have an invitation from Willie and Fritz here. We're all riding down together to Stuttgart."

I figure he can't talk while he's swallowing. And he doesn't. But he starts coughing, so I bang him on the back. Maybe a little harder than normal.

"Slow down," I tell him. "I know you like this stuff, but you're going to drown in it."

The boys laugh. They're three sheets to the wind. High when we got there and out-and-out drunk now. Willie and Fritz. Fritz and Willie.

So we're sitting there drinking, and people are singing, and I know Gottfried's mad. But at least he knows to keep his mouth shut. I'm guessing the Bremen boys think my brother's the quiet type. If they think at all. Which I kind of doubt.

We stumble out of there about midnight when the crowd starts thinning out. The Bremen boys, they offer to show us the hostel where they stayed last night. Both of them puke in the streets on the way.

Some good-looking girls pass by and make faces. We hoot at them, laugh, whistle. Gottfried too, you know. We're all looking them up and down. One thing always cheers up Gottfried, and that's a pretty girl. Sometimes it's any girl at all.

We finally get to the hostel, and it's real nice. Clean. We get in cheap too, being Hitlerjugend and all this. Cheap is good, no? Ought to make Gottfried happy. But when we get in our own room, Gottfried lets loose on me.

"What the hell were you doing?" he shouts. "You'll get us killed, you dummkopf!"

"Look," I say, "calm down. Take it easy, okay? Willie and Fritz are going to give us great cover. Who's going to suspect us when we're together with these guys?"

Gottfried scratches his cheek, but he doesn't talk.

So I go on. "I make a good point, right?"

"Maybe," he says. "But what if they figure us out? They do that, we're dead." That's Gottfried, right? He's always saying what if this, what if that.

So I say, "How do you think they're going to figure us out?"

"Well…"

"Look, nobody figures us for Jews. Am I right?"

I'm looking at Gottfried with his even features, his straight, little nose, his big brown eyes. He's looking back at me. Truth is, we look as Gentile as anybody. He says, "I know, but…"

"Only way is if you let them know."

"Yah, but what if they figure it out anyhow?"

"Gottfried," I say, "these two little schmucks? They're dumb as rocks. I'm not going to tell them. You're not going to tell them. Just act normal, like we did in Giessen around the boys. You know how. Easy."

He goes on. What if this? What if that? Blah-blah-blah...

"Look," I say finally, "don't talk too much, okay? Say yes, say no. Be the quiet type."

Finally he says, "Okay. But if we end up getting caught, don't blame me."

Next morning, we meet up with the Bremen boys and take off. They never shut up, so it's not too hard for Gottfried to keep quiet. Not too hard for me either.

We ride most of the morning. Only time we stop is to take a leak or get a beer and maybe something to eat. But in the afternoon, things get interesting, because near Sinsheim, we start seeing girls around our age, riding on bicycles. Some of them look very good to us about now.

This is something all guys understand.

So Gottfried rides up alongside me. "Maybe we can get some," he says, waving his hand in the general direction of some girls. Willie and Fritz hear him too.

Fritz says, "Hey, the ice man's got blood." They both laugh.

A little while later, we spot a couple of girls sitting on a blanket under a tree by the side of the road. They're having a picnic. So we stop and get off, go over there, ask if we can sit down with them. They giggle, make some room for us. We talk.

Now these girls, they're dressed to ride, no? They've got no place to stay tonight. And they're flirting with us, liking our uniforms and all this. Couldn't be better. Willie, he's a smooth talker, I give him that. Talks them into coming along with us.

"Yah," he says. "Better for you girls. Safer than by yourselves." Gottfried and I, we catch each other's eyes. He laughs. He's got one arm around a brunette, so he's looking cheerful now. This girl, she's not my type, but she's okay. Kind of short with short, curly brown hair. Big, dark brown eyes. Dimples. Big tits, big ass. I like a slimmer girl myself. The other girl, she's more my type. Blonde, tall. Voice like Marlene Dietrich in *The Blue Angel,* which we saw at the movies after I won some money beating my father at skat. But Fritz and Willie, they're all over the blonde. That's okay. I'm not all that particular in the dark.

One good thing we've got in common, my brother and me, is girls. They like us. Back home, sometimes we went out with the same girl. Him one time, me the next. We have no problems with finding them. And they tell us they think we're cute, whatever that means. Gottfried, he doesn't look so cute to my mind. I don't look so cute either, to tell the truth. We're both of us a good height. I'm a little taller, I guess. He's got regular-guy looks, straight black hair that falls down his forehead sometimes, big eyes, small straight nose, nice smile. Good teeth. Some girl said he's got a whispery voice "like feathers," whatever the hell that means. More like light sandpaper, if you ask me. Sounds pretty funny when he's mad.

To my mind, like I say, I'm nothing to look at. Best thing I've got is lots of hair. Thick and curly. Papa was always on my back to cut it off. People also say I have a lopsided grin, which I do. Looks strange to me. But girls, they seem to like it for some reason or other. My nose is not too big, but it's not small like Gottfried's. I've been accused of having a smoky voice. I have brown eyes, like Gottfried's, but they say I've got heavy eyelids. Maybe I do. Maybe I'm sleepy all the time.

We both get told we look good, but to me, we look average. But hell, what do I know? I'm going by what girls tell us. We're not girls. Who knows how they think anyhow?

So like I said, it's a beautiful day and a nice ride. The four of us take turns riding back and forth between the two girls. Don't ask me what for. Making small talk. Nothing much, I guess. Later on, we stop off to watch the sun go down. Romantic, no?

We have four boys with their arms around two girls. Gottfried and I have the little brunette between us. We're taking turns kissing her.

"Mmmm," she says and giggles.

Willie and Fritz, they have the blonde between them, and they're doing the same.

"Oh, I shouldn't," says the blonde, wiping away a fake little tear.

"There, there," Fritz says. Willie gives her his handkerchief. A gentleman.

We stop in Sinsheim and get something to eat, some beers. We keep telling the girls how sweet they are, how pretty, all that. And they go straight from loving our uniforms to loving us.

Now, I can see there's got to be some negotiating. I mean, the blonde is between Fritz and Willie, and they're going to do what they're going to do. But it looks like the brunette, she's not sure whether to go with Gottfried or with me. To me, it looks like she's maybe sweeter on me than on my brother. Why I say this is because when we're walking, she's walking between us and holding both of our hands. But she's batting her eyelids mostly in my direction. Giving my hand extra little squeezes. Laughing at Gottfried's jokes but looking at me when she laughs at them. Gottfried acts like he doesn't see all this, and maybe he doesn't. He's trying hard with this girl. Wants to impress her.

Now, I wouldn't mind getting lucky tonight. But when we stop walking, I take the girl's hand out of mine, turn her so she's facing him, and put her hand in Gottfried's free hand.

"You kids have fun. I'm going to find me a card game in town." Then I turn and walk away. I can hear Gottfried talking to her. She's laughing. She likes him well enough. After this, I go into town, walk around a while. Couple of hours later, I go back to the hostel where we're staying, and I get a room and go to sleep.

Next morning, I knock on Gottfried's door. The brunette is gone, and he's whistling and getting dressed.

"You win some money?" he says.

"No," I say. "You have fun?"

He's got his back to me, putting on his shirt.

"Rudolf," he says, not turning around. "Thanks."

I'm surprised. But in a pretty good way.

"Age before beauty," I say. We both laugh.

A couple of minutes later, we're waiting downstairs to see what's what. Fritz and Willie come down, ready to get going. The girls are long gone, and the Bremen brothers are beaming. Seems like they both got lucky with the blonde, but we don't ask. I admit I'm feeling a little sorry for myself.

Well, the riding weather's not too good today. Kind of misty. But it's cool, so we ride a little while. Finally, we decide to stop for breakfast in some small town. Afterward, Gottfried is checking the bill. Checking, checking, checking. Drives me crazy how he's got to always do this. Does it every goddamn time.

"Look," he says, tapping the ticket, "she overcharged us."

He calls the waitress to come over. Now, this woman is not the kind you argue with over a couple of pfennigs. Old, crabby woman. Gray hair in a tight bun, nose nearly touching her chin. She snatches the bill from Gottfried. Stares down at the bill. Glares up at Gottfried.

"It's correct," she says. "Pay up!" Slams the thing down on the table.

Last thing we need right now is Gottfried arguing with some small-town waitress about a few pfennigs. I grab him by the arm and twist hard.

"Pay the goddamn bill, Gottfried."

He does, but he doesn't leave a tip. She's cussing us out when we go. The way she looks, though, it's kind of comical, so the Bremen boys and I, we all start laughing.

Now Gottfried gets mad, and I guess he thinks we're laughing at him. Which, I have to admit, we are. So he rides behind us all the way to Stuttgart. I look back at him, and he sticks out his tongue. What a baby.

After this, I tell Willie and Fritz we'll go with them to meet their big-shot uncle. Gottfried hears me, but he's not talking.

So then we meet this guy. Uncle Heinz sure doesn't look like the Aryan heroes in Nazi pictures. He's kind of short and boxy with a squarish face and curly black hair. Pressed uniform. Brownish-green shirt, grey jacket, swastika armband, knee breeches, boots.

The works. He says he's a higher-up in the *Sturmabteilung*, which most people call the Brownshirts or Stormtroopers—SA for short. Supposed to be Hitler's bodyguards, but they're mostly bullies and thugs. This guy, he's shorter than Hitler, and that's short.

Anyhow, Uncle Heinz says he's buying us lunch. Takes us to a nice place. I know, because it says so on the door. It says, "No Jews Allowed." So we go in. We get some green-pea soup, spaetzel dumplings, smoked cheese. Delicious. But for dessert, we have to listen to Uncle Heinz. What's the question? Doesn't matter. Hitler's the answer. He'll get rid of all the non-Nazis, make Germany clean and pure, full of pure-blood guys like him and us. Hitler's going to put the German people, his *volk*, back to work. He's going to give the volk more living space. He's going to build up the best army in the world. Everybody who is not Aryan, they can't be part of the volk. Jews and communists, they've got to go. And losing the war? That was all their fault and blah-blah-blah.

So now, what I'm doing is tuning myself out. This guy, he's insane. So I'm smoking my Kurmark cigarette, drinking my Lowenbrau, making sure I keep looking interested. But the truth is, his blabbering goes in one ear and out the other. Gottfried, he's eating real slow with his head down so he doesn't have to look at the jerk. Can't blame him. Suddenly, Fritz starts sneezing, so Uncle Heinz quits blabbering and fishes around for a handkerchief.

"Beer's good," I say. Just to say something.

"Yah," Uncle Heinz says. "It's the law, the *Reinheitsgebot*. When you brew German beer, you can use only pure ingredients—hops, barley, water. Other countries, you know, they use all kinds of trash to preserve the beer. Soot, henbane, stinging nettle."

"No kidding," I say. "Shocking."

"Yah," he says. "And the German volk, we also have to cut out the junk—the Jew soot, the communist stinging nettle, the rest of the trash. As the führer says, we must get rid of the blood poisoning in the body of the volk." He raises his glass.

"To an Aryan *volkskörper!*"

"Heil Hitler!" says Willie, who's had a few. Fritz finishes wiping his nose. Then Fritz and Willie, they raise their glasses. They're impressed, happy to show off their Uncle Heinz. I copy them, naturally.

"Heil Hitler!" People all around us nod approvingly.

Now through all of this, Gottfried's mostly keeping his head down like I said, so he doesn't stop to toast Herr Hitler. Uncle Heinz, he picks up on this. He suddenly gets real quiet. Stares hard at Gottfried. Then he looks directly at me.

Says, "Your brother, he doesn't approve?"

I don't waste time. I give Heinzy a big grin. Then I nudge Gottfried on the shoulder, friendly-like. "Sure he does," I say.

Gottfried looks up. His face is red. He tries to cover. Says, "Great food."

"He's got a big appetite," I say. "Makes him forget his manners."

"Yah," Willie says excitedly. "Gottfried's got bad manners, Uncle." Then he wags a finger back and forth and grins. "But not with the fräuleins." He and Fritz burst out laughing.

Gottfried manages to laugh and raise his glass to them. The moment passes, and I'm breathing again. Uncle Heinz shrugs, goes back to his beer, goes on with his bullshit. He says he knows all the hotshot bankers and industry guys like Thyssen, Krupp. and Schacht. Knows all the old military guys too. Hitler's going to give them all work to do, so we'll have the best army in the world.

And I'm thinking, I'll bet Uncle Heinz is right about that. Hitler is nuts, but he's not a dummkopf. You can't expect rich big shots who lost everything to sit around on their hands. The big bankers, the steel makers—the junkers. Hitler's got to put them back to work. How? Build up the army, naturally. What else can those guys do anyhow? Give dancing lessons?

After lunch, we say our good-byes. "Bye-bye, Uncle Heinz. We hate to go, but we have to move on." And the four of us, we start riding again. After a while, we stop for a short break. Willie and Fritz drank too much at lunch. They want to lie down on the grass and rest for awhile. Gottfried and I go for a little walk.

I say to Gottfried, "I know a good way to make some money," and I tell him my idea. I wait a couple of seconds, but he's not talking. He shakes his head no.

"You scared?" I say.

Now, this is something nobody says to my brother. Not ever. You say he's scared, and he's got to prove he's not. Even if he is. Especially if he is.

"Of course not," he says.

His face is getting hot and red. He's working his jaws. I can practically see the blood throbbing in his temples. "Only, I'm afraid we might miss seeing the Graf Zeppelin."

"We won't."

I lay out the whole thing again. My idea, the timing, everything.

"We can leave here before sunrise," I say. "We'll be long gone before they ever wake up. We'll still have plenty of time to get to Friedrichshafen. And afterward, we'll have money to enjoy ourselves and to eat."

He knows I thought of everything, but he looks down, shakes his head, acts like he doesn't like the idea. But he does like it. I know he does. He wishes it was his idea, that's all. Why? One, it's a goddamn good idea. And two, we've got no money right now, and this will keep us eating and sleeping under roofs for a while.

"Okay," he says finally. "But if we get caught, it's your fault."

"Okay."

"And from now on, you run all your crazy, mixed-up ideas past me first. And no more buddy-buddy with Nazis."

"Okay."

Pretty soon, the four of us get back on our bicycles, and we ride to Tübingen, which takes a while. It's not good riding weather. Too hot, even with no shirts on. When we get there, we go and find some nice grass along the Platanenallee next to the Neckar River. We sit down on the grass under a big plane tree and relax.

"I need a beer," I say.

Says Willie, "Me too."

Says Fritz, "Me three."

"I'll go get some," Gottfried says. Fritz and Willie give him some money, compliments of Uncle Heinz. So Gottfried walks off, and after an hour, he comes back with a big sack. He walked to the marketplace, the Kronenstrasse. Got some guy who was selling out his stock to give him a bargain.

"How could I say no?" Gottfried laughs. "I got us some sandwiches too."

I can see Gottfried is getting into it now. He's starting to enjoy my plan.

So we start eating and drinking. The sun is going down. Gottfried, he starts telling dirty jokes. To make all of us laugh. Gottfried is a dirty-joke specialist. Anyhow, we keep on drinking, and now it's dark. Stars coming out. So then I suggest we stay here, drink our beers, leave in the morning. Why not? The park is quiet, the night is mild. Nice breeze. No rain. So we all agree. And we keep on drinking, joking, taking breaks to go pee on the bushes.

But after a while, I stop drinking beer. I pour some water from my canteen into a beer bottle. I'm watching Gottfried. He doesn't drink any more either. But the Bremen boys, they don't notice what we do. They're getting good and soused, which is how we want them. We start singing drinking songs. After a while, Fritz throws up. Then I go off in the bushes, make vomiting noises, come back. Must be about 2:00 a.m., and Fritz falls asleep. Then Willie goes off, pees, and comes back. There's a whole pile of empty beer bottles lying around us.

"Let's knock off, get some rest," I say.

Nobody objects. We take off our boots and help Willie take off Fritz's boots.

But I don't go to sleep. Neither does Gottfried. I can feel him twitching, even though he doesn't butt up next to me. Finally, in spite of himself, he sleeps for a while. About 4:30 a.m., I shake Gottfried awake, real gentle. Don't want to startle him.

"Let's go," I whisper.

The Bremen boys, they're dead to the world. We put on our boots. Then we tie their boots on our handlebars, and we take off. We take the back streets through town, stop at a quiet café, get some breakfast. We're both happy. We find some water and clean up the Bremens' boots.

Then Gottfried says, "Let's do it."

He asks the café owner for directions to Nazi headquarters, which is near some coffee house, and we ride over there. We still have on our uniforms, naturally, and we ride over there. Outside Nazi headquarters, we see some young guys. They want to be Nazis, but they've got no boots. There are lots of guys like that right now, but they have to get in line and wait. Why? The Nazis can't take them in fast enough. They don't have enough supplies for so many guys. So these young guys, they hang around Nazi headquarters and wait for somebody to call their names. Right now, there's a few of them talking about how happy they are, because the university here in Tübingen already fired all their Jewish professors. Being free of Jews—*Judenfrie*—that's the goal, right? When we hear this dreck, this is when we decide to make our move. Gottfried decides he'll do it.

He says, "Go and wait where they can't see you. Was your idea, Rudolf, so let me do the work. I can sell better than you anyhow."

He thinks I'll mess up. He thinks he's got to protect me. But he also wants to show me he's not afraid.

"Okay," I say.

So we take the boots off the handlebars, and Gottfried walks over to the guys there. He's got the boots. He gives them all a smart "Heil Hitler." Then he makes up some silly, cockamamie story that he bought these boots in Munich to give to some buddies, but now he's short on cash, so he's got to sell them. He asks, would they like to buy them cheap? Yah, yah! You bet they would!

After a couple of minutes, Gottfried comes back grinning. Shows me the thirty marks he got.

He says, "Give a German a pair of boots, and he's happy. Even if he has to buy them!"

"Good man!" I say. I give him a friendly smack.

"Was easy," he says. He shrugs. "Anyhow, you can't sell things the way I can, and we need the money."

I don't answer him. Why? One, he's right—we need the money. And two, let him think he's better than me at whatever he wants. Who gives a damn?

Right away, we start biking again. We get out of town. Too bad we couldn't wait and see Willie and Fritz wake up though.

Along the road, we meet a couple of girls. Turns out they're on their way to Friedrichshafen, so we ride along with them. This one girl, she's my type. Tall, slender with pretty hair, like a reddish blonde. She's got a cousin, she says, a rich widow. Owns a guest-house in Sigmaringen.

Gottfried, he's feeling good now. We've got no Nazis with us, and we've got money in our pockets. Well, in his pockets anyhow. And we still have enough time to get to Friedrichshafen.

So this evening, we decide to go with the two girls to their cousin's guesthouse. Turns out to be a fancy-schmancy place. To show off. Big, heavy furniture, plush. Heavy mirrors with silver frames hanging on the walls. Our appetites are very good, and we get a good, big German supper—fat schnitzel cutlets with brown gravy, red sauerkraut, asparagus, a nice bok beer, the works. They even have a cute maid to serve us. Naturally, we don't tell them who we are. Why should we? Anyhow, by this time we're getting pretty good at passing for Nazis.

III

GOTTFRIED

The next morning, we leave the girls in Sigmaringen and go. Rudolf wants to stay longer. See, he likes one of these girls. He thinks if we stay another night, we can both get some. Now I can always use it, so I'm tempted. But what if they want to come along with us afterward? If they do, we'll have to spend money on them. So I tell Rudolf we need to go on without them.

Lake Constance is a beautiful place, but it's a place for tourists, very expensive. And there are girls down there too. There are always girls. Besides, I'm getting sick and tired of wearing these uniforms and the few clothes we took from home. So I tell Rudolf, "Let's buy some new clothes," and we find a small store there in Sigmaringen.

We each buy shirts, trousers, vests, neckties, jackets, and new shoes. We get a good deal, but now we're low on money again.

We put on our new clothes and go for a little walk. On a side street near the clothing store, we pass by a few Orthodox Jewish men in their big, black hats and long, black coats, with their prayer shawls hanging out. They all have beards, mostly grey. They're very friendly—smiling, nodding, saying, "*Gut Yontif!* Happy holiday!"

What holiday this is, I don't know. The Orthodox have too many of them, and who can keep them straight? But I like to be friendly. So I say, "Gut Yontif."

I can see they don't expect those words to come out of my mouth. They're surprised, smiling.

One of them, he claps me on the back. Says, "Where are you *boychicks* from?" *Boychicks* is Yiddish. Means "little boys" but in a loving kind of way.

Now in our hometown, most Jews didn't talk much Yiddish. Mama did sometimes, because her parents talked Yiddish. But not Papa. See, after the war, Germany suddenly started getting a lot of Jewish immigrants from the East, especially from Poland, which is a poor country, where they hate Jews worse than Germany ever did. There were thousands of Polish Jews starving to death. Anyhow, these people started coming to Germany when we were kids. This made the regular German people nervous, even some of the German Jews. For instance, Papa had no use for them. When they came to our shul, he always pointed them out, told us to leave them alone.

"We're Germans, not Polacks," he'd say. "Remember that."

Mama didn't feel the same. She's strong, but she's got a soft heart, and she felt sorry for the Polacks. They came to our hometown practically starving, with nothing. So she tried to help them out. She used to cook food and take it to the shul for them. She took us along with her sometimes, and we would listen to the adults talking Yiddish. Sounded something like German, but funny. We liked the funny words and picked them up. So did the few other Jewish kids we knew.

So now, here we are in this little town far away from home, and what do we see? Polacks from the East. I'm very surprised. Who would expect this here? Polacks in long, black coats with their high hats and their side curls and beards. One of them says, "Come and pray with us, boys."

Right now, I'm feeling—I don't know—homesick or something. Maybe I'm kind of religious still. Matter of fact, I never ate pork. At home, we always ate kosher. Rudolf, he laughs at me. He says pork is delicious. But one thing I can tell you—he wouldn't dare say that to Mama.

Anyhow, at home, I would sometimes go to shul with my parents. Was an Orthodox synagogue—men in one place, women in another place—and I sat with Martin and Papa. Martin liked shul for some reason or other, even if he doesn't understand Hebrew and never learned how to read in any language. My father liked shul too in spite of the Polacks who came there. He loved to close his eyes and listen to the chanting and sway back and forth like the other old men, and he liked to sing the Hebrew songs. He always looked happy there, peaceful.

See, our family is not well off, but our name is Kahn. This means we came from the tribe of the high priests in the olden days. The *kohanim*—the high priests—they're always honored during services. So sometimes, the rabbi would ask Papa to read from the Torah, our bible. That made him feel proud. Matter of fact, when he was up there on the altar reading, you'd never know there was anything wrong with his head.

So now, when the old Polacks see us and invite us to come and pray with them, I want to go. I know Rudolf doesn't though. He's got no use for any religion. But I make him a little proposition. If he comes along, we'll go to a rathskeller afterward. He likes this idea, so he says okay. My brother, he loves his beer.

So we follow the Polacks to their little shul. There's no rabbi or cantor today, but the place is nice. They have an ark and a Torah with a beautiful, blue velvet cover and a gold crown sewn on the front. I'm very surprised to see this. See, Torahs are handmade. Every word written by hand on parchment, not paper. They're very expensive to buy, and this is a small shul in a small town.

"Where did your Torah come from?" I ask.

One old man laughs, looks up, and points. "He provides."

I see Rudolf roll his eyes, but I don't think anybody else saw him, thank God.

We all sit down. The service, it's in Hebrew, just like at home. The same melodies we're used to. After an hour or so, they pick up the Torah and ask us our last name, and when I say "Kahn," they get very excited. They want us to read from the Torah. Rudolf shakes his head, taps a finger on his throat like he's got a sore throat. The liar. But I go up there to the front. To me, it's an honor.

When I get back to my seat, Rudolf is grinning at me. I know that look. Sure enough, he leans over and whispers inside my ear,

"Good thing you did that, Gottfried. Now God will forgive us for stealing those boots."

"Shut up, Rudolf!"

Well, I didn't mean to, but I said that much too loud. All the old men turn and stare at me. I try to pretend it wasn't me, but they know it was, and I'm very embarrassed.

After services, we're supposed to go for a beer, and since I promised, we go. But after what Rudolf said, I'm in a very bad mood. We sit there, and I don't talk. I order a stein of Furstenberg, and he orders a couple of them. He keeps trying to cheer me up by telling jokes. Me, I like a good joke, and I have to admit some of his jokes are pretty funny. But I don't feel like laughing, so I don't. Rudolf acting like a baby in shul—it's aggravating. We sit there a long time.

Finally, he apologizes. Says, "Look, I'm sorry, Gottfried. Okay? Let's go and see your Graf Zeppelin."

So since he apologized, I start to forget about it. I pay up, and we ride our bicycles into Friedrichshafen, where the Graf Zeppelin is supposed to land tomorrow. We get a good night's sleep in a clean hostel, and when we get to the airfield the next morning, we see hundreds of people walking around. It's very exciting, seeing so many people talking to each other, everybody happy, everybody excited. When we look up at the sky, it's very bright, and we have to shade our eyes from the sunshine. But everybody still wants to look up while we're waiting. There are people singing and dancing, and bands playing. I don't know how many bands, but there's a lot of loud music. A lot of people too—more than we ever saw in one place before.

When the zeppelin finally shows up, everybody cheers. Looks like a smooth silver whale swimming in the sky. I'm guessing it's more than two hundred meters long and thirty meters across. It's also very noisy. It has enormous motors and spinning propellers. Matter of fact, the motors get so loud when the zeppelin starts to come down that we can't hear the band right next to us. Then the zeppelin stops. Hovers in the middle of the air just above the ground. A couple of hundred guys with strong ropes pull it the rest of the way down and tie it onto stakes in the ground.

The whole time, everybody's yelling and shouting—everybody! Kids too. They're working the crowd, selling souvenirs. We also see Nazis—SA men in their brown uniforms. One of them catches a skinny kid, a pickpocket. He hauls him up off the ground, shouts at him, slaps him up and down. A woman standing next to us, she shakes her fist angrily.

"Good!" she says. She's clutching her pocketbook tight to her chest. "They finally got one of those filthy little gypsies!"

He's just a kid, see. Maybe eight or nine years old. He shouldn't steal, but I feel sorry for him. It's not right, the way they are beating him up.

Just then, we see the passengers stepping down off the gondola, walking along the ground, waving at the crowd. If their ride from South America was long or hard, you wouldn't know it. They're all dressed up like big shots at a party. Who they are, I can't say. But to fly on the Graf Zeppelin from South America, that takes good money and connections too.

After the landing, Rudolf and I walk around. This whole place is a tremendous enterprise. In a museum here, they show

how they build the zeppelins—all the different models—from the beginning to this one here. People have been riding in it back and forth over the Atlantic Ocean for four years. After we see all the exhibits, we go back outside to walk around the Graf Zeppelin, to see the whole thing up close. But when we get to the port side, all of a sudden I get a sick feeling, like a fist in my stomach. On the tail fin and rudder, there's a big, black Nazi swastika in a white circle with red in it. The way the sun is hitting it, with all the shine on the paint, you can tell the paint job is pretty new.

That swastika on the Graf Zeppelin—all lit up in the sun like that—it's very tough for me to see. I was always proud to be German. But seeing the Nazis' swastika up there, I'm upset.

When other people see the swastika, they stop too. A couple of people salute and shout, "Heil Hitler." Most people definitely like what they see. They're pointing at the swastika, and they're nodding and smiling. Makes me sick.

Nearby, we hear a couple of loudmouths. Middle-aged men, businessmen maybe, wearing nice, gray suits and good-looking homburg hats. Both of them are puffing on cigarettes and talking loud enough for everybody to hear them.

"A dirty Jew," one of them says. He flicks a long ash off his cigarette onto the ground.

"Nah, a communist," says the other guy.

"A Jew and a communist, both. What's the difference? Only a jackass would try to burn down the Reichstag."

"They're all the same dirty bastards. Like the führer says—cancers on the volk."

Me, I can't stand to stay there anymore. I say to Rudolf, "Let's go."

But Rudolf, he's grinning from ear to ear.

I say, "What the hell's so funny?"

He doesn't answer me. Instead, he walks away from me, right up to these two jerks, and he says, "Don't you gentlemen know our führer has outlawed smoking?"

The two guys in homburgs laugh, ignore him.

So then he shouts at them, "You bums! What? Are you a couple of Jews or something? You filth!"

He turns around and stomps off, heading directly over to a bunch of SA men, who are standing around, talking.

Well, now the two homburgs, they suddenly stop laughing. They're watching Rudolf, and he's walking straight over to where the Nazis are. The homburgs are starting to get a little nervous. One of them is shuffling his feet.

The other one says, "What? Is smoking illegal now?" He's looking all around him.

As it turns out, nobody around there is smoking except the two of them. This was something I hadn't noticed myself, but I guess Rudolf must have noticed it.

Anyhow, Rudolf just keeps walking over to the SA men, and when he gets to them, he salutes and starts talking to them like he's their best friend in the world. They all laugh together. Then Rudolf starts to gesture in the direction of the loudmouths.

Now these guys are looking plenty nervous. One of them drops his cigarette, grinds it out in the dirt, and says to his buddy, "Put it out. Let's go." His buddy tosses what's left of his smoke on the ground and stubs it out with the sole of his shoe. They walk off in a big hurry.

Rudolf hangs around with the Nazis another minute or two and then comes walking back to me, grinning that crooked grin of his. I burst out laughing. I'm proud of him.

"You're nuts," I tell him. "What the hell did you say to those SA guys?"

"Oh, it's a beautiful day. Isn't this terrific? Nice weather. Blah-blah-blah... Told them a couple of jokes. Maybe I asked if they knew the time." He points at his wrist and shrugs. "I've got no wristwatch, right?"

"But is it true Hitler has outlawed smoking?"

"Huh?"

We both start laughing, and I have to admit I'm feeling a lot better now. It's getting late in the afternoon, and we both feel like relaxing, so we go for a walk, and then we ride our bicycles around for a while, looking at all the people. We see a couple of pretty girls walking by, and Rudolf and I get the same idea at the same time. So we stop and talk to them, invite them to have a bite to eat. These two girls, both of them, are very cute blondes about our age. Sisters from Munich taking a little vacation. Tonight is their last night here, and tomorrow they're going home. They act very happy to meet us. We take them out for some green pea soup with spaetzel and cheese, and then we go dancing at a place they know. Afterwards, we go with them back to their hostel. We're hoping to get lucky, but we're disappointed, especially Rudolf, because it's been a long time. But we take a room at their hostel anyhow.

The next morning, we talk to the man in charge at the hostel, and he tells us some places to visit. We're visiting, but we're also looking. We want to figure out the best way to cross over the border into Austria. We ride a boat to the town of Konstanz, which costs seventy-five pfennigs. It's a good value, but we're almost out of money again.

We get breakfast, some rolls, coffee. It costs only one mark, but now we're completely broke. But we have our own boots still. So we get back on our bikes and ride over to Lindau. We find out where Nazi headquarters is, and we ride there. Why not? And there are a couple of guys standing outside there, so we start talking with them.

"I would like to buy them," a guy says, "but all I have is twenty marks."

I figure we can get more than that. Didn't I get thirty marks for two pairs before? I'm ready to say something, but Rudolf takes my arm and twists it, so I keep quiet.

Then he says, "You guys can have both pairs for twenty marks." Why he does this, I don't know. But as soon as we leave, he says, "I didn't like the feeling I got there. Didn't want to hang around for a few more pfennigs."

Sometimes Rudolf gets a certain feeling about somebody. Me, I learned a long time ago not to argue when he gets that kind of feeling.

Now Lindau looks to us like a nice little town, like a little island sitting out on the lake. The streets, everything—all of it—nice and clean. We decide to go and find Mama's friends, the Nordlingers. Somebody tells us where to find the house, which isn't hard. See, there are only three Jewish families in the whole town, so everybody knows where they live.

Anyhow, from the Nordlinger house, it looks like the sky and the water are swallowing up the whole world. But pretty as the town looks, the Nordlinger house looks like the opposite. Matter of fact, the whole place is completely worn out—paint peeling, furniture falling apart. The Nordlingers look worn out too. Frau Nordlinger—maybe she was pretty once, which Mama said, but now her face looks like a hard little raisin. Herr Nordlinger, he's skinny and hunched over, like he's going to fall on his face any minute. He's wearing worn-out pants, which he holds up with thin, red suspenders.

The Nordlingers live here alone. They have three kids, grown and gone, but pictures of them when they were younger are on the mantle. Two serious boys and one plain girl with a sweet smile. One boy in Berlin, one in Munich, and the girl married and living in the United States.

Being in this house is depressing, but of course, the Nordlingers invite us to have supper. We're hungry, so we stay, but they don't have much to eat—just some boiled eggs, some bread, and some milk. She warms up the milk and adds a little sugar. We dip the bread into the sugar-milk to soak it, and after we eat it, we tip the bowls up to our mouths and drink out what's left of the milk. Mama used to fix the same thing for us sometimes when times were hard. After this, we thank them and get up to go.

"No, no, please sit down," Herr Nordlinger says. "We have a letter for you from your mama. It came a few days ago by way of Jacob Gessner in Frankfurt."

Frau Nordlinger says, "We'd like to hear it if you don't mind. I haven't had any news from your mother in quite some time. You can read it to us."

Me, I don't like to read out loud. The teachers used to hit me at school, because I did a bad job with it. So I start reading Mama's letter to myself. Then I stop and tell them afterward what I just read.

"Mama says they're waiting to hear when they can go to America. She thinks it won't be a problem for them, because the government wants Jews to go. She also says an hour after we left home, some Hitlerjugend came to our house, looking for us. Mama recognized some of them—boys from our old school—but they acted like they didn't know her. They asked where we were, and she said she didn't know. So they called her all kinds of names, and one of the bastards spit on her face."

"Can you imagine?" Frau Nordlinger says. "Boys you went with to school? My God!"

She and her husband start talking about this, so now I can't concentrate, and Rudolf wants to shut them up.

Says, "Nobody's going to hit you, Gottfried. Read it out loud."

So I take a deep breath, and I do.

Of course, I walked out of the front room after the boy spit at me. I went into the kitchen and washed off my face. Papa was standing in the front room in his army uniform with the Iron Cross on it. Those boys made a mess out of everything. They tore our telephone out of the wall. They took knives and shredded the cushions of our sofa and Papa's big chair. They picked up the table and smashed it to pieces. They broke everything made of glass. Anything they could get their hands on. I went into our bedroom and closed the door. Papa stayed in the front room with them the whole time, but they didn't touch him. When there was nothing left to destroy in the front room or the kitchen, they wanted to come into the bedroom, but Papa was standing in front of the door, and he started to yell about his Iron Cross. Then he screamed he was Captain Adolf Kahn, a German war hero. Who the hell were they? He was yelling about the war and the fire trenches. Then all of a sudden, the Hitlerjugend left. They slammed the front door and left.

"Oh, thank God!" Frau Nordlinger cries.

Rudolf shakes his head. "The bastards busted up the whole place, goddamn them."

"There's more," I say, and I go on reading.

Your poor father couldn't stop shaking the whole night. But I was proud of him. I think they didn't dare to touch us because he was a war hero. And I thank God every day that you boys were not here. Our friends gave us some dishes, some furniture. And people at the shul also helped us out. Someone even brought over a new telephone.

"They were so lucky," Frau Nordlinger whispers. "So lucky."

But just when I thought everything was quiet again, the Nazis beat up poor Martin.

I stop reading. Rudolf and I stare at each other. Justus Nordlinger and his wife, almost together, say, "Oh no!"

It happened in front of an apartment building a block away on our street. Our friend, Jakob Hirsch, was waiting nearby for someone to pick him up. Later on, at the hospital, he told me what happened. He said Martin was doing nothing wrong. He was just standing and looking up at a window on the second floor of the building. Some people up there were having a little party. You know how Martin loves to hear people laughing and singing. While he was standing there, some of those Hitlerjugend came up to him.

One of them said to him, "What do you think you are looking at?"

Martin said, "Nothing. I'm only enjoying the music."

Then another one said, "Hey, isn't he the brother of those Jews who beat up our friend?"

Well, to make a long story short, they beat Martin very bad. They broke his nose. They also knocked most of his teeth out. The dentist could not save the few teeth he had left.

Jakob said the people from the party knew what was going on. They were watching the whole thing from their window, but they did nothing to stop it. Thank God Jakob was there, even though he could not stop them by himself. When his friend arrived with a car, they drove Martin to the hospital. He was there for a week. After they let Martin come home, I asked your uncle Josef to take him to Zwesten. That way, they won't find him if they try to look for him here. Now I pray all will be well in Zwesten. Josef said right now, it's quiet there. He is respected as a cattle trader, even though he is a Jew. The people in town still buy from him, even though the Nazis have made rules against this.

"Sons of bitches!" Rudolf shouts. "If I was there…"
"But we're not," I say.

In this letter, you will find a little money from Siegfried in New York. He is making a living there painting flowers on plates and tablecloths. Please leave a letter for me with the Nordlingers. They will send it to Jacob Gessner in Frankfurt. He will make sure I get it. Do not send letters to our house. They might be looking for anything from you. Also, remember you have relatives in Basel, the Haas family. Maybe they can help you go to America. God willing, we will be together again soon.

Hugs and kisses,
Mama

IV

RUDOLF

Mama's letter is very upsetting. Also, it makes Gottfried start worrying out loud. What will happen to Mama and Papa? Why did we leave them? What if the Nazis come back and kill them? What if they find out where we are? What if they kill Martin and our relatives in Zwesten?

I'm worried too, but mostly, I'm frustrated. I want to go home. Beat the shit out of them. Cowards. I want to take my family away from there. They can't get Gottfried and me, so the cowards took it out on Martin, a kid who wouldn't hurt a fly.

And that's the truth too. He wouldn't. Martin started crying one time when Hubert smashed a goddamn fly on the kitchen table. Hubert did it to make him cry. Mean. Another time, Hubert pushed Martin into the river with his clothes on. Gottfried and I, we pulled him out, and Mama whipped Hubert, but it didn't help. With Hubert, nothing helped.

Well, anyhow, we're talking about all this when Frau Nordlinger says, "Boys, we don't want to upset you more than you already are. But we think you need to leave Germany. Tonight."

Then she tells us two Nazi Stormtroopers came to their house yesterday.

She says, "We don't know why. They didn't knock. They banged. They came in and looked around, like they were looking for someone or something. They said they'll be back."

Herr Nordlinger nods slowly. "Yah," he says. "They also went into the houses of our neighbors. One of our neighbors had some books, which they took away with them."

"Thugs," Frau Nordlinger says. She tells us the Nazis burned up a lot of books by Jews and other people, which was the first we heard about it.

"You didn't hear?" she asks. "They had big bonfires all over the country."

Then she says, "You know, our son in Berlin was high up in the government, a lawyer. Last week, the Nazis fired him and all the other Jewish men there."

So I ask, "You and your kids, are you going to leave?"

Both of them shake their heads. Herr Nordlinger says, "We're too old to start over, boys. About our sons, I don't know. Both of them are married to Christians, so we don't think the Nazis will bother them."

"Anyway, all of this trouble is temporary," the frau tells us. "The German people are good people, decent. Soon, you'll see, President von Hindenburg will throw the Nazis out."

"But you boys need to get out of here tonight," Herr Nordlinger says. "We're afraid the Nazis will come back again to our house. It's not safe for you to stay here."

Then old man Nordlinger asks us if we can swim.

Now that's a good one. What we did every summer at home, all of us kids, was swim and swim and swim. When it got hot, and when we had a little time, we would swim. Had a special swimming hole in the Lahn River. Gottfried and I got a biology lesson there a few years ago. We were coming to take a dip, and what did we see? Our sister, Clare, swimming in the river. Had that guy, Alfred Roper, in there with her, acting all lovey-dovey. Then the two of them came up out of the river with nothing on them—and I mean nothing. Now, this was something we had never seen before. A first. So we were whistling and clapping and shouting, "More! More!"

Clare, she screeched. Then she and Roper, they jumped back down in the water. Couple of minutes later, their heads popped up, and we watched them talk. Then she swam over to the shore where we were standing.

She said, "Don't tell Mama. I'll give you whatever you want."

We couldn't think of anything we wanted, but we said, "Okay, we'll keep quiet," and we did. Why? One, it might keep Clare from bossing us so much. And two, now we had this IOU from her, and IOUs come in handy. But like I already said, you can't pull the wool over Mama's eyes too long, and she figured out about Clare and her boyfriend. Not from us though.

Anyhow, that was then. This is now.

Herr Nordlinger, he gives Gottfried a pen and some paper to write back to Mama. While he's writing, the old man gives me directions to the Lieblach River. He says it's a small river, and we should swim across it tonight. On the other side is Austria, and nearby is a small town, which is Hörbranz. He tells me how to find the house of a shoemaker there, name of Schuster.

"Catholic people," he says. "We've known them a long time. Good people. They will help you."

So Gottfried finishes up the letter, and we say our good-byes. We walk to the east, to the edge of the town, and there's the Lieblach. We need to leave our bicycles here, so we hide them in a small forested area by the river. Strange though. Feels kind of like we're saying good-bye to good friends. Both of us stand there a couple minutes looking at those beat-up old bicycles. We spent many hours with them, no? And before that, so did Clare and Siegfried. Pieces of junk, really. Don't know why we feel so sad to leave them here.

Well, the Lieblach River, this is another surprise. Tonight is full of them. It's a very small river, so small you can see the other side. We never saw a river as small as this one. Hard to believe it's a border river on top of that. Seems dumb to me to use this little river for a border between two big countries. But right now, I'm glad they do.

So we take our shoes off and stick them inside our rucksacks. We step into the water, which is goddamn cold even if it's not much of a river.

And Gottfried says, "You know, I feel like I'm leaving home again."

"Not me," I say. "I feel like I'm leaving hell."

Of course, I don't tell Gottfried this, but it's hard to say how I'm really feeling. Guess I've got mixed feelings myself. But so what? One, it doesn't make any difference how I feel, because we still have to go. And two, what's done is done. Can't go back and undo it.

So we slide down into the water. Hold our rucksacks over our heads the best we can. Walk when possible. Try to paddle when it's deeper. We have to be very quiet, very careful. Watch for the spotlights they've got there, moving back and forth, back and forth. Guess they put the lights there to keep people like us from crossing over. A couple of times the lights do hit us, and one time, we think maybe we hear a guy shouting at us. Makes us both nervous, but we keep going anyhow.

Finally, we make it across. We're out of Germany, and that's okay with me. Germany doesn't want us, and we don't want to be there. But we get a hell of a bad welcome from Austria. Because now, we're soaking wet from swimming, and on top of that, a cold rain is starting. It's mostly farmland we have to slog through, and with the rain, our shoes go sinking down in the mud. Wet, heavy, very slow going.

I think I know the direction we are supposed to go, but I get lost. So we're going around in circles in the mud for a good hour. We're soaked through, shivering. Gottfried's mad at me, yelling.

"He gave you directions, goddamn it! Can't you ever pay attention?"

I'm mad at myself too, but what can I do? We have to keep going. Nothing else we can do. Can't sleep in an open field in the pouring rain, can we?

It's the wee hours of the morning when we finally get to Hör-branz, and it's still pouring down rain. Little town, little houses there, shutters all closed up. We stumble around till we find Lindauer Strasse, which is the main street. We see signs, but it's not easy to read them through this heavy rain.

Anyhow, we follow the main road along just like old man Nordlinger told us to, and finally, we find the shoemaker's house. There's a big painted wooden shoe on the outside wall, hanging up next to the door. So we go up on the porch and knock on the door. It's a big, heavy door, thick wood with a lot of stuff carved in it. I know this, because we stand there shivering, waiting. To me, it seems like a long time, so maybe they don't hear us. I knock again—harder this time.

Finally, the door opens a crack, but kind of slow and squeaky. And there stands a sleepy old man in a long, heavy nightgown and a nightcap. He's holding a lit candle in a cup, and he's got dark shadows under his eyes. Looks like a ghost in some scary movie.

"Yah?" he says. He's got a deep voice, soft.

"Herr Schuster?" I say. My teeth are chattering. "Herr Nordlinger in Lindau said for us to come here. Can you help us out?"

The old man opens the heavy door wider and lets us in. I never felt so happy to get inside before. Gottfried and I, we're wet and filthy. We're shivering and dripping mud on their nice, clean wood floors.

Then the wife, she comes out of the bedroom. Tall, straight old lady, skinny, long white hair in a braid hanging on her back. She's wearing a long white robe. To me right now, she looks maybe like one of those angels Clare used to sing about. She doesn't ask questions. Helps us get ourselves cleaned up, gives us some blankets to wrap up in. Afterward, she tells us to sit down and rest. She feeds us some bread, some lentil soup. And then she fixes up a nice stack of blankets in the back room there on the floor and tells us to sleep. We don't need to be told twice.

Next morning, I wake up and see the sun coming in through a window. I'm happy to see there's no more rain. But Gottfried is lying there with no blanket, sweating, and his teeth are chattering.

"I feel like hell," he says and coughs.

He's not alone. I'm coughing for the last few hours too. I can't believe it. We're both as sick as dogs. Sweating, freezing, sweating. Something in the river water, maybe. Who knows? Sick is sick. It doesn't matter why.

But the Schusters, they don't blink when they see how it is with us. They take turns feeding us and washing up after us, helping us out every way they can. Strangers, no? Not Jewish, but they treat us like we're their own kids.

It takes us a long time to get well, maybe a couple of weeks. Days, we can hear the old man in his shop at the front of the house. He's fixing shoes, making shoes. There's that familiar smell of leather, that sound of knives stropping on leather.

Makes me think of Mama's shoe shop and another place too, the one where I worked after I quit school. It was called Leopold & Herz. Mama got a job there for me, helping out, making shoes, selling leather, sharpening knives—little stuff. After a few months, I helped my friend Ernst Bloch get a job there too. And when Herr Leopold wasn't around, Ernst and I played cards—pelotte, skat, whatever. We got paid zero— *bubkis.* Worked hours and hours for practically nothing. Why? We were kids, that's why. They took advantage of kids.

Every day after work, Herr Leopold made me walk with his kid to their house. The Leopold boy, he was maybe six, seven years old. Fat little kid, sad. Never smiled. Thick glasses. Got teased all the time. Anyhow, after school, the kid came over to the business and hung around there until closing time. It took me twenty minutes to walk this kid over to Herr Leopold's house, which was a fancy place in the other direction from my house.

We always had to stop in front so the kid could pet Snowball. Who was Snowball? The stone lion, which was standing up on a pedestal at the entrance, right next to the Leopolds' cement wall and their fancy wrought-iron gate. The Leopolds had plenty of money, but they had only this one lonely boy. Seemed like Snowball was his only friend. As for Herr Leopold, he was a busy man. Busy, busy, busy. He didn't go home after work, right? Whatever he was doing, it was female, but it wasn't his wife.

Anyhow, on my say-so, Herr Leopold hired Ernst Bloch. This was the same guy who called to warn us to run away the night we left Giessen. This is how IOUs can come in handy.

Well, now we're in Austria, so at least there's no Hitlerjugend after us. But we're pretty goddamn sick. On top of everything else, I come down with boils all over my body. Full of pus. Hurt like hell. Frau Schuster uses warm water on them, breaks them open real gentle, squeezes them out. Never complains either, even when she's taking care of squeezing out boils. Makes me feel disgusted with myself. Embarrassed too. I keep apologizing to her.

But all she says is, "I'm glad to help you, Rudolf. Please relax. Let me help you." That's it.

It's hard to do, but I try. I owe that much to her at least.

I had boils like this one other time when I was little. Clare cut them open with a knife. I was crying, and she was screaming at me to shut up the whole goddamn time. And now I've got the same problem. And guess what? It's a stranger, not even a Jew, who's taking care of me. Treats me nicer than my own sister. You figure it out.

The whole time the Schusters are taking care of us, they don't ask us a single question. Finally, we decide we have to tell them who we are, where we come from, why we're here. We're guessing they'll kick us out when they hear all this. Why? Helping out Jews like us, Jews on the run—that's asking for trouble. But they sit there and listen and nod. Seems like they already know. I'm thinking maybe they talked to the Nordlingers, but they don't say so. And I get the feeling they would have acted exactly the same way even if they didn't know the Nordlingers.

But they do know the Nordlingers. And a few days before we're feeling well again, Frau Schuster comes and sits us down, folds her hands in her lap, and tells us the Nordlingers got arrested.

Says, "All we know is the Nazis came back and took them away. The SA was there before, you see. At their house."

"They told us," I say.

She sighs. "But sadly, they were not the only ones. They also arrested the other two Jewish families in Lindau."

She tells us after the Nazis left, one of their neighbors went into the house to find their children's telephone numbers. He also found the Schusters' number and called them. He said the Nazis were arresting all the Lindau Jews. For hiding criminals.

"Criminals?" I say.

"Must mean us," Gottfried says.

Frau Schuster sits, wringing her hands, sighing now and then. Gottfried and I are upset. We think this is all our fault. Frau Schuster, she seems to know this is what we're thinking.

"Listen, my dears," she says, "it's not your fault. The Nazis wanted an excuse, that's all. They want a Jew-free Germany, and in a small town with three Jewish families…"

"But what if they come here next?" Gottfried asks.

"They won't," she says. "This is Austria. Anyway, my husband and I aren't going to stop helping people like you, no matter what happens."

"There have been others?" I ask.

She smiles like she's explaining something to a little kid, which is what I feel like right now.

"Yes, Rudolf," she says. "Of course. You're not the first ones to run. Sad to say, you won't be the last ones either. But you're two of the lucky ones."

She's right. At the time, though, we have no idea how right she is.

V

GOTTFRIED

It's very lucky for us to be landing up in Austria with such nice people, and they take very good care of us. I feel terrible about what happened to the Nordlingers and the other Jewish people over there in Lindau. Rudolf and I are sorry we stopped off there. Right now, all we can do is hope they will make it back home again.

The Schusters try to get us to stay here longer, but we want to go. The longer we stay, the more we worry, even if they say no Nazis will come over here. So the day after we get the terrible news about the Jewish people in Lindau, we pack up. We thank them for all their help, and we say we're leaving.

But Herr Schuster asks us to sit down with him before we go. Says, "You boys should at least take a few days to look around this beautiful area here. It might be a long time before you get a chance to come back."

I'm not too excited about the idea. I want to get out of Austria and go over to Switzerland. But Rudolf wants to stay. He wants to hike in the mountains. See, we both like to hike, and we both love the woods and the mountains. We always dream about seeing new places too. So naturally, we would like to take a few days, see the sights here, the beautiful mountains. But this isn't a good time to stay in Austria. Germany and Austria were like one big country in the past, and Austria is Hitler's home. On top of that, most Austrians hate Jews as much as the Nazis do.

Then Herr Schuster says, "Gottfried, I have a nice camera, a Voigtlander Basser 6 x 9. Would you like to have it?"

"Me?"

"Yes, you. I heard you tell your brother you would love to have a little camera."

"Well, thank you. But I wouldn't take your camera, Herr Schuster. I should be giving you a gift, not the other way around."

"Please take it, Gottfried. It would make me happy. I don't use it anymore."

"Why not?"

"I don't go out too much. As a matter of fact, I would love it if you would send me some pictures of the mountains around here. I would love to see the Vorarlberg area and the mountains again. You know, I can't climb anymore myself."

So I take the camera, and I tell Rudolf, "Well, after he gave me this nice camera, and they took such good care of us, I hate to disappoint him. So maybe we can stay around here for a couple of days anyhow."

The next morning, Frau Schuster makes us a delicious breakfast of fresh bread and butter, coffee, and cheeses, and she packs us a lunch too. We say our good-byes, and we go. We walk a little. Then we put out our thumbs and hitchhike, and we get a ride in the back of a farm truck. When we jump inside there, we wish the damn truck hadn't stopped for us. The back, where we are, is full of all kinds of junk, like stinking bits of chicken guts and feathers and rusty farm tools.

When we get into the town of Bregenz, it's a big relief. The town smells good and looks clean. It's very old and very beautiful, sitting up there over the lake. So we climb up a hill, and Rudolf and I take turns taking pictures with my new camera. From the top of the hill, you can see Germany on one side and Switzerland on the other.

"Over there," I tell him, "it's Germany. Over here, it's Switzerland. We can see our past and our future at the same time."

Rudolf laughs at me. "What? Now you're a philosopher? You got your crystal ball too?"

What a dummkopf.

We walk down the hill and over to the Martinsturm, which is a very famous old building. Some of it was built in the Roman days. I find it very interesting—especially the onion-shaped steeple. So I take some pictures to send to Herr Schuster. Afterward, we eat the picnic lunch Frau Schuster made for us, and from there, we decide to find a place to stay. A man points out a nice-looking hostel, which is half-timbered, like many places in Germany. We don't have much money left, so I don't want to spend a lot. But we decide to go inside and take a look, and a scrawny guy at the front desk says he's got a room for us.

Says, "You look like good boys. I can make you a deal." And he does.

Then he sticks out his chest like a rooster and says, "You know, you boys are lucky to get a room here. Matter of fact, Herr Hitler is coming to stay here in a couple of weeks. His man Goebbels was just here to arrange it."

He points to a page in the fancy leather guest book on the counter.

"Look," he says proudly, pointing to Goebbels's name, which is signed in heavy black ink.

Rudolf grins. "That's terrific!" he says.

Now, I don't want to stay here. But Rudolf quickly grabs the fountain pen on the counter, dips it in the inkwell, and signs us in. Then he sticks out his hand.

"I'm Willie Bremen," he tells the manager. "This is my brother, Fritz."

Damn it, I'm thinking. Here we go again.

"I'm Herr Brunn," the guy says, pumping our hands, one at a time. Big show-off. Then he takes us to our room and leaves us.

I lock the door. I'm furious.

"We're so lucky, Willie? You like to stay where Hitler stays, Willie? That feels good, Willie?"

Rudolf shrugs.

"Don't be silly, Gottfried. One, Goebbels's signature—it's probably a fake. Anybody could sign anybody's name. Didn't I just do the same thing? And two, who gives a damn if Hitler's going to stay here? It's a nice place. Cheap too. Cheap should make you happy."

I'm so mad I can't talk. When he sees how mad I am, he starts backing off.

"Oh, come on, Gottfried," he says. "Relax. Let's go for a hike. Take the camera and get some pictures for th Schusters."

Well, what can I do? The last thing I want to do right now is stay around this goddamn place. Makes me a nervous wreck, to tell the truth. If Hitler's going to stay here, Nazis can show up anytime. So I decide we'll stay outside all day, then we'll stay inside our room tonight, and we'll leave early in the morning.

We go out. Back to the base of the Pfänder, which I figure is maybe three hundred meters high. I take some nice pictures, and then we decide to do a little tree climbing. Rudolf gets himself up into a tree without falling, which is a surprise to both of us. But since he made it, I decide to climb into the tree next to his and take a picture of him. I climb up maybe ten meters when the branch suddenly cracks under my foot. It's a sickening feeling. I drop my camera, and I land very hard on the ground. Right away, my left knee starts bleeding and swelling up. Hurts like the dickens.

Rudolf climbs down from his tree, takes off his shirt, and tears off some strips of cloth.

"Gottfried," he jokes, "You see how much I love you? Look, here's the shirt off my back."

"Very funny."

He ties some pieces of his shirt around my knee and helps me to get up. Gets his arm around my waist. I get my arm around his waist to lean on him.

"Pick up my camera," I say.

"It's broken," he says. "Leave it."

"No! I can fix it! Don't leave it!"

He shakes his head, but he scoops it up.

When we get back to the hostel, the manager tells a maid to come with a pan of warm water and some soap and bandages. She's pretty rough, cleaning me up. Mostly what I'm thinking is two things—this hurts bad, and she should shave off that mustache of hers.

Then the manager pats my back. "You'll be fine, Fritz," he says.

I'm confused for a second, because I completely forgot Rudolf told him we are Fritz and Willie Bremen. Then the schmuck roughs up my hair.

"Strong boy like you," he says. "Good Aryan stock. You'll be fine!"

"Goddamn right!" Rudolf laughs.

Me, I look the other way. My knee hurts like hell, and all I want is to get this night over with and get out of this goddamn place.

I'm not hungry for supper, and I tell Rudolf we shouldn't go out again, but he ignores me and goes out.

"Relax," he says. "Keep your leg up. I want to go out, have a little fun."

He says he'll come back soon, but he doesn't. He's gone half the night. I don't like it. Why did he have to go out? Just to prove he can? What if something happens?

Finally, I fall asleep, but it's a very light sleep.

When he gets back, he slams the door and throws up on the floor. He's drunk.

"Where the hell have you been?"

"G'night," he mumbles.

He lies down—maybe he falls down—on his bed and starts snoring right away, which keeps me up the rest of the night. Next morning, he's got a terrible headache, which serves him right.

We get dressed and check out, which is a relief. We go out to find some coffee and rolls for breakfast. It's a nice morning, so we sit down on a bench in a park. The sunshine feels good. After a while, we both feel better. My knee is still sore, but I can walk.

"Best thing to do now," Rudolf says, "is catch a bus to St. Gallen."

This, he says, is according to some guys he met last night in town.

"What guys?"

"Some guys who know what's what."

He says he played a couple games of cards with these guys, and this is what they told him. He takes a sip of coffee, pulls out a new pack of cigarettes and some matches.

"Hey," I say. "American cigarettes?"

"Yah. I won them," he says. "Want one?"

We smoke. Then he reaches into his pocket again and takes out some Austrian schillings. "Here," he says. "You keep them for us."

Now, I'm never surprised if Rudolf finds himself a little card game. I like to play cards too, but I don't like to gamble the way he does. I hate to lose—that's why. But my little brother, he loves to gamble, win or lose, and anyhow, he usually wins. He's very lucky at cards.

When Papa came home from the war, that's when it started. Rudolf, Papa, and me—we would play skat. Mama thought it might help calm Papa down. It didn't, though, because Papa hated to lose, and Rudolf was very good from the beginning. He was only a little kid, but somehow he knew how to get the grand hands. He was always wanting to play for money too. It was only a little bit of money, but he always won. So after a few hands, Papa usually quit. Then Rudolf and I would take what he won and go into town to see a movie. We saw *Tarzan the Ape Man* three times on what he won from Papa.

Later on, we started playing other games. Rudolf was very good at all of them, especially pinochle and poker, which we learned from our school friends. In pinochle, he almost always got the most melds and tricks. In poker, nobody could bluff better than him. How he knows all these things, I don't understand. I guess he was born knowing them.

We can use money right now, so I start to count what he gives me.

"Rudolf," I say. "You were out almost the whole night. Where's the rest?"

He gives me a sheepish look. "Gone."

"You spent it all?"

"I bought some identification papers," he says. "They were expensive."

"But couldn't you save *some*thing? How will we eat?"

"How's your knee?" he says.

Now all of a sudden, it's getting cloudy out—dark, black clouds. So we grab our stuff and head over to the bus station. Naturally, on the way, it starts raining cats and dogs, and we get soaking wet. On top of that, the goddamn bus is late.

Once we get on the bus, the ride goes pretty fast, and I'm glad to get to the Swiss border. But at the Swiss border, a guy in a uniform asks to see our papers. He's on the bus, walking up and down the aisle, and everybody is waving papers up in the air for him. He stops and looks at some papers, ignores other ones. When he gets to us, he holds out his hand, and Rudolf gives him the identification papers he bought. The guard is going nowhere fast. He's taking his time with us. He looks at the papers, squints like he can't read them, looks up at us, looks down at the papers, looks up at us again.

Finally, he says something. "Where are you two from?"

"Frankfurt," Rudolf says. "We're taking a little holiday."

"Willie and Fritz Bremen, huh?"

We nod.

For some reason or other, he's not buying it.

"Wait here," he says.

He walks to the front of the bus and gets off. My heart falls into my stomach. Rudolf gets up and goes to the front of the bus. He follows the guard off the bus, and I'm sitting there thinking, This is it. We're finished.

But after a few minutes, Rudolf comes back by himself.

My mouth is completely dry, but I manage to whisper, "What happened?"

Rudolf gives me his crooked little grin. "The rest of the money I won last night? Well, it wasn't all gone before, but it is now."

VI

RUDOLF

We get off the bus in St. Gallen, and now it's late in the after-noon. We don't know anybody, and naturally, we've got no money, and we're hungry. We have to get inside someplace tonight too, because it's colder here, close to the Alps. So Gottfried's idea is to see if there's a synagogue, and maybe we can get some help there.

This isn't a big town, and we get lucky. We find the synagogue, and we meet the rabbi. Short guy, big black beard, big belly. He's holding a big handkerchief, which he waves around and uses to wipe his face every couple of minutes.

So he's wiping, and we're talking. Telling him our story. When we get done, he says we're not unusual. Ever since Hitler took over

Germany, Switzerland has been getting thousands of refugees, mostly Jews. The Swiss higher-ups are afraid we're going to take jobs away from the Swiss people. Which is nuts. Why? One, there are hardly any Jews in Switzerland. And two, even if you add in thousands and thousands more Jews, ninety-nine percent of the people here *still* won't be Jews. Same thing is true in Germany. But none of this matters. It's easy to scare people when times are hard.

Then the rabbi says, "I'm afraid I have some more bad news. You can't get asylum here. You can't work here, and you can't stay here. You can only stay long enough to find someplace else to go. So most refugees are having to turn around and go back to Germany."

"But we can't go back there," Gottfried says. "They'll kill us."

The rabbi nods. "I understand, but what can I do?"

"So," I say, "you can't help us?"

"Not really," he says. "But go over to Basel anyway and talk to the people at the at the Swiss Federation of Jewish Communities."

He takes out a piece of paper and a pencil. Writes everything down, gives Gottfried the address. Then he tells us this is a group which has organized to help refugees, so maybe they can help us.

Well, Gottfried and I are very surprised by what the rabbi tells us. Disappointed too. We thought we could stay in Switzerland either until we could safely go back to Germany or if not, until we could go to the United States. We thought Switzerland was supposed to be neutral. Not antisemitic either. Turns out we were wrong all the way around. There are Nazis everywhere around here. Winning elections, making speeches, putting money in the Swiss banks. And on top of that, Switzerland is the Nazis' all-time favorite holiday place.

For some reason or other, Gottfried decides to tell the rabbi what a beautiful building this is. Don't know why he's got to do this. It only means this rabbi's going to blab our ears off. Which he does. Famous building, famous architects, blah-blah-blah-blah. Then he's got to tell us about other buildings here. Who gives a damn? A building is a building. Once you see it, you see it. But not Gottfried. He's got to hear all about every little bitty detail and take a lot of boring pictures.

But maybe the rabbi likes us after all this blabbing, because now he decides we can sleep inside here if we want, and he even gives Gottfried a map and a few francs for our bus tickets to Basel. So that night, we sleep on a rug on the shul floor. We don't get much sleep, but it's better than what we get later on.

Next morning, we're heading out when we see a little shop selling fabrics and embroidery. Pretty blonde girl standing at the door. Reminds us of Clare. When we were little, Clare looked soft and beautiful like this girl. She had blue eyes and blonde hair, and she smelled sweet, which this girl does too. Maybe we're missing Clare, so we start talking to the pretty girl, and we buy a couple of fancy handkerchiefs from her for Clare and Mama. The blonde girl, she sews their initials on: "CS" for Clare Simon, which is her married name. And "EK" for Mama. But when or if we'll ever see Clare and Mama again, who knows?

When we get done, Gottfried takes out the map the rabbi gave him. It says Basel is maybe one hundred-seventy kilometers away. Gottfried wants to walk and try to get rides to save money. When we start out, it's already the middle of the afternoon. We stick out our thumbs, but we don't get any rides, and by sunset, we're still no place. We pass by trees and trees and trees. We walk through little rolling hills and see cows and fields. Looks to us like the only stuff they grow out here is flax and hemp, which we can't eat.

About sunset, we stop at a farmhouse and knock on the door. We can see the farmer's wife inside, but she goes into a back room. Maybe she's scared of us. Maybe her husband's gone. Who the hell knows? Meantime, my stomach's growling, and seeing all this flax and hemp reminds me of something Siegfried once told us.

He told us during the war, his class in school used to go inside the forest and take the leaves off the trees, and the teachers would grind them up for the kids to eat. They called this "spinach." Siegfried said they also took dirt—clay—and mixed it with a little water, rolled it out on a big table, and made it into "noodles." While he was telling us about this, Siegfried made disgusting sounds to show us how eating these things made him vomit. After I think about this story, I'm not hungry anymore.

We keep walking, and it's not too long before we find another farm. Windows closed, curtains closed, all dark inside. But we see a barn. The door is falling off, and the whole thing looks like it's falling apart. But right now, it's getting dark, and it feels like rain. Also, there's no moon, no stars. We can't keep walking when we can't see, right? And if it rains, it's going to be bad. We already found that out when we crossed from Germany into Austria. Besides, we're both tired out.

So what we do is go inside the barn and lie down on the dirt floor with our jackets under our heads. There's no hayloft, nothing. All they've got in there is a couple of stalls. Two cows in one of them, an old horse in the other one. Lying up against a wall, we see some hoes, shovels, and other junk. Filthy place. Cold too. And the stink!

"Whoo-wee," I say.

"Goddamn cows," Gottfried says. Then he cuts a loud one. "I'll show them!"

The horse in here, he's not our friend. Doesn't like company. Stomps his feet, snorts, sneezes. And between his racket and the cows farting, it's a long, long night. On top of that, it pours all night. And naturally, the roof leaks.

When morning finally comes, our stomachs are growling out loud. But there's no place to get breakfast. There aren't too many farms out here, and the roads look mostly empty, so all we can do is keep walking.

Then Gottfried starts talking about food.

"Do you remember during the war when the French prisoners got packages from home?"

"Not really," I say. "All I remember is sitting on their laps. Didn't they sing to us?"

"Yah, but remember when they got packages from home, like hard rolls and chocolates? They soaked the rolls in warm water, squeezed out the water, and then cut them open and filled them up with shavings from the chocolates."

"Don't talk about food, Gottfried."

"See, they knew we were hungry, so they shared what they had with us."

"Don't talk about food, goddamn it."

"That chocolate was delicious. They always gave extra to Clare too. But she earned it, haha!"

"Shut up, will you?"

He likes to drive me crazy.

Finally, about noon, we see a farmer working in a field. Hard-looking guy in overalls and a beret, pushing a hand plow. This guy looks miserable. Hot and tired, with sweat rolling down his face. We come up to him slow. We look like bums, and we don't want to scare him. We stink pretty bad too. But to tell the truth, he doesn't smell like a bed of roses himself.

When he sees us, he stops working. Takes a dirty rag out of his pocket, wipes the sweat off his face. Tall guy, maybe forty or so. Strong looking. Red, wrinkled face, close-set eyes, nose like a hatchet. Uses his rag again. Blows his nose. Sticks the rag back in his overalls pocket. He looks us over, looks us up and down.

Finally, he says, "Where are you boys from?"

I say, "We're on holiday. From our school in Munich."

He considers this, then shakes his head. "You don't fool me. I see plenty of guys like you. Refugees, right?"

We turn around and start walking off. But then the farmer yells after us, "Hey, boys! I don't give a damn who you are. Hey! You're hungry, aren't you?"

We stop and watch as he waves a tired arm over an acre or so of dirt. He spits on the ground.

"Listen, I could use some help, boys. Can't pay you, but I can give you some food, let you clean up."

Gottfried whispers to me, "What if he reports us? We better go."

I look the guy over. "Nah," I say. "I'm not worried."

Gottfried doesn't say anything.

We stay where we are, and the farmer walks up to us.

Gottfried isn't looking at him. He spots a fancy farm machine sitting idly in the field.

"Wow!" he says. "That's a beautiful rototiller." He looks at the farmer. "Why aren't you using it?"

"Can't," says the farmer disgustedly. "She's brand new too. Just got her last month. She was working fine when she came, but now she's quit on me."

"Can I take a look?" Gottfried asks.

"Wish you would," the farmer says.

So Gottfried walks over. He whistles. "Wow! A Simar tiller. Five horsepower." Looks up at the farmer. "Must have cost plenty."

"No kidding," says the farmer. He spits on the ground. "Good for nothing too."

Well, Gottfried gets interested. He fools around a minute and gets the thing to start up. Then he messes around with this and that, and after a few minutes, he says, "See, it should have two forward speeds, but one of them isn't working like it should." He turns off the machine. Considers a minute or so.

"If you have some tools, maybe I can fix it," he says.

The farmer is grinning like he just saw Jesus.

Then I say, "Look, my brother and I could use a place to stay tonight and some food and a wash. If he fixes this thing, can you give that to us?"

"You bet," the farmer says. "Tell me what tools you need. I'll get them."

Gottfried tells him, and he goes off.

I say to Gottfried, "You ever see this kind of machine before?"

"You kidding?" he says. "This is a brand-new tiller, very expensive too. I'm surprised to see it at a place like this."

I have to hand it to my brother. He never saw this thing before, but he's thinking, So what? It's a machine, right? Doesn't it have parts? Don't they move?

So pretty soon, the farmer comes back with some tools and says, "The wife made a nice lunch inside. Come and get something to eat first."

When we go in the house, the farmer's wife gets a whiff of us and excuses herself, leaves the room. Can't blame her, but hell, who cares? We're getting coffee and a good meal—salad, sauerkraut, potatoes. She even baked *basler leckerli*, which are delicious cookies with honey.

We're feeling good now, so after lunch Gottfried goes to work on the guy's tiller. Turns out it's not such a snap job. Takes him all afternoon. First couple of hours, he's got to look at it, turn it this way, turn it that way. Takes all three of us to move it, and we sweat like pigs doing it. The goddamn thing weighs as much as the three of us put together. Also, Gottfried wants tools the guy doesn't have. He tells us it's going to take him a lot longer without them. For the next few hours, he does a lot of cussing and farting.

There's nothing I can do though. So I sit down under a tree, close my eyes, take it easy. I'm feeling good. Nice breeze, nice day, puffy little clouds, blue sky. Little song running through my head which we used to like…"Lustig ist das Zegerunerleben, Far-ia, far-ia, ho…" It means, "Happy is the gypsy's life…"

That's us right now. Gypsies.

Finally, maybe four, five hours later, my brother gets the machine to work. The farmer is so happy he gives us both big hugs.

Kind of surprises me. First time a man ever hugged me. And for no reason too. What did I do? Nothing.

We get a washtub and hot water and towels to clean up with. Then we go inside to eat another delicious meal. This time the farmer's wife stays in the room. Afterward, she offers to wash our clothes. Then she hangs them on a line outside and gives us warm blankets to wrap ourselves up. We go to their barn to sleep, but this barn isn't too bad. Clean straw—and no cows or horses. Just some little mice rushing around and waking us up now and then.

The next morning, we're feeling much better. We're singing and walking, and finally, we see some trucks. We catch a ride, walk some more, ride some more. Takes us the rest of the day, but we finally get into Basel around sunset.

VII

GOTTFRIED

When we get into Basel, it's the Sabbath again. So I tell Rudolf, "Let's find a shul," which we do. It's a big, beautiful synagogue— two stories with onion domes on the roof and round windows at the bases of the domes. We get a beautiful surprise in there too. During the services, there's a premier *hazzan*—a very famous cantor. He's known in Germany and everywhere else, and he's also an opera singer.

Me, I always loved opera. We used to hear it on our first radio, which Siegfried bought for us in Munich. We listened to this radio for hours, no matter what was on it. See, it was something new to hear human voices coming from a box. Of course, I had to figure out how it worked, so I looked around for radios to take apart. One time, I fixed a broken radio and gave it to Clare so she could listen to opera in her room. She wanted to be an opera singer in the worst way.

Sometimes, Clare saved enough sewing money to go to the opera theater in Giessen, and one time she took me along to see *Der Singend Teufel* by Franz Schrecker, which was an opera she loved. The night we went, SA men were standing outside the opera house, shouting at people not to go in, because Franz Schrecker was Jewish. But most people went in anyway. See, this was before Hitler took over, so most people weren't too afraid of Nazis yet.

During the services at the shul in Basel, I think about Clare. Is she happy with her fisherman in New York? I hope so. Will we ever see each other again?

After the services, we find the rabbi and tell him our story, and he listens. Seems like there are already quite a few refugees in Basel and all around here, and he knows of a place we can stay—but only for one month. It's a house across the border in Mulhouse, France. So that's where we go the next day.

The Ullman house is a large half-timbered home, which is owned by a rich woman—a German Jew who came to Switzerland many years ago. She lived here until her husband died. Then she moved to Basel and rented the house to other people. But when Hitler took over in Germany, the old lady decided to use her old house for German refugees. She doesn't charge refugees to stay here, but everybody has to help with chores, and nobody can stay more than a month.

Right now, about twenty of us are staying at Mrs. Ullman's house, and we're from all over Germany—Berlin, Hapsberg, Heidelberg, Munich, Frankfurt, Hamburg. Most of us are Jewish, but not all of us. For instance, we meet a German skier here, by the name of Hannes. He's a friend of the famous American skier, Dick Durrance, who lived in Germany before Hitler took over. Hannes says he hates the Nazis, and all he wants is to go to America to teach skiing.

We also meet a very nice woman, a social worker. She left Berlin because the Nazis wouldn't let her work with handicapped children anymore. The Nazis came into the place where she worked and kicked everybody out. They put the handicapped children into a van, and when she objected, they told her they had the parents' permission, and they would arrest her if she argued. So she went home, packed up, and left. She's waiting for money from her brother, and when it comes, she's going to England.

We also meet a couple of professors and a medical doctor. All these guys are Jewish. The Nazis fired them in April. The doctor, he's very depressed. His wife and kids are still in Berlin. She isn't Jewish, and neither are their children, and they want to stay in Berlin. The poor doctor sits around with his head in his hands all day.

Over and over, we hear sad stories like these. We also hear a lot of people say the Nazis are only a passing fancy—thugs, degenerates, can't last, won't last. Some Jews we meet, they say they're going back to Germany as soon as things calm down.

But a few Jews here are strong Zionists, who want to go to Palestine. At home, most Jews didn't believe in Zionism. We sure didn't. Here in Mulhouse, we have long talks with one of these

Zionists—a guy our age by the name of Sol. He's a big shot in the Zionist Federation, which is a large Jewish outfit. They think Jews shouldn't live in Germany, because Palestine is the country God gave us.

"That's crazy," I say. "We're German citizens. Our father fought for Germany in the war. He got an Iron Cross. How can you say Germany isn't our country?"

"Then why are you here? Why don't you go back to Germany?"

"Well," Rudolf says, "right now, there's a problem. But after the Nazis leave, maybe we will."

Sol laughs. "After the Nazis, there will be others like them. There always have been. Besides, the Nazis aren't going anywhere soon. And if Hitler gets his way, there won't be any Jews in Germany or anyplace else in Europe. Didn't you read *Mein Kampf*?"

We hadn't read it.

Sol tells us the German Zionists have a new deal with the Nazis. He says German Jews can pay to go to Palestine on ships with kosher food and Nazi crews. We think he's nuts. We hear all kinds of stories here. How much is true, who knows?

To stay at the Ullman house, we have to do chores. We take turns peeling potatoes, cooking, cleaning. They also have a lot of rules. Too many, if you ask me. We're supposed to write down the times we come and go and tell them where we're going. Men and women are not allowed in the same room. We're not supposed to stay out late at night. And so on and so on.

Gottfried (front), Rudolf
Summer 1933 Mulhouse, France

Rudolf and I do our chores, but otherwise, we don't pay much attention to their rules. Curfews, for instance, we ignore. We use the windows to come in and out whenever we want. There are quite a few girls at this place, and they like to have a good time. One that I like very much is a teacher from Berlin. A *shikse*—not Jewish. Maybe about five years older than me. From her, I learn the ropes.

Rudolf also has a shikse girlfriend by the name of Karolin. I remember her name, because Karolin was the name of my father's mother. She was a beautiful woman, my grandmother. Only eighteen years old when she died having my dad and his twin brother. Anyhow, Rudolf's Karolin, she's our age, and she's from Munich. Very pretty in the face, and tall like a model—almost as tall as my brother. She tells Rudolf some Nazis were trying to have their way with her. I don't know if they did or not, but that's why she left.

One rule of the Ullman house, we can't ignore. We can only stay here for a month. More refugees keep coming, and everybody here has to find another place to go. Us too. Every morning, we go into Basel to talk to people at the Swiss Federation of Jewish Communities.

The first time we tell them our story, they give us ten Swiss francs and thank us for our information. They tell us to come back and see them. We want them to think about us, not to forget about us. So we go back every day. This way, maybe some guy on the committee will find a place for us to stay until we can figure out how to get to the United States. We don't like living where anybody can kick us out anytime.

Gottfried and Rudolf
Summer 1933 Basel, Switzerland

On the Sabbath, we go to shul with a couple of other Jewish boys. The second week, we meet the Haas family, the cousins Mama told us about. They used to have a kosher butcher shop in Zwesten, so of course, they know our Uncle Josef. Anyhow, some years ago, they moved to Basel with their son, David. They opened up a hostel and a butcher shop, and they made good money here. Then David married a Jewish girl, who also came from Zwesten. She went to Germany to visit Zwesten soon after we came to Basel. She would like to move back to Zwesten, because she is pregnant and her parents still live there.

Left to right: Rudolf, David Haas, Gottfried, ?
1934 Mulhouse, France

David says we can come and stay with him, but his house is small, and he has his parents there, so we say no. He also offers us a room in his family's hostel, but I tell Rudolf we can't stay there either. See, their hostel happens to be popular with the Nazi Hitlerjugend. Me, I've had enough of Hitlerjugend. But David doesn't care if they stay there. He says he's happy to take their money.

For Rudolf and me, money is getting to be a big problem, and naturally, we don't want to ask David for help. Rudolf finds some card games and gets us some money this way, but nothing regular. Then one of his buddies, by the name of Fritz, tells Rudolf he knows a way for us to make a little steady money.

Now, this Fritz is an ex-cop, a tough guy inside and out. Lifts weights. One time, when Rudolf and Fritz got drunk, I saw Fritz pick up Rudolf like a rag doll. Fritz, he's a brawler too, always getting in fights. But Rudolf says he's good protection, and the way Rudolf likes gambling, I guess he can use protection. Fritz also has a good nose for business, but he's more Rudolf's buddy than mine.

Anyhow, Fritz finds us a little deal here in Mulhouse. It seems like some Swiss people like French bakery stuff and French coffee. But some people in Basel don't like to go to Mulhouse for some reason or other. Fritz tells us we can buy this stuff in Mulhouse, then bring it to Basel and give it to him, and he'll sell it in Basel for much more than we pay for it. We can split the profits with him, he says.

"Why does he need us?" I ask Rudolf. "He can do all that without our help."

"Yah, he does it," Rudolf says. "But he has more customers than he can handle on his own. Anyhow, he wants to help us out. He knows we need the money."

"But what if we get caught?"

"So what? We leave. Look, we can't stay here forever anyway."

"What if they turn us over to the Germans?"

"Fritz says they won't. He says the Swiss like to give refugees a chance to leave on their own. If they catch you, they give you twenty-four hours to get out. If you don't leave, then it's trouble."

Me, I don't like to count on Rudolf's friends. He has two other buddies like Fritz here—Pacher and Justus. This Pacher, he's an odd duck. He never talks. Rudolf says he's just quiet, but to me he seems too quiet. He stares at people and doesn't talk to them. Justus, though, is the complete opposite. Nobody can get a word in edgewise around him. But at least I have things in common with Justus. He likes a good joke, likes to play around with girls. Sometimes, when Rudolf is busy, Justus and I get a couple of girls and go over to Basel or Zurich to go dancing.

Anyhow, I figure I better check up on what Rudolf's friends tell him, so a couple of days later, I ask our cousin David about this smuggling business. He tells me a lot of refugees do some smuggling. He says most people don't pay too much attention. David says right now, if they catch you, they do give you a day to get out.

So when I hear this, I tell Rudolf, "Okay, let's do it," and Rudolf, Fritz, and I start our little smuggling business. We don't make much, but it's better than nothing, and it's steady money.

But except for visiting the Jewish agency every day and the little work we have, there's not much to do. So one day, we go and visit Zurich with David. The weather is very good, so David drives us to see the Sihtal river valley, and we stop and walk around Langnau am Albis, a small town on the slopes of the Albis Mountains. We leave the car and go for a short hike. We're all in good spirits. We get an hour's rest in the high mountain air, let the sun shine on us.

We're relaxing there when we hear a guy cussing in German. He keeps on cussing, getting louder and louder. So we get up and walk down onto the road to see what's going on. We see a car parked on the right-hand side of the road, and not just any car. A beautiful 1933 Rolls-Royce Phantom II. It's the best Rolls-Royce ever made. With a chauffeur in a uniform and man standing next to him, cussing a blue streak.

This guy, he has his wife and two kids in the back seat, but he's cussing anyhow. I'm disgusted, hearing him cuss in front of his family. The poor guy he's cussing out, the chauffeur—he's almost in tears.

So we ask what's going on. Turns out, the chauffeur speaks English only, but lucky for everybody, David knows how to speak English. The chauffeur tells us he has a problem with the car, but he doesn't know what's wrong with it. But that's his job. He's supposed to know. Matter of fact, Rolls-Royce won't sell a Rolls-Royce unless you furnish a chauffeur, who knows what to do. This model is made to be driven by a chauffeur who knows how to fix problems.

Me, I'm very excited. I want to see this car close up, see the engine. Of course, Rudolf knows this. So Rudolf and I walk over to the German guy, and Rudolf introduces us as Fritz and Willie Bremen. This is something we do now all the time until we get to know somebody. Then Rudolf tells the German guy I know a few things about cars, so maybe I can help.

"Do you mind if I take a look?" I ask.

"Be my guest," he says.

So I check it out, and the car is magnificent inside and out. The problem turns out to be something very simple in the carburetor, so I fix it.

The owner, by the name of Schmidt, is very happy. He calms down, gets very friendly. Tells us he's here on holiday with his family, and he invites me to drive him back to Zurich. What a pleasure for me! But he makes the poor chauffeur go back with Rudolf and David.

When we get into Zurich, Schmidt says he would like to take me out for lunch. We take his wife and kids to a hotel, and Schmidt directs me to a famous beer hall, the Zeughauskeller.

This place used to be an armory. There are big stone pillars, heavy wood beams on the ceiling, weapons, armor, oil paintings. Very impressive. We order some sausages and beers. The sausages taste good, but they can keep their wheat beer. During our meal, we talk. We talk a little about his Rolls-Royce. He tells me he also used to invest in Mercedes-Benz automobiles.

"Yah," I tell him. "I was very disappointed when they decided to get out of German motor racing."

" So was I," he says. "But things are getting better, so they'll be getting back into it again. Maybe even next year."

"Maybe Caracciola will come back and race," I say. "He's getting old though."

He nods. "Tell me, where did a young man like you learn so much about automobiles?"

I tell him to help support my family, I quit school and went to work for Opel. "That's how I learned," I say. "But what I would really like to learn is how to fly."

"You should," he says. "And you should fly the new airplanes. Don't bother with the zeppelins. You won't like flying them. They're too slow for you." He smiles. "I know that personally—from riding in the Graf Zeppelin."

"No kidding?" I say. "I would love to ride in the Graf Zeppelin one day. As a matter of fact, I saw the Graf Zeppelin land in Friedrichshafen not long ago."

"In May?" he says. "I was there. I was one of the passengers on that flight."

Our lunch is very pleasant. We don't talk about politics—only about cars, planes, and zeppelins. And I'm thinking, This guy and me—we have a lot in common. I like him very much, and I think he likes me too, because after lunch, he offers me a real treat.

"How would you like to go for a little ride outside of town? You can see how my Rolls *really* drives."

Naturally, I would love this! So we get in the car, and I drive, and he sits there and relaxes.

"Can I go faster?"

"Certainly," he says. "Go as fast as you like."

I take the car almost to the limit, which is close to a hundred sixty kilometers per mile. This car is a dream. Rides as smooth as a baby's tush. Finally, we drive back into Zurich.

When we get into town, Schmidt says, "I like you, young man. I would like to send you to England, to Rolls-Royce, so they can give you their training. And then you can drive my car for me and be my chauffeur."

"I wish I could," I say. "But I can't. See, my brother and I have to stay together. We're trying to get to the United States."

"Why?"

"Our family is over there, and right now, we're refugees."

Schmidt, he suddenly clamps his mouth shut. He gets completely quiet. He stares hard at me. His eyeballs look like they're about to pop out of his head.

I feel a sudden shiver go straight down my back.

He almost whispers, "You're a goddamn Jew?"

Now I'm scared. This guy is suddenly like another person. The hate in the air—I can almost touch it. He gets completely red in the face, and before I know what's happening, he's shouting at the top of his lungs.

"Goddamn you! Stop the car, you swine! Stop the car right now!"

I'm shaking. I pull over, and as I turn off the ignition, he suddenly leans over and spits at me.

"Get out of my car, you piece of filth!"

I wipe off my face with the back of my hand. I get out and slam the door, and I start running as fast as I can.

Behind me, I hear his car doors banging and his engine turning over. I look back and see him in the driver's seat, and he's coming after me. I can't believe it. This guy is trying to run me down in broad daylight in the middle of Zurich.

I jump off the street and onto a sidewalk, where I trip and fall flat on my face. Schmidt stops the car, rolls down the window, leans out, and screams, "You goddamn dirty Jew!"

Then he sticks his head back inside the car. To me, it looks like he's trying to reach for something. I'm sure he has a gun in there, and when he finds it, he's going to shoot me.

Now I'm tasting my own blood. I feel my forehead and my nose, and I'm bleeding very bad. But somehow, I manage to pick myself up. By this time, people up and down the street are watching what's happening. A couple of them look shocked, but nobody makes a move. Nobody says a word.

Schmidt sticks his head out the car window again. His face is all hot and twisted, but if he has a gun, he doesn't show it—maybe because he can also see how people on the street are watching us. But he leans out the window as far as he can and shouts again.

"You filthy Jew! Soon *we* will take over, and all of you will go straight to hell!" Then he shrieks, "Heil Hitler!" at the top of his lungs, and he speeds off.

This whole thing probably takes no more than a minute or two, but to me, it feels like time has stopped completely. My heart is beating so hard I can't hear myself think.

People start moving again on the street. A man comes up to me and asks if I'm all right. Gives me his handkerchief to hold on my bleeding face. Two women come up and take my arms. Tell me to come with them inside a little restaurant. They talk to somebody, and soon I'm sitting down at a back table, and somebody is washing my face with soap and water. Somebody puts a couple of bandages on my nose and forehead. Somebody gets me a warm roll and some hot coffee.

"Thank you," I say to them. "Thank you." But the whole time, I can't stop shaking.

I stay in the café for a long time. Finally, I step outside. I walk to the bus station and catch a bus back to Mulhouse.

I'm thinking, What if Schmidt comes after us? In my mind, I go back over everything I said to him. What did I tell Schmidt about us? Not much, thank God. He doesn't know where we're staying, and I remember he doesn't know my name. The only name I gave him was Fritz Bremen. Thank God for that.

The first person I see when I get back is Pacher. He stares at me like he always stares at people. Then he says, "What the hell happened to you?"

It's more words than he's ever said to me before, so I tell him what happened.

He shakes his head. "Goddamn Nazis. You okay?"

I nod. "I'm not hurt bad," I say. "It was goddamned scary, but I'm okay."

Pacher looks at me a minute. He shakes his head. "No place is safe from those bastards."

He's right, but it's still hard to believe I almost got killed by a goddamn Nazi on a beautiful day in Switzerland. The whole world is going to hell.

I'm a little cheered up by Pacher, though. At least he's talking to me for a change. He even seems sympathetic. Maybe he's okay after all.

A few days later, David Haas' wife comes back from Germany. She tells us about a Jewish cattle dealer the Nazis beat to death.

"But that happened six months ago," she says, and it's been peaceful since then."

"What about Uncle Josef? Is he all right?" I ask.

"He's fine," she says. "The Nazis keep trying to get people to stop trading with Jews, but most people in Zwesten—they're still doing it. Things are definitely getting better."

But David isn't convinced, and he isn't ready to move to Zwesten. He tells her more people are leaving Germany than are going back, because the Nazis are passing one new law after another against Jewish people.

We've now been at the Ullman house for one month, which is the longest we're allowed to stay. A lot of people who were here when we came have already gone. Sol, the Zionist we argued with, got passage on a ship to Palestine. Our girlfriends are gone too. They decided to go to Paris. Fritz is also in Paris now. He told Rudolf he couldn't pass up a good business proposition there.

"What was it?" I ask Rudolf.

"He didn't say, and I didn't ask. Maybe it's not kosher."

The committee finally gives us a little good news. They have found some work for us as farmhands, but it's temporary—only until after the fall harvest. Then we're supposed to leave the country. The farm is near Mulhouse in the little town of Lauterbach. We'll get beds, food, a small salary, and weekends off. Sounds good to us. We pack up our rucksacks and walk to the farm. We figure we can keep doing a little smuggling too if we want to—maybe on weekends. But right now, it feels good to have any kind of steady work, even if it's only temporary, and even if we have no idea where to go from here.

Left to right: Henri,
Rudolf (on fence), Marie
1934 Lauterbach, France

VIII
RUDOLF

We end up in Mulhouse and Lauterbach in the area of
Alsace-Lorraine in France, which used to belong to Germany
before the world war. Then it came back again to France, but
there's fighting over it all the time. The people here speak both
French and German. Same thing in Switzerland too. French, we
don't speak yet. But the friends we make—they're trying to teach
us. Comes easy to Gottfried, not so easy to me. Reading, writing—these things don't come easy to me either. Numbers are a
different story.

The Jewish agency gets us jobs on a nice French farm, but we're
still illegal here. And the French government—they're not too dif-

ferent from the Swiss government. Nobody is exactly welcoming us with open arms. But still, the French people like to hire us. Why? One, they can pay us practically nothing, because we're illegals. And two, illegals can't complain, because nobody's listening.

So we take the farm jobs, and we're glad to have them, but the truth is, we don't know any more about farming than we do about speaking French. We told the agency we had worked on our uncle's farm in Zwesten, but we didn't tell them what we had done there, which wasn't much. We were just stupid little kids. But anyhow, it doesn't take Henri Ladner too long to figure out Gottfried and I are no farmhands. Too soft. Henri, though, is a good guy—a *mensch*. He decides to gives us a chance.

So we get up at four o'clock in the morning and milk the cows. Which seems easy the first few minutes, but it's not so easy. It's a lot of work. Then we feed the chickens and the pigs, clean up their messes, take the sheep out to the pasture, clean out the barn, brush the horses, saddle the horses, pump the water out of the well, chop up the wood.

At six o'clock in the morning, we head into Mulhouse, because the Ladners own a little café there, and it is popular with farm workers in the area. We work inside this café for two hours, making coffee and breakfast for the workers. Serve them cognac too. All of them need their morning cognac. But we don't eat there ourselves. We clean up the café, close it up, and then go back to the farm. Out to the fields.

And then the farmer's wife with her little daughter—they come out with the baskets, with the wine, with the breakfast. Breakfast is a big French bread and sausages and wine. It's always a big breakfast. And then we work through the whole day, pitching hay, putting hay on the wagons. At lunch, another bottle of wine, sausages, cheese, and meats. At sundown, we quit. Then Gottfried and I clean up, and we eat some supper out in the barn. Sleep there too, up on a hayloft. It's okay up there. We have blankets. And at night, we fall asleep fast. Maybe it's not a hotel, but we get used to it. Used to all the smells there. Our own too. Which is not so sweet.

After a couple of months at the Ladner farm, Gottfried and I have muscles we never knew we had. It's hard work, but I like it. Gottfried doesn't, though. He says it doesn't pay enough. He also thinks the days last too long, because he doesn't have enough time to read his books and study his French, which he loves to do.

One day at the café, Gottfried hears about a job opening for a fishmonger. Packaging and selling buckling, which is a kind of smoked herring fish. To sell them, he would get to drive a car. So he takes this job, and soon he's making more money and working less than me, and he's driving around the countryside, meeting people. Taking plenty of pictures too. But the truth is, I don't care. Why? One, I can't stand fish. And two, I like working in the fresh air. Feels very good to me.

When Gottfried gets his new job, he starts renting a little apartment in Mulhouse, the town where they keep the fish. He has to get up early, take the fish out of the barrels where they get smoked, hang them up on hooks, unhang them from hooks, then package them up. Then he has to drag the packages of fish from town to town to sell fish all day long. This doesn't give him time to come out to the farm on weekdays. I miss him, but I don't want a job like his.

On Saturdays, we keep doing our smuggling. Then on Saturday nights, I stay with Gottfried in Mulhouse. Sometimes we go over to Basel, sometimes to Zurich. Gottfried and I have plenty of fun on Saturday nights. There are always girls around. They come and go, come and go. Refugees plus French girls teaching us French, showing us a good time. I have regular pinochle and poker games in Mulhouse too. To sleep, I go to Gottfried's place. I don't come back to the farm until Sunday nights.

Henri Ladner, the farmer I'm working for, is a big, strong guy in his thirties. Suntanned, naturally. Dirty-blond hair, blue eyes, white teeth. Looks to me like a perfect Aryan, but he's no fascist. It seems Henri and his buddies hate the Nazis. They have no use for Herr Adolf Hitler. Henri spits on the ground when anybody says the führer's name. Sometimes Henri's friends say "Adolf Hitler" just to get Henri to spit on the ground.

Henri and I, we get to be good buddies. Like I said, he's a mensch—a very good man. We work hard, but we always work together. He's the boss, but he doesn't put on high-and-mighty airs. I learn a lot from Henri and the way he treats the people who work for him.

Henri's got a wonderful family too. He grew up on a farm near here, and sometimes his parents come over to play with their grandkids. The Ladners have three boys and a girl. But they're all under twelve years old, so they're not big enough to help out much. Ladner's wife, Marie, is short and round. Round face too. Always laughing and singing.

Henri, Marie, and the kids like having me there. The kids call me Oncle Rudi and laugh at my French. Little by little, I learn to speak it. It's hard, but at least I can get by.

After a couple of months, I don't sleep in the barn anymore. The Ladners take me into their house just like a son. I share a room with the boys. Marie and Henri Ladner. Beautiful people. Second time now I've been this lucky to be helped by good Christian people. I work all day in their fields, but at night I go to their home. And it's my home too. We—all of us—sit at home together. And I'm like one of the family.

Nights, after dinner, the kids ask me questions about my uncle's farm in Zwesten. So I tell them stories. Some of them might even be true. For instance, I tell them our Uncle Josef grows cattle, which he calls kosher pigs. When they get big and fat, he takes them to his friend, the kosher butcher, who kills them kosher style. This is something new to the Ladners—what kosher is, how they kill the animals. So I tell them the whats and the hows.

"It's quicker, and it doesn't hurt the animal as much."

But the Ladner boys, they're boys, right? I have to tell them all the gory details, like how the knife slices the jugular vein and so on. I've got to give a little demonstration with my finger sliding across my throat. I tell them how they chopped up the dead cows and hung up the pieces on hooks. Boys, they like to hear these things. But not the little girl. She claps her hands over her ears and shakes her head. She doesn't like gory stuff. So I have to tell a different story. Like how, every summer for a few years, Uncle Josef gave us the job of making the calves come back to the barn. We put ropes on their necks, but they were very stubborn. They wouldn't walk. Stupid too, I guess. One of the calves kicked me, so I kicked him back. Surprise, huh? But if I sang a lullaby to this calf, he would come along with me.

But mostly, I tell my stories to the boys. They love my story about when we found a cat in a puddle. Skinny, all dirty, and wet. We took the cat and put it in the oven to dry off. Turned on the heat. Then our aunt came home.

She sniffed and said, "What's stinking up my house?"

Then she opened the door to the oven, and out jumped the cat. And my aunt started screaming, so naturally, Uncle Josef came running. Now, my uncle, he was very strict but also good natured. He got a big kick out of seeing that cat run off and seeing my aunt pointing to the oven and screaming.

The two boys, they like this story a lot, naturally. But Marie warns them they better not try anything like this here.

Uncle Josef didn't always think we were so funny though. He caught us slicing off pieces of sausage in his smoking room one time. And he caught us poking holes into new-laid eggs, which we liked to drink raw, right out of the shell. Those times, he didn't laugh. He had a heavy leather belt, which he kept hanging up on a hook, and he took that belt down. Smacked us pretty good with his belt, let me tell you. Big, strong man too. We didn't go inside his smoking room or take eggs out of his henhouse after this.

Now the Ladner boys, they don't like this story. But I tell it to them anyhow, mostly so they will listen to Henri and Marie when they say don't do something. But the truth is, I never see Henri or Marie hit their kids, no matter what. This was something completely new for me. The Ladners don't hit the kids, and the kids say their teachers hardly ever hit them either.

In Giessen, our parents hit, and our teachers hit. With parents, there was usually a reason. But not with teachers. They could hit for any reason or no reason, and that's what they did. Sadistic, no? I had one teacher who smacked the side of my head or pulled my ear every time he passed me. He liked to hit me. I could be sitting and minding my own business, and suddenly, out of nowhere—bam! If I cried, he would make me stand up, and he would call me a baby in front of the other boys. Sometimes, he would tell the other boys to call me a baby until I stopped crying. So what did I do? I stopped crying. You get tough pretty quick that way.

I hated this teacher so much that one time, I decided to get even. I made a little slingshot with a pen and a rubber band, and I wadded up a hard little ball of paper. I waited until the bastard was standing with his back to me, looking out a window. Then I set off my slingshot, and my little paper ball smacked him so hard in the back of his head he howled. Boy, was I happy! But not for long, huh? He didn't see me do it, but somebody told him. So he made me stay after school, and when everybody else was gone, he closed the door and made me take down my pants. Then he took a cane— more like a very thin wooden stick, which bent like a whip—and he whipped me hard. He beat me on my back and on my butt and on my legs. But I never cried. I wouldn't give him the satisfaction.

Every day for a week, he did the same thing to me after school. I never said anything at home, but one day, Clare decided I was not walking too well, and she made me show her my back. She went screaming for Mama, and when Mama saw the terrible sores, she marched to the school and put a stop to the whippings. But I was always getting into trouble, so it happened again later on. It was better not to tell, right? Because when you did, the beatings got even worse the next time.

But that was then, and this is now. And here and now, they don't hit the kids, which is good. Because if anybody hit one of the Ladner kids, I might have to kill them.

I love these Ladner kids. They're the little brothers and sister I never had, huh? Sometimes I put them on my knee like my Uncle Josef used to do with us and bounce them up and down. I teach them the same little song he used to sing to us when he did this.

Hopp, hopp, hopp! Pferdchen lauf galopp!
Über stock und über steine,
aber brich dir nicht die beine, Immer im galopp!
Hopp, hopp, hopp, hopp, hopp! Pferdchen lauf galopp!

The song means something like this: "Hop, little horsey. Gallop over sticks and stones but don't break a leg." All kids love it.

Gottfried and I manage to live and work in Mulhouse and Lauterbach for more than a year. We learn French, live pretty well, and have fun too. We know we might have to leave suddenly one day, but right now, we stay put, and the longer we can stay, the better. Maybe things will change in Germany. If not, we can try to save enough money to get over to the United States.

But I guess we've been lucky a little too long. One day at work, Gottfried takes a herring off a hook. He's going to wrap it up and put it in a box, but he suddenly feels a stab on the palm of his right hand. It's a sharp, little fish bone, which he pulls out. It's not bleeding much, so he doesn't think about it again. But pretty soon, his right hand gets swollen and red. And after a couple of days, he's too sick to get out of bed. I don't find out about this until the fish boss finds him in bed and comes out to the farm.

Right away, Henri gets his wagon and his horse, and we go to Mulhouse. Henri helps me get my brother out of bed and over to the hospital. Gottfried, he's pretty bad. He's got yellow jaundice, fish-poisoning from that cut. They don't know any way to stop the infection from spreading, so it spread all over his body.

Naturally, the French people we know, they help us out any way they can. My friends, Gottfried's friends, the whole Ladner family, David Haas and his family—even Gottfried's boss and some of his customers—everybody comes to visit. They bring food, books, little gifts.

I stay with Gottfried all day, so naturally, I can't work right now. After a couple of weeks, Henri says he's got to hire somebody to help him out, which he does. He tells the new guy it's only temporary until I can come back, but naturally, the new guy wants my job. There are a lot of people like this guy now, and Henri tells me he's a good guy. Been out of work a long time.

Then one night, when I come back to the farm from the hospital, I see a French policeman—a gendarme—sitting in the kitchen with Henri and Marie.

The gendarme says, "Sorry, buddy, but you have twenty-four hours to get out."

I don't know, but I'm guessing the new guy told the gendarmes about me. Was no secret, and anyhow, I can't blame him if he did. Sometimes, one guy's got to step on top of another guy to survive.

I'm not too surprised to get caught. We knew this could happen, right? The Ladners don't get in trouble, thank God. They get a bawling out, but that's it. The gendarmes and the farmers around here, they're all friends or relatives, so they look the other way when somebody does something not exactly kosher. Besides, like I already said, most French people don't care for Hitler, and they don't like to make it hard for people who run away from the Nazis.

I'm not worried about me, but I hope the gendarmes won't come for Gottfried. I'm sure the people we know well won't report him, but I don't know about anybody else. But what can I do? There's nothing I can do to stop them.

In the morning, I say my goodbyes to the Ladners. Henri has tears in his eyes, and Marie is bawling into her handkerchief. The kids are in school, so I don't have to see them crying, which I'm glad about. But I admit I'm wiping tears off my face too.

After this, I stop at the hospital and tell the nurses what's what. Gottfried is asleep, and I don't want to wake him up and upset him. The nurses promise to explain everything to him when he feels better. They tell me not to worry. He's going to make it. I have to trust them, that's all. Nothing else I can do.

Now what? I can't go back to Germany, and I can't stay in Switzerland. And now, I'm supposed to get out of France. But I decide to stay anyway. Why? One, I can finally speak the language—not good, but okay. Two, France is a big country. And three, I'm only one little guy.

Most refugees are going to Paris. But I don't like the idea of going there, even if Fritz and Pacher are there. There's too much trouble in Paris right now. There's a bad depression over there and riots in the streets. I decide I'll go anyplace that's not Paris and not too close to Mulhouse.

So at the railroad station, I get in a line to buy a ticket some-where. I hear the guy in front of me say he wants a ticket to Lyon, so I ask him a couple of questions. I find out Lyon is pretty far away from here, and it has nice weather.

So when I get up to the window, I say, "One-way ticket to Lyon please."

The girl gives me a ticket and says, "Bon voyage."

And that's it. I'm on my way to Lyon, France. What the hell I'm going to do there, I have no idea.

Gottfried
1934 Paris, France
Driver's license photo

IX

GOTTFRIED

I'm in the hospital in Mulhouse a long time, for a month at least. My hand—my right hand too—it takes a long time to heal. I try to work on my fingers all the time to get them straightened out. I guess they got crooked from the blood poisoning. I can move them, but not like before, and I can't feel things too well with my fingers. I can't write with my right hand anymore either, so I'm trying to practice writing with my left hand. So far, it's not too hard, which is a surprise to me. Maybe I was born left-handed, but I always used my right hand to write. See, we were not allowed to write with the left hand. The teachers used to hit us if they saw us trying to do this.

When I find out Rudolf is gone, I'm very worried. One of the nurses tells me what happened. Seems like everybody knows—the nurses, the doctors, Rudolf's friends, my friends, everybody. So I expect them to come and arrest me too, but for some reason or other, nobody comes. David Haas says maybe they caught Rudolf because he was gambling all the time, and somebody was a sore loser. But maybe I made somebody mad too, and I just don't know about it yet.

David is trying to help me. He brings me newspapers to take my mind off my worries. But the newspapers don't do the trick, because they say things are getting worse, not only in Germany, but here in France. For instance, when we came here, the French people were very friendly. Wanted to help us in any way. But for refugees coming here now, it's not the same. The French politicians want France to close the borders. Some rich Jewish Frenchmen are saying the same thing. The government wants to get rid of refugees who are already here too—even people who can help them, like Jewish doctors from Germany. Stupid, if you ask me.

I ask David if he can bring me good French books to read. Maybe if I read some books, I can practice my French and take my mind off my worries. So he brings me *The Hunchback of Notre Dame* by Victor Hugo. After this, I spend my time reading and exercising. I love to read, and now I can understand and speak French much better than when we came here. Not perfect, but pretty well.

After Victor Hugo, I read other books too. I learn some interesting things in a book about German heroes. My parents, both of them, are very patriotic—used to be anyhow. This was the reason they gave all of us boys the names of German heroes. Turns out, though, that the names they picked were as crazy as Papa calling himself Adolf. For instance, the name Rudolf. That guy was a German hero in the Christian crusades. He killed Jews right and left. Martin, I think, was named after Martin Luther, who started the Lutheran religion and hated all Jews. Hubert was the name of a Catholic hero. He was a thief who became a Catholic saint. Now, my brother Hubert is a thief, but I'm pretty sure he won't ever be a Catholic saint. Siegfried and Gottfried were both heroes in operas. But the guy who wrote those operas was Richard Wagner, a big antisemite. Hitler loves him. So now, I have learned these things, but my parents, naturally, never knew them. See, they had very little education, and they don't read much. Matter of fact, in my family I'm the only one who reads all the time.

The days I spend in the Mulhouse hospital pass very slowly, and every day I think about Rudolf. We were always together before this, and I worry about him being all by himself. Also, I would like to know more about what he's doing, but he's no good at writing. He sent me one short letter a few weeks after he left, and that was it. He said he went to Lyon, which I can't figure out. Why there? He said he's washing dishes and living with a nice woman and her daughter. At least he sent an address for me to write back to him, which I do. Matter of fact, I write him every couple of days. I remind him to watch his money, because he always depended on me to do that.

Mama writes to me one time too. David Haas brings her letter to me. She says the authorities finally gave her and Papa passports to go to the United States. But they would not give a passport to

Martin for some reason or other. See, I think they know he's our brother, so they are giving him a hard time. They're still trying to get even with Rudolf and me. Mama and Papa won't leave Germany until they know Martin will be safe. So, of course, I worry about all of them.

Finally, they let me out of the hospital. I want to go back to work and save a little money, but my old boss can't use me. I try a few other people, but I have no luck. It seems like people everywhere hate to hire refugees now.

So I go see the agency in Basel, and I ask them for advice. They tell me to go to Paris and apply for passports at the American embassy. But they warn me it's rough in Paris now. Most agencies that were helping Jewish refugees have been closing, and France has been sending Jewish refugees back to wherever they came from— even back to Germany. Also, there are a lot of strikes and riots in Paris, because many people are out of work there too.

Nothing they say makes me happy, but what choice do I have? I decide to go to Paris, because in spite of all the problems, we might have a chance to get into the United States from Paris. I don't like hearing about all the trouble there, but Paris is a big city, which might be a good thing. Maybe it would be easier for me to get lost there if I have to. I would like Rudolf to join me there too. It would be better for us to stay together in case something happens to one of us. I decide to try and get settled there and then convince him to come.

The committee gives me travel papers and money to buy a train ticket, but that's it. There's no extra money for food, so I don't eat. The next day, I take the train to Paris, and when I get there, a guy at the train station tells me I can get food and a free bed at the Salvation Army. So this is where I go. It's a strange place to go, because it also happens to be the evening which begins Yom Kippur, the holiest day of the Jewish year.

Turns out there are a couple of other Jewish refugees here at the Salvation Army. One of them is a guy my age from Munich, by the name of Arnold Schwartz. When I introduce myself, he wishes me a happy new year, which is a surprise to me, because he's a great big guy with green eyes, a little nose, freckles, and a curly red beard. Then he tells me his mother was Irish and his father was a German Jew. His mother died a long time ago. The Nazis arrested his father and his older brother last week and threw them both into a concentration camp. He was here in Paris visiting some friends when he found this out, so now he is going to stay in Paris.

A guy in a uniform comes over and tells us to take a seat.

Arnold says, "Are you going to eat?"

"I don't know. It's Yom Kippur," I say.

Me, I would like to fast, which is what I have always done. Jews are supposed to fast from sunset of the evening before Yom Kippur until sunset the next day.

We're both staring at the food and debating whether to eat it when the guy in the uniform asks us to bow our heads. He says a prayer, which he ends in the name of "our Lord, Jesus Christ." Then they bring us bowls filled up with lentil soup with ham. Arnold and I look at each other.

"Are you going to eat this?" I ask.

He shrugs. "I'm not religious. I'm hungry, and ham is good."

He takes his spoon and starts eating.

I feel very guilty about eating any food, but ham is not just any food—it's *treyf,* not kosher—and that's something I always avoided. But now I'm feeling kind of light-headed on top of feeling guilty. After a whole day, I'm very hungry, plain and simple.

Rudolf would be laughing his head off right now. I can almost hear him telling me I won't get hit by lightning for eating ham. Finally I give up. I eat the soup, and to be honest, it does taste good. But I guess anything tastes good if you're hungry enough.

Later on, I'm lying on a cot, but I can't sleep. I keep thinking about my family, all the problems. And I think about Yom Kippur too—the way things used to be. About my family at home and how happy we were on every holiday, even when things were hard.

How the hell did I end up on Yom Kippur eating ham in a Christian mission in a foreign country?

So I'm lying on the bed, feeling sorry for myself. I'm exercising my stiff fingers to keep them from hurting. I'm wishing Rudolf was here with me. But somehow or other, I manage to take a deep breath and give myself a good talking-to. See, I know I'm very lucky. Lucky to be alive and lucky to be at this place. If not for the Salvation Army, where would I be? Here, I have a roof over my head, food to eat, and a cot to sleep on. The Christians who run this place are good men—*mensches.* They don't care who you are, Jew or anything else. If you need help, they give you help.

But the truth is, I feel guilty about eating that ham. So the next morning, when they give us breakfast, I decide not to eat—to fast the whole day. I guess I'm not ready to give up Yom Kippur altogether.

Arnold comes and sits down with me, and we talk. He's a smart guy, and he has some friends here in Paris. He invites me to come with him to meet them, which turns out to be a good idea. Arnold and I get to be good friends here. He's a guy I can always count on. Likes to laugh too, likes my jokes.

Arnold's friends tell both of us about an outfit in Paris that helps refugees. We go over there, and right away they offer a job to Arnold. He has a good education, so they can use him right there. But for me, they can only find a little job—cleaning up in a biscuit factory. It's a hard job, but it's work, so I'm happy to have it. I clean up whatever they say, including the toilets.

Me, I save every franc I can. I wait in lines and eat at soup kitchens. Once in a while, I buy myself a tin of sardines and a baguette at the market, and it tastes like manna from heaven. Sometimes I take a few biscuits from the factory where I clean up. These biscuits taste like cement, but they fill my stomach, so I'm glad to have them. I have to be careful though. If they catch you taking biscuits, they fire you.

But this is not the first time I've been hungry, so I ignore the risks and keep up my spirits. That's what we had to during the war too. See, even with Mama's shoe-making business, there wasn't always enough food for us. Farmers had to sell everything to the army. It was illegal for them to sell food to civilians or to trade food for goods. But we had to eat, so we took our chances. Once a week, at night, Mama would send Siegfried to farms to trade shoes for eggs, butter, and cheese—even for chickens.

To me, these nighttime adventures sounded very exciting. Siegfried was my hero. Compared to Rudolf and me, he was grown up.

I was only four years old, but I always begged him to take me with him, and he always said no. Finally, one time, he said okay, but he warned me not to make a sound.

"If the soldiers catch us, they'll shoot us. Especially you, Gottfried. They hate little Jews."

I was very excited, so I did my best to keep quiet. But at the farm, Siegfried traded shoes for a live chicken. He tied the chicken up in a gunny sack with a hole for air, but it was squawking anyway. So the whole way home, I was scared to death.

Finally, Siegfried heard me whimpering and stopped. "What the heck is wrong with you, Gottfried?"

I whispered, "Why can't you kill that chicken so it will be quiet?"

"Don't be silly," he said. "It wouldn't be kosher. A good Jew can't be caught dead eating a dead chicken that's killed wrong."

At the time, I had no idea what he was talking about. Now I realize he was kidding me, but it wasn't funny at the time.

So now, I'm by myself in Paris. But at least I have a job, which a lot of people don't. Even so, I don't have enough money for an apartment. Arnold stays in a place with his friends, and I can leave my suitcase there. But there is no room there for me to sleep.

So naturally, I ask about the places the government has for refugees. But I soon find out the people in these places live like animals. The government places are old army barracks. They're filthy with rats and lice, and there are families with babies who cry night and day. I decide I would rather stay anywhere else. So when the weather is nice, I sleep in a park or I go to the Salvation Army. If they have long lines and not enough beds, I sleep on the metro trains. I meet all kinds of people there too—other refugees. All kinds of people.

Once in a while, I sleep in the factory where I work. They have a big closet for their brooms and mops. I go inside just before the place closes up. Then after they close up, I come out and lie down on the factory floor. I don't do this too often though. Don't want to get caught and lose my job.

Days, I keep to myself. I like to talk to other people, so it's very hard for me to keep my head down and keep quiet. But at my job, the only person who knows about me is my boss, Monsieur Girard. If anybody else finds out I am not legal, I can lose my job and maybe my life. See, the gendarmes, have orders to arrest refugees with no papers and throw us in jail or hand us over to the Germans at the border.

Anyhow, one day when I'm cleaning up, I see a toilet is broken. I know where to find some tools, so I fix it. Another day, I find out there's some trouble with the electricity, so I fix that too. This is when Monsieur Girard comes to talk to me.

Says, "Kahn, I've got a broken machine on the floor. Think you can fix it?"

"I can try." I fix it for him. I don't ask for money.

Later on, he asks, "You know anything about cars?"

"I can drive them and repair them. I used to work as a mechanic in Germany."

Girard looks up at the ceiling, then back at me. Says, "That's interesting."

A couple of days pass by. Then Girard tells me he's got a proposition for me. He needs a chauffeur at night, and if I take the job,

I can quit this cleaning job. He says he's going to get me a license and a uniform, and he'll pay me good money—in cash.

"One more thing, Kahn," he says. "You do your job. You drive the car, but you don't ask any questions."

I get a nervous feeling in my stomach, but I ignore it, because right now I need money, and if I can get it, I can find a place to live.

The next day, Girard sends me to a place to get a driver's license. He gives me money in a sealed envelope to bribe somebody. So this way, I get a driver's license with my picture on it, and I'm very excited about it, because now, I can get driving jobs. It's not a work permit, but it's close enough. It's something official to show people, so maybe I can survive here.

All the refugees with a little money live in cheap hotels. We get low rates and maybe some furniture. The first hotel I move into is so cheap that whores use it. Refugees and whores. That's who I live around now. The girls, they're always inviting me to come to their rooms. But now that I have free time during the day, I figure I can get my own girls for nothing if I want to. Besides, I don't want to get sick from a whore.

Now, every night during the week, I drive Monsieur Girard around Paris, so he can pick up and deliver whatever it is. First, I meet him at his apartment building in a fancy-schmancy neighborhood not far from the Arc de Triomphe. I wear a chauffeur's uniform, and I drive him around in his Peugot 601. It has a powerful motor with six cylinders. Naturally, I love driving his car.

I don't know what Girard is doing, and I can't ask. He never talks to me except to give me directions. Every night, he goes into rundown places and comes out with bags. Then I take him to nicer places, and he takes in the bags. This is every night until one night when he goes into a dumpy place and comes out running.

He jumps into the car with his bag and shouts, "Step on it!"

I'm driving away in a hurry when I hear a popping sound. Then more popping sounds.

I say, "Is somebody's shooting at us?"

"Just drive."

But I'm very nervous. A crazy Nazi almost ran me over in Zurich, and now somebody's shooting? I decide no matter what, I have to find out what's going on. What's he up to? What's inside those bags? Am I going to get killed?

There's a big house where we go maybe once a week, and when we go there, Girard always stays inside quite a while. I figure the next time we're over there, I'll try to find out what's what.

We go there a few days later, and after Girard goes into the house, I get out of the driver's seat, open the back door, and take a look inside a bag on the back seat. Money, paper money. That's all I can see in there—a lot of money. Not French francs, though. Foreign money. German marks, Italian lira, British pounds, American dollars. I close the bag as quick as I can, and I get back into the driver's seat and wait.

At the end of the night, Girard fires me. I guess he saw me nosing around.

"You're fired, Kahn," he says. "And you better keep your goddamn mouth shut. If you don't, I'll find out. I'll come after you, and I'll make goddamn sure you go back to Germany. And that will be the end of you."

"I don't know anything," I say.

I swear up and down I'll keep quiet. He scares the hell out of me. But he lets me go. The truth is, I was going to quit after what I saw anyhow. But now I'm really worried. A guy like this—what if he changes his mind? Decides he better get rid of me? He knows my name, where I live. So I figure I better move, and the next day I find another cheap room in a hotel on the Rue Reaumier in the Second Arrondisement.

After a few days pass by and nothing happens, I go out and start asking if anybody knows of a driving job. A guy who lives at the hotel tells me I can get work driving a taxi. This guy, he's not a refugee. He's more like the hotel busybody. He knows everybody and everything going on.

So with my driver's license, I get a job driving a taxi with no problem. But all the other drivers come from Russia, and the Russians don't want anybody else driving taxis. A week later, when I walk in, I see a couple of gendarmes talking to the boss, and I hear one of them say they're looking for somebody by the name of Kahn. Naturally, I turn around and run like hell. But I can hear the gendarmes coming after me.

Before long, I start to run out of breath. I'm thinking I'm as good as dead. Then I spot a very crowded side street filled with shouting people. They're carrying communist banners and signs, jumping around, screaming, throwing their hats in the air, shouting slogans, pumping their fists up and down. Some of them are throwing rocks at buildings on the street and smashing the windows. I run to this street and push my way into the crowd.

I'm trying to catch my breath when a guy standing there sees me huffing and puffing. I pump my fist up and down like I see other people doing, and he sticks two fingers in his mouth and whistles. A bunch of his buddies come and surround me—bury me in the crowd with the rest of them. The guy who whistled, he winks at me. I'm one of them now, see. So I raise my fist, throw my beret in the air, and shout along with the others.

The strikers stay out there on the street until it starts getting dark, and when they break up, I figure it's safe for me to leave too. But when I get close to my hotel, I see a couple of gendarmes standing there, and I'm afraid they're waiting for me. See, I gave my address to the taxi company when they hired me. So now, I turn around and walk away as fast as I can. All night long, I ride the trains, moving from one train to another and worrying the whole time.

The next morning, I find Arnold and tell him what happened to me. We agree I better move again, but I don't have any money, and I need work again.

"I have an idea," he says. "I just heard the Michelin Tire Company needs stunt drivers for some advertising films."

"What do I know about stunt driving?"

"Listen, Gottfried, you need work, and I bet they'd hire you. Can't hurt to ask, can it?"

I'm thinking, Why would a big company like Michelin hire me? Plenty of people drive cars. People with papers—not refugees. But I'm desperate, so I go to meet them. Their insane idea is to film somebody driving down the steps of Sacre Coeur to show off Michelin tires—how good they are.

Now, Sacre Coeur is a famous church sitting high up on a hill. You can get a terrific look at Paris from the top there. And from the bottom up to the top, there are around three hundred steps. I look up at the top from where I'm standing—which is down at the bottom of the steps. It's a long, long way. How fast would a car go down those steps? What if the tires blow out? What if the car rolls over?

The guy I'm talking to is grinning. "Doesn't it look like fun?"

I'm thinking, Yah, it does look like fun. It looks like suicide too.

I ask the guy, "Anybody ever try this before?"

"No, but we're sure it will work."

"What makes you so sure?"

"Simple. Our tires are the best!"

He sees me scratching my head.

"Look, buddy," he says, "it's only an hour of work, and we'll pay you more than you can make in a month someplace else."

My heart starts pounding. I'm nervous, but I follow him up the hill to the back of the church, and I get into a French car, a Citroen. I feel like I'm in a dream while I'm doing this, but I'm still doing it. They give me a helmet, and they tie me up in the car. Tie me up altogether, so I won't get hurt. I have one hand on the wheel, one hand on the gearbox, one foot on the brake, and one foot on the clutch.

They get everything going, cameras and all that, and then they yell, "Go!"

I'm dripping through my clothes. Whether it's my nerves or all the stuff they wrapped me in, I don't know. Maybe both. But I say a little prayer, and then I go.

I get lucky again. Nothing bad happens. I drive the car down the steps and, thank God, I make it down in one piece. I have a sore tush for a week. But they pay me right away, and it's enough money to last me awhile.

A couple of weeks later, I get a letter from Mama. She and Papa want to leave for the United States, but for some reason or other, Germany is refusing to let Martin go with them. The only way they'll let him leave Germany is on a tourist visa to France. Uncle Josef is putting Martin on a train to Paris, and Mama tells me to take care of him until they get to New York—until the family figures out how to get Martin there.

What can I do? I have to move again. I need a little more space for Martin. I look around, and on the Rue de Poisonnier, I find a cheap place. I also buy a used bed from some Jewish guy who is moving to Australia. Why, I don't know. Are there Jews in Australia?

When I pick up Martin at the train station, he's shaking like a leaf. It's been a long time, so I'm surprised all over again to see him acting like a little kid and looking like a normal man.

"Want to see my take out my teeth?" he asks. Then he opens his mouth and pops out his dentures. He sucks in his cheeks. He looks like an old man.

People passing by are staring, and I'm embarrassed.

"Put the dentures back in your mouth," I tell him. "That's not a polite thing to do in public."

He puts them back in and hangs his head.

What I feel now is stuck. Martin is like a baby. I can't let him go out by himself, because he might get lost or hurt or something. And I can't leave him alone, because he's scared to be by himself.

Me, I'm not easygoing like Rudolf. When Martin comes, I feel like I have a big burden I don't want. It's not Martin's fault, but he's like a heavy weight on me. Another mouth to feed when I can hardly feed my own mouth. I have very little patience with kids, which is what he acts like, so I'm yelling at him all the time. Makes me feel terrible, but I can't stop myself.

Arnold is a nice guy though, and he helps me out. He finds Martin a chef's hat and an apron, which makes him happy—like a kid playing dress-up. Arnold also finds some kitchen stuff—some baking supplies, so Martin can keep himself busy making cookies and pastries all day. I can sell what he bakes, which helps us out. We even find a bakery, where they let Martin work now and then.

Martin Kahn
1935 Paris, France

One night, something funny happens. Wasn't funny at the time, though. I'm feeling bored stiff, and Arnold can't come over. So I decide to take Martin with me to a bar where they have a dance hall. See, Martin is a big guy—good-looking too. You don't know he's simple-minded unless he opens his mouth. But I figure it's so noisy in this dance hall, with all the people and the loud music, nobody can hear anybody too well.

Anyhow, we go inside, and pretty soon I pick up a couple of girls. They like our looks, and they're drunk, so it's easy to talk them into coming with us to my hotel. Martin, he knows some songs, and he can sing, so we sing our way to the hotel.

But after we get to the room, nothing happens. Of course not. Martin never grew up down there, and he has no idea what to do. He lies down and goes to sleep. I try playing with both girls, but it doesn't work. Last thing I see is the girls slamming the door on their way out.

Naturally, I should have known better, because nothing can happen between Martin and a girl. I don't know what the hell I was thinking.

But I'm going completely crazy taking care of Martin. Every time I open the mail, I'm hoping there's a letter saying my family figured things out for him, and finally, thank God, after three long months, I get that letter. I'm very relieved. But Martin is scared to death, and he gets worse and worse as the day comes closer for him to leave. I try everything I can think of to make him feel better, but nothing helps. The poor guy keeps crying he doesn't want to go. Makes me want to tear my hair out and cry too.

When the day finally comes, I pack him up and borrow a car. Then we drive to Le Havre, and I put him on a ship heading to Mexico. Siegfried is supposed to go there to meet the boat and take Martin from there to New York.

In Le Havre, I try my best to get Martin settled down on the boat, but he cries like a baby, even though a nice lady there promises to stay with him. He looks at me like I'm killing him, and I feel like that's exactly what I am doing. Finally, he seems to wear out. I hug him, say good-bye, and leave. Maybe I should feel relieved, but I'm shaking when I walk down the gangplank. I get in the car, drive into Le Havre and get good and drunk. I sleep it off in the car, and the next day, I drive back to Paris. I feel like somebody tore me apart and patched me up again, but the pieces don't fit together anymore.

What have I got in Paris? No family, no job, no nothing.

Gottfried
1935 Paris, France
Luxembourg Gardens

Rudolf
1934 Lyon, France

X

RUDOLF

It's maybe 7:00 p.m. when the train gets me into Lyon. First place I go when I get off the train is a tavern, which is opening up for business. I walk inside and order a beer. And I say to the bartender, "Je suis un refugie allemand." Don't say it too well, but at least I say it.

This guy, he's a big, fat fellow. Thick black mustache and three, four, five chins. Dirty apron. He looks me up and down, then he says, "You want work?"

Yah," I say. "I used to be a bartender."

Well, I kind of was a bartender, huh? Didn't I pour cognac for the workers at the Ladners' café in Mulhouse?

"I don't need a bartender," he says. "I can use somebody at closing time to clean up the place and wash the dishes."

"Nights?"

"Nights only," he says. "That's when I need help."

Maybe I look pathetic to him, because then he says, "You got a place to stay?"

I shake my head.

"Look," he says, "I have no room at home, but you can sleep over there."

"Over there" turns out to be a storage room, which is filthy with a lot of junk everywhere. But I thank him. Why? One, I'm lucky to get any work and a roof over my head right now. And two, there's no other choice tonight. But the next morning, I start thinking about what else I can do.

At noon, I take a couple of francs that I have on me, and I stop at a little café, by the name of "Le Petit Café." No kidding.

I order a baguette, some cheese, some fruit. The girl waiting on me, she's maybe ten years older than me. Plain-looking, but very friendly. Brown hair, nice figure, quick smile. Tells me her name is Francine Fregonara, and I tell her I'm Willie Bremen. But Francine is a pretty smart girl. She takes a good look. She walks back and forth to talk with me all through lunch.

Then she says, "Willie Bremen—that's not your real name, is it? You're a Jewish refugee, aren't you? Well, that's okay. I'm Jewish too. I hate the Nazis."

Francine and me, we get to be friends right away. Not like a girlfriend, more like a big sister. Like Clare. Every day, I come back to this café. The third or fourth time, I ask Francine to go out, and we go to a movie. After this, she wants me to meet her mama, and she invites me to come over to their house. And naturally, I go. Just she and her mama are living there. Francine's father, he died fighting against the Germans in the Argonne area of France during the war. This is the same area where Papa was fighting, which I don't tell Francine.

The next time I visit the Fregonaras, we play skat, and I teach them a little poker. We have a lot of laughs. And after I come over a few more times, Mama Fregonara asks me a question.

"Would you like to stay here with us? We have one extra room, which nobody uses, and we can use some help around the house."

So I say, "That would be wonderful. But I better warn you I can't fix anything. I have two left thumbs."

Francine laughs and says, "Oh? You deal cards and shuffle them pretty fast!"

I don't think they care if I can fix things or not. It makes them feel good to help me out, and they like the idea of having a man in the house. I don't have enough money to pay rent, so Francine says I can teach her German instead of paying rent. Naturally, I can't teach anybody, but she knows this. So I say *oui* and *merci*. It beats sleeping in a dirty storage room, right?

The next day, I move over there, and right away, Mama Fregonara sits me down. "Rudolf," she says, "You need to write letters to your mama and to your brothers. You need to tell them what's what."

I don't like to write letters, but she's right. So I write to them, send my address.

Francine—she's going to be Clare, and this old lady—she's going to be Mama. But that's okay. I kind of like it.

But it's not right if I live here and don't pay rent. So I go to some restaurants and ask for work. And at one café, the owner says he's going try me out washing dishes. Says if I'm there long enough, maybe I can be a waiter later on.

So I'm there working, and one day a regular waiter doesn't show up. It's busy too, so the manager asks if I would like to take the guy's place today. All I have to do is take the orders from the table and call down the orders to the kitchen. There's a loudspeaker, and I call the order down there through the loudspeaker. Simple, right?

So some guy orders smoked goat cheese, which is, "Fromage fumé de chèvre." I go to the loudspeaker and shout, "Fromage fumé de cheval!" Which is what I thought he said. But all of a sudden, it's completely quiet in there, and people are sitting with their mouths hanging open. Then my boss runs over to me, grabs my arm, and starts yelling at me.

"You idiot! You ordered horseshit cheese, not smoked goat cheese!" And he puts me back to washing dishes. After a while, I get promoted to waiter, but I have to be very careful about what I say.

Now I have a steady little job and a nice, clean bed. Francine and her mama find out I'm not lying about my two left thumbs. But I give them most of the money I make, and they feed me and take care of me. Pretty soon, I start making some extra money I can keep, because I make friends at the café, at the tavern, wherever. I find some card games, and I join up with one of my new buddies, by the name of Ernest Moos. He's been selling used clothing, trinkets, and junk at flea markets, and he needs a little help. We go around here and in Nice, and buy out all kinds of stuff, anything somebody else can't sell. We take it to flea markets and sell it there.

Left to right: Rudolf, Ernest Moos
1935 Lyon, France
Flea market

Ernest, he's got a good head for business. Teaches me some stuff. Like when he buys, he offers half of what somebody asks. When he sells, he sets his price twice as high as what he wants. I watch him making deals. Sometimes to get something he really wants, he acts like he doesn't want it at all and walks off. Pretty soon, the seller runs after him, lowering the price. It's bluffing on another stage. That's all it is.

Gottfried, he writes to me all the time. He's in Paris, which is where he went after he got out of the hospital. But now, Martin is staying there with him, and he's got to take care of Martin. Later on, Gottfried writes that Martin is finally going to leave Paris. Gottfried wants me to move there, but I'm doing fine right here. I have a nice place to live, a job, and a lot of friends. And to tell the truth, I kind of like being on my own. Not having him bossing me around all the time.

But I wish Gottfried and I could get out of Europe already. We've been gone from home over two years, and things don't seem to be getting any better. Here in France, for instance, one government comes in and another one goes out. Back and forth, back and forth, back and forth. Like goddamn seesaws. The government that's in right now, it's giving orders to deport refugees. But where I'm living, the gendarmes don't try too hard to catch us. Whoever they do catch, though, is out of luck. Two Jewish buddies of Ernest's, they got caught, and the gendarmes took them to the German border. The Nazis shot them in front of the gendarmes, right there at the border. So naturally, Ernest keeps telling me to watch out, be careful. But I have to live, right? I'm not going to walk around inside my own shadow.

I meet a few Jewish refugees in Lyon and Nice, but most of them go to Paris. The ones who come here usually have friends or relatives here. For instance, a cousin of the Fregonaras just came here. He left Germany because the Nazis made new laws again, and now, Jews can't be German citizens.

"How can they do that?" I ask. "We have been citizens all our lives. Our fathers and grandfathers have been citizens. We have done everything in the world for Germany."

"I don't know," he says. "But they did it."

"Didn't anybody say anything against this?"

"Not really. The non-Jews—they have work, food in their bellies, clothes on their backs. The Nazis blame the Jews for everything bad, and things are better for the majority of people. So they don't pay much attention to these new laws."

I think about what he says. What do most people want? A place to call home, a few clothes on their backs, a full stomach. A job, some friends, some fun. That's all I want too. But I don't get what I want.

One night, I'm playing cards at a place with Ernest and his friends, and in through the front door come a couple of gendarmes. They walk straight over to my table and tap me on my shoulder.

"Your papers, Monsieur."

Which naturally, I don't have.

"Come with us."

Ernest tells them I'm his cousin, and he takes out some money to bribe them, so they'll go away. But it doesn't work. They take Ernest's money, and they take me too. It's a big night for them, huh? They take me out to their car, and they drive me to the jailhouse.

How they found out about me, I don't know, but I'm scared stiff. I'm sure they're going to take me to the border like those friends of Ernest's. The last people I'm going to see in my life are going to be goddamn Nazis. Waiting for me at the German border.

At the jailhouse, they bring me in, take me to a cell, and lock the door. The gendarmes who brought me, they leave. So now there's only me in a cell and three guards sitting in a little room nearby. They have nothing much to do. Why? I'm the only prisoner in here right now, so they're bored stiff. They're drinking wine and wishing they're someplace else. I wait an hour, let them get some more wine in them. Then I take out my deck of cards, which I always carry with me. Start doing some fancy shuffling. Playing some solitaire.

When I see them watching me, I say, "How about we play some pinochle or poker? I've got no big plans tonight."

So they laugh and talk it over. They decide, Why the hell not? Four guys—we can play some cards, pass the time. They know I don't have any weapons, and there's three of them and one of me. So they let me out of my cell, and the four of us, we play cards all night long. We drink, have some laughs, have a good time. Pretty soon, they're calling me Rudolf, telling me their life stories. By morning, they're my good buddies.

When the sun comes up, we finish a last game, and I get up and go back in my cell. I close the door. Seems to make them feel sorry for me. They stand out there talking to each other for a long time. Then two of them go out the front door, and the third one opens my cell door.

Says, "Rudolf, listen. We all put some money in the cash box, and we're saying your friend came with your papers, and he put in money for you to leave. So go. But leave France right now. Today. If somebody catches you again, we'll get fired, and you'll be back in Germany."

I thank the guy, but I tell him I have no idea where to go from here. Best bet, the guard says, is Spain. So I go from the jailhouse to tell Mama Fregonara what happened. She's wringing her hands, crying. I don't go to Le Petit Café to tell Francine. Why? One, I need to pack up and get out before they catch me again. And two, I don't want to see Francine cry.

Now, the jail guard, he told me exactly what I have to do. First, I catch a train to Cerbère, which is the town on the border with Port Bou. The train goes very slow through the Balitres Tunnel. When the train gets in the middle of this tunnel, that's when I jump out. On the other side of the tunnel is Spanish territory.

I'm thinking somebody's going to stop me over there too. I have no papers except the fake ones I bought to get into Switzerland. But I have no choice anyhow. So I get on the train. When it gets to the tunnel, I stand between the train cars and wait until the train is moving very slow. Then I throw my rucksack down, and I jump out. I'm lucky I don't get hurt.

I wait in the tunnel until the train is gone, and then I walk out and look around. There are a few people, but nobody is checking papers, and there are other guys like me, walking around with rucksacks, so it's not too hard to blend in. But I'm kind of scared to talk to anybody.

So I start walking on the road like I know what I'm doing. Which I don't. Seems like I'm walking for hours and hours and hours. I get tired and stick out my thumb, but no cars stop. Finally, an old truck. A farmer, he takes pity on me and points me to the bed of the truck. I have no idea where he's going, but right now, I don't care. I'm too tired to walk anymore.

I'm sitting in the bed of this truck on top of some farm junk, and I start thinking about my family, my friends. I'm wondering if I'm ever going to see Gottfried again. Or Mama. Or anybody else I love. I try to rest and watch the fields, the cows. What else can I do?

The truck keeps going and going and going. Finally, after a few hours, we stop. The driver gets out with a big basket and sits down on the grass at the side of the road. Tells me with his hands to come over and offers to share some food with me. He's a little guy, tight like a wire. Maybe sixty or so; I'm not too sure. A lot of leathery wrinkles on his face, especially around the eyes. He's got a big smile, and he's very friendly, so naturally, I start feeling better.

He gives me some soupy stuff in a bowl. Smells like fish, which I hate. There's a lot of red sauce in the bowl and some little things that look like tails swimming around. He's trying to tell me what I'm eating, but I can't make out what he's saying. Anyhow, I don't exactly want to know.

Listening to this nice old man talking, I feel like I landed on the moon. I'm in Spain, but he is not talking to me in Spanish—at least not the Spanish I heard from tourists when I lived in Lyon. But we're both trying to communicate, so we wave our arms and point a lot. At least he understands me when I say *merci* for the food. I don't like it, but I eat.

When we get back in the truck, he's got me riding up front with him. Which is nice but kind of stupid if he gets stopped and somebody asks questions. But this farmer, he's singing and laughing. Guess he doesn't much care. I like this guy. Easygoing. Anyhow, nothing happens. We smoke some terrible cigarettes of his. He sings me some happy songs in his language, and I sing him a couple in German. Finally, we come to a big city, and this is where he stops.

"Adeú, amic. Bona sort."

I figure the words mean, "Good-bye, friend, and good luck." What else can they mean, right? I wave, say, "Merci." Don't know what else to say anyhow.

I'm wishing I was a lot smarter. Gottfried, he picks up new languages easy. Not me though. Turns out this new language I've been hearing is Catalan. Something like Spanish, but not Spanish.

So now, my life is upside down again. I'm in Barcelona. In my pockets I have a little money, thanks to my gambling night in jail, and I'm thirsty. So I go to a tavern and get a drink, muscatel. Try to pay with French money. The bartender takes it, but I think he's trying to tell me I need different money. It's nighttime though. No banks open.

Finally, I'm yawning. I move my hands around, trying to ask where I can go to sleep tonight. The bartender understands and draws me a little map. So I go and walk over to some flea joint, sign in, and climb up a bunch of stairs. The hallway is completely dark.

I'm trying to see where the keyhole is to unlock the door to my room, when somebody hits me hard on the back of my head and knocks me out completely. I guess some guy must have followed me from the tavern. I wake up later, lying on the dirty rug in the hallway. I have a goddamn knot on my head and a terrible headache. There's nothing left in my pockets. The little money I had, somebody took it. I don't bother going inside my room. I just lean against the wall with my pounding head, and I wait. In the morning, I get up. When the desk clerk isn't around, I leave. I have no money, and I don't want him to call the police, right?

On the street, I see people walking, enjoying the warm day, the sunshine. I decide to follow a couple of them. What else am I going to do? We come to a big, wide street. It goes on and on and on. Beautiful old shade trees on both sides, big hotels, restaurants, shops, flowers everywhere. People walking, stopping, talking, buying, selling. And all along the street, there are guys sitting on the side, shining shoes. They all have on little red caps and little red coats.

I walk over to a group of them. An older guy, bald, with a dirty shirt hanging out over his big stomach, he stands there doing nothing. I figure he's in charge. So I move my hands like I'm shining shoes.

I ask him in German and then in French if I can work there.

The boss, he looks me up and down, nods like he knows all about me. Gives me some clothes, some polish, a little stool. He says something in Catalan. Maybe he's saying something like, "I can always use a good boy like you." But maybe not. Maybe he's saying, "Sit there, keep quiet, and shine shoes, you little shit."

So I go and sit down there, and I start to work. I'm a bootblack shining shoes on La Rambla. A very famous street, I find out later. The other shoeshine boys here are mostly young, dirty, skinny kids. Look like they never eat, most of them. But we shine shoes together. I take out my deck of cards and show them some tricks, make them laugh. The boss starts to watch me and enjoys himself too. Pretty soon, he brings me something to eat—a banana. I make faces, sounds, scratch, act like a monkey, make them laugh. Then I show them a few more card tricks, and in no time, we're all good buddies.

That night, a couple of the shoeshine boys take me to the place where they sleep. They've got some space under a bridge, like a little shack they made out of cardboard, pieces of tin, and junk they found. One of them shares a blanket with me. Torn and dirty. They have big, ugly rats crawling around, but the kids don't try to kill them. They only cuss out the rats and throw stuff at them. Guess they think the rats have to live too. Who knows? I teach the kids some cuss words in German, and they teach me some in Catalan. Like *merda*, which means "shit." I need to learn the important stuff first, right?

After a couple of weeks living like this, I play some cards and scrape a few coins together. I find a cheap room in a building, a filthy place that rents to anyone. But this is how I have to live right now. At least, I'm not on the streets. The kids on the streets, they're disappointed when I leave the bridge, but I let them stay in my room when I can sneak them in.

It's maybe a month later when a big guy sits down in front of me for a shine. You can tell this guy doesn't miss too many meals. Looks rich, fat—like a businessman. Two chins, big belly, clean shave, nice gray suit, good-quality homburg hat. No Spaniard though. He's got a German newspaper, which he unfolds with a snap and starts to read. So I'm sitting way down there on my little stool, shining his shoes. But I'm also looking up, trying to read the guy's newspaper upside down. For me, it's hard enough to read right-side up. So that's why I guess I don't notice when he stops reading. Suddenly, he takes down his paper and looks at me. I don't look at him though. I keep my eyes down and shine his shoes.

But then he starts to talk to me in German. "Who are you?"

Now, the Nazis, they've got agents in Spain picking up people like me. I don't look up. I don't say a word. I keep shining, shining...

He says, "I'm talking to you, young man. The way you look, the way you act—I know who you are, what you are."

I'm scared stiff, but I don't look up. I keep shining, pretending I don't understand him. I can't let anything show on my face.

Then the guy says, "Listen, brother, I'm not a Nazi. I'm an attorney. I work for a company in Holland. The owners are Jewish. Talk to me. I can help you."

I don't believe a word he says. I just keep shining, but he keeps talking.

"I'm from Frankfurt," he says. "I can tell you're German. You're a German refugee, aren't you?"

He says he's been watching me, asking questions about me. "I like how you work, how you get along with people. I need a good worker. Somebody I can talk to, somebody I can trust."

I don't look up at him. I'm listening, but I don't look up.

"My clients own a chicken farm nearby. I can get you a job there, outside the city. You'll eat and sleep well, and you'll be safe there."

Finally, I finish shining his shoes. I hold out my hand so he can pay me. He gives me a big tip. Too big. This is when I finally look him in the eye.

"Listen, brother," he says, "I'm leaving now. But you should come with me. I can take you to a safe place. A chicken farm. I can get you a job there. I guarantee you will live well there. You're not in Germany now, my friend, and I'm not a Nazi."

He's talking and I'm thinking. Maybe he is what he says, maybe not. But what have I got right now? Nothing. I have no future shining shoes on La Rambla. The way I see it, I've got two choices. One, I can stay here, shine shoes and wait. For what, I don't know. Or two, I can take a chance and go with this guy. To where, I don't know.

I decide to go with him. I stand up and give the boss my red cap and coat. The German guy, he sticks out his hand.

He says, "My name is Max Glauber."

I shake his hand. "Willie Bremen," I say.

He doesn't blink an eye. "My car is over there," he says.

We walk a couple of blocks to his car, a big black Mercedes Benz. Merda. It looks like the same kind of car the Nazis drive. But I already decided to go with him, so I get in. Just in case, I keep my hand on the door.

So we're driving through town, and he tells me again that he's an attorney, and he's driving me to a chicken farm. Says it's nearby, on the coast, outside a little town, name of Vilassar de Dalt. Says the chicken farm is sitting back behind the town, and there's another town nearby, by the name of Vilassar de Mar, which is on the ocean. Then he goes on talking about the chicken farm—what it is, the operation, what they want to do there. I tell him I don't know about chicken farms.

I say, "Herr Glauber, the only chickens I ever saw, I ate them or their eggs."

He laughs. "Well, my friend, you can learn."

Then he tells me his clients are Jewish brothers out of Holland, who own some successful chicken farms.

"They started a farm here, but it's not making any money. That's the problem, Willie. It *is* Willie, isn't it?"

Then comes an amazing sight—an ocean. Right here, outside this car. I never saw anything so beautiful in my life. I roll down the window and stick my head out, and Glauber stops the car.

Says, "Magnificent, isn't it? It's the Mediterranean Sea. Why don't you get out and look?"

I do. I forget about everything. I stand there a long time, listening to the sounds of the waves, watching the water. There's nothing else in the world I think about, nowhere else I want to be. But Glauber finally says, "Let's go. You can come over to this beach whenever you want."

After a couple of minutes, he drives up into the hills nearby, and sure enough, we come to a fence and a gate. There's a little sign there on the gate. It's a chicken farm. I can't believe it, can't believe my good luck. This guy is who he says he is, and the chicken farm is real. Finally, I can relax, and I do.

"My name is not Willie Bremen," I say. "It's Rudolf Kahn. I'm Jewish."

He nods. "Yah, I know."

The chicken farm is exactly what he says it is. Glauber takes me in and shows me around. He tells me he wants me to learn the work here, whatever goes on, so I can tell him what's what.

He says, "We aren't making any money here, but we should be by now. I want you to keep your eyes and ears open, tell me what you see. I'll come back for a report every Sunday."

We walk through the farm. To me, this looks like a very modern place. Every chicken has a number. And to lay an egg, they go in a little compartment, and the minute the chicken goes in, the door comes down. The chicken lays an egg, and then they pick up the chicken and mark down every chicken that lays an egg. Thousands and thousands of chickens and eggs.

After this, Glauber shows me a little house where I can sleep.

"Rudolf," he says, "go up to the big farmhouse this evening, so you can meet the foreman and his wife and have supper with them. I'll tell them you're coming."

So he leaves me in the little house, and later on, I go up to the farmhouse to eat. The foreman's wife is a great big woman. Ugly too—with black whiskers. I see an empty chair next to her, so to be polite, I sit down there.

But when the foreman comes in and sees me sitting there next to his wife, he goes crazy. I have no idea what he's saying, but he's looking from me to his wife and shouting. Takes a full plate of food and throws it at me. Then he takes a full glass of wine and throws that at me too. He misses both times, but there's broken glass and food and wine all over the goddamn place.

I jump up as quick as I can and run out of there, back to the little house where I'm supposed to stay. I don't go back up to the big farmhouse to eat after that. But there's no problem with eating anyhow. There are more chickens and eggs here than I ever saw in my whole life. Every meal, it's going to be eggs and chickens and eggs and chickens and eggs and chickens.

The next day, I try to start learning. Try to keep out of the foreman's way. I follow the other workers around, do what they do, and after a while, the foreman acts like he doesn't think about me anymore.

Every Sunday afternoon, Glauber comes by, talks to the fore-man, looks around, then asks me to go with him for a little walk or a ride. I'm supposed to watch and tell him what I see, which isn't much at first. But after a month or so, I start to ask questions, and I find out about all the little markets in the towns nearby. In the middle of these little towns, on Sunday mornings, the people have markets with vegetables and fruits, other stuff to sell—little markets. And every Sunday morning, the foreman and his wife leave the chicken farm. They're not dressed up to go to church either. They take the truck and they go. What they're doing is driv-ing to these nearby towns and selling eggs from this farm at all the little markets. Lots and lots of eggs. And then they're bringing the money back with them to the chicken farm. The farm should be making money from this, right?

So this is when I ask Glauber, "What happens to the money for the eggs they sell at the markets on Sunday mornings?"

"What markets? What money?"

"Every Sunday, they open up markets in the towns nearby. And the foreman and his wife, they go there—to all different places. They sell eggs there."

So we get wise to them. Glauber goes and sees them, finds out they've been keeping all this egg money and fires them both, the foreman and the wife. Then he makes me the foreman. He also hires a woman from a school in Dresden, by the name of Eva, a specialist in chickens and whatever. Looks like a professor in a skirt. She has a tight little bun at her neck, thick glasses. But nice. And right away, she gives me books to read about hatching, about feed-ing chickens, their sicknesses, how to treat them.

Now, numbers I'm pretty good at, but reading and writing? Not for me. Too stupid. But Eva makes me read the goddamn books. Every day I have to read, study, learn something new about chickens and farming. Their food, their grains, their mix—even their shit, which is something I never figured to learn. But I know this is good for me, to learn about growing chickens and to get some education like this. Maybe it can help me later on.

Anyhow, we're working hard every day, and the farm is making a little money but not much. Glauber tells me we need to make more.

One Sunday, he's got some bad news. "Rudolf," he says, "unless the farm makes a lot more money soon, the owners won't be able to repay their bank loan."

"How soon is soon?"

"In about three months, if things don't pick up, they'll have to close the farm."

Now, this is a big problem for me. Finally, I'm catching onto Catalan, little by little. I'm living good here, learning too. I need to figure out something I can do to help the farm make more money. So all week long, after Glauber gives me the bad news, I think about what I can do. And the next Sunday, I give Glauber my ideas.

"Suppose I get some of my German friends from Mulhouse to come over here and help me build up the farm."

I tell Glauber about Fritz, Pacher, and Justus. Tell him I'm in touch with them, and I'm thinking they will come.

Then I show Glauber some figures, which I wrote down about how we can improve production, sell more eggs. If my plan works, then the owners can pay off their bank loan little by little.

He says, "Renegotiate the loan, huh?"

I say, "Better than to lose the whole thing, right?"

Glauber, he looks at my plan, and he likes it. "I'll give it a try," he says.

So he takes my proposition to his clients and to the bank in Holland, and they go for it. They'll hold out for four more months and see how it goes.

Right away, I write to Gottfried and ask him to come. But he's got to stay in Paris. He's working with some Jewish agency that helps Jews get out of Europe. He says he'll let me know when I should come to Paris to see somebody at the American embassy.

Next, I get in touch with my friends from Mulhouse. Right now, two of them are in Paris. There's my buddy Pacher, who is an anarchist—from Prussia originally. Pacher—he's kind of quiet, but he's smart and very musical. In Mulhouse, Gottfried and Pacher didn't get along at first, but after Gottfried almost got run over by that screwball Nazi, they started to be friends. Right now, they're still friends in Paris. Pacher got Gottfried into an outfit that's raising money. They're helping get people out of German concentration camps. The Nazis throw in anybody who says something against them, but if you bribe the right big shot, sometimes you can buy a man's freedom. Pacher's gang, they get money some way or other, and this is what they do. Help get guys out of the camps and over to Paris.

Then there's my buddy Fritz, who is in Paris right now too. He's a strong guy, a wrestler, and a weight lifter. Used to be a policeman in Germany, but he left because he is an anarchist, and the Nazis don't like anybody who disagrees with them. Fritz is the same guy who helped Gottfried and me earn a little smuggling money. He doesn't tell me what he's doing in Paris right now, but maybe it's not exactly kosher.

So I write letters to Fritz and Pacher, and both of them like the idea of coming to Spain and helping me build up the chicken farm. Then Glauber fixes it for them to come here legally as students. Gets them some papers that say they are coming to study. Fritz is going to study Spanish history, and Pacher is going to study bugs. Pretty funny, huh? I don't know where Glauber gets his crazy ideas, but they give us a lot of laughs when we finally meet up again at the farm.

The last one to come is Justus, the only Jew in our gang. This guy, he's kind of like Gottfried. Was a mechanic in Germany, in Munich, but he was also putting out flyers for the communists. Which is why he left. Hitler was arresting communists and throwing them into prisons after the Reichstag fire.

Justus is the only one of us who stayed in Switzerland. He's been hiding out there, moving from place to place to place, trying not to get caught. I catch up with him through my cousin, David Haas, and Glauber sends him some papers so he can come here. Supposedly to study Spanish architecture. I have to hand it to Glauber. The guy can fix up pretty much anything.

My friends come to help me build up this farm, because they have no future where they live now, and they have no better place to go. All of us are revolutionaries, you know.

Left to right: Rudolf, Justus, Fritz, Pacher
1935 Vilassar de Dalt, Spain
Chicken farm

So when they come, I explain it to them, what we're going to do. After this, we all work like dogs. The main thing we need to do is raise more chickens, sell more eggs. So we work hard and do this. Every day, a couple of us get the old truck, put some eggs in the truck, and go into the little towns around here. We sell the eggs, and we give the money to Glauber on Sundays. He gives it to the Dutchmen, and they start paying off the bank.

When my buddies come to the farm, we naturally talk about what's going on everywhere else. How the Nazi Party keeps growing. Even Spain has big troubles. But here on this farm, we can be happy. We can have a good life. And we get to be like a little family—Eva, Pacher, Justus, Fritz, and me. Pacher, he's a hell of a music man. Yodels and sings and plays guitar. Every night, we're singing and dancing, and we play cards. We've got everything we need. We even get ourselves a puppy. We call him Gustav.

This little dog, he's very smart. I never had a dog before, but I always loved them. Dogs and horses both. Anyhow, we have fun training Gustav. He can walk over a table with a bunch of open beer bottles on top of it. Won't spill even one drop from one bottle. We train him to help us too—to watch who is coming and going. We have a big gate down by the main road. You can't see it from the farm. But we don't lock it, because Gustav always lets us know whenever somebody is coming. We train him to protect us.

One day, Gustav starts barking when he sees a stranger coming down the road. Turns out to be a priest, who lives in the mansion on the hill behind the farm. He introduces me to a beautiful girl, by the name of Carme. Carme Sabater. By now, I already had quite a few girlfriends. But this girl is different from all the others. She changes my whole life.

Gottfried and friends
1936 Paris, France

XI

GOTTFRIED

One day, I get a little letter from Rudolf. He says he's in Spain, working on a chicken farm. A chicken farm? What the hell does he know about chickens? Wants me to come and work over there. Says he thinks Fritz, Pacher, and Justus will come too, which I'm happy to hear. Guess I'm going to miss Fritz and Pacher. Well, Pacher anyhow. We got very friendly in Paris, helping each other out, getting some people in Paris to give us money. Pacher sends it to some friends, who bribe the Nazis to let a few people go.

I'm very happy to hear from my brother. We've been apart a long time already, and I miss him—miss his wisecracking too. I think about him all the time, and naturally, I worry about him doing something stupid. Like getting himself caught again and getting sent back to Germany. He's been caught twice already, and he's been very lucky to get away both times. But how many times can he be so lucky?

Me, I don't count on being lucky. I try to pay attention and watch my back every minute. Here in Paris, I see open hate on the streets—signs saying, "Jews get out!" Matter of fact, if they catch me right now, they'll take me to the border and hand me over to the German police. It happens every day, so maybe it's a good thing Rudolf isn't here, or I'd have to be watching out for him too. It's hard enough to take care of myself right now.

It would be nice to go to Spain and be with my brother, but I shouldn't leave Paris. Not now, when I finally found some people to help us get over to the United States. These guys work for a Jewish outfit, which is trying to help Jewish refugees. My job is to write letters and talk to people—get us as many affidavits and recommendations as I can. So I write back to Rudolf and tell him I can't leave right now. When we get an appointment with the American ambassador, I'll let him know, so he can come here.

Meantime, I remind him to be careful over there. As bad as it's getting here, my friends say it's even worse in Spain. Maybe it's okay where he is, on his little farm. But we are hearing how Hitler and Mussolini are helping the rich people and the Catholic Church start a war in Spain. They want to kick out the government, which is a republic, and put in a dictatorship. What if my little brother gets caught in the middle of all that? But if Fritz is going to be with him, I'm worried anyhow.

See, I did some business with Fritz here in Paris. Ex-policeman, tough guy, always has some sort of deal cooking. But I wouldn't trust him again. Not after what he did to me here in Paris. I was supposed to sell some mirabelle, that was all. But that's not what happened.

Now, mirabelle is a tasty, sweet fruit. Something like a plum. It comes from Alsace-Lorraine, and it's very popular in Paris for eating and cooking. Fritz told me there was a shipment of mirabelle that nobody wanted. Dented cans. If we went and got it, we could have it. But we had to pick it up at night. I wondered about this, but I didn't want to ask too many questions. So one night, we met at the railroad yard.

Fritz said, "I'm taking care of everything. All you have to do is help with loading the stuff on our truck, and we'll divide it up and make a little money."

We walked up to the front gate, and a guy inside unlocked it and let us in. Fritz bribed him—gave him a bundle—and the guy took off.

"Good buddy of mine," Fritz said. I was thinking, He's some buddy if you have to bribe him.

Then we sat and waited. It was completely quiet in there. Pretty soon, though, a dump truck came to the gate and flashed its lights. Fritz opened the gate, let it in, and we jumped into the back of the truck, which drove us over to a corner of the yard. There were a lot of pallets stacked up there. We jumped off, and two more guys got out of the cab. Then the four of us started to look for a pallet labeled "Mirabelle." When we found it, Fritz gave us some knives, and we cut the ropes around the pallet and loaded the boxes in the bed of the truck. Naturally, they were very heavy, so it took us an hour, working hard. We finally finished and drove the loaded truck up to the front gate. But a van was sitting there, blocking us from going out.

"Godamn him!" yelled Fritz. "I gave him plenty! He was supposed to stop them!"

Fritz told the rest of us to stay put, and he hopped out and started to walk up to the van. But the front doors suddenly flew open, and two gendarmes pointing guns jumped out.

One of them just stood there pointing his gun at us. The other one shouted, "Out! All of you! Keep your hands up!"

None of the rest us moved, but Fritz got out with his hands in the air and said, real slow and loud, "My—name—is—Fritz."

"Keep your goddamn hands up," shouted the same cop. "The rest of you, get out of the truck. Hands up in the air!"

But just as we started getting out of the truck, the quiet cop suddenly wheeled and shot his partner through the head. We all jumped. Who expected this? The guy dropped. Blood poured out his nose and mouth. I saw pieces of his skull and his brains scattered on the ground. I couldn't believe my eyes. The shooter didn't blink.

"Fifty percent, Fritz," he said. "And get rid of the evidence."

Fritz nodded. The gendarme glanced briefly at the rest of us. Then he got back in the police van and drove off.

"Stay here, Gottfried," Fritz told me. "Come down from the truck and wait right here."

I was shaking like a leaf. I got down and stood there. Fritz and the two other guys— they threw the dead gendarme in the back of the truck on top of the boxes, and the three of them drove off. After an hour, they came back without the body, but they had a few shovels. They gave me one, but I just sat there. I was sick to my stomach. They shoveled up some dirt and made some holes. They buried what they could and threw dirt around to cover up the blood.

Finally, I said to Fritz, "I didn't come here for this."

"Nobody did," he said. He shrugged. "It happened. So forget it."

"All I came for was to make a little money off some mirabelle."

"Mirabelle?" Fritz burst out laughing. "Are you kidding?"

"Mirabelle—that's what you said. What the boxes say..."

He laughed again. The others laughed too.

"What?" I asked. "What's so damn funny?"

"We've got guns here, stupid. Guns. Good, new rifles. We're going to make a lot of money, Gottfried." He swept his hand around. "You, me—all of us!"

I looked from one guy to the other. "A gendarme got killed, Fritz. *Killed.*"

"Look, Gottfried," he said. "Calm down."

He put his hand on my shoulder. "It wasn't supposed to happen this way. But take it easy, will you? We ended up doing everyone a favor. That bastard was a Nazi. A spy."

Me, I had no way of knowing if anything Fritz said was true. But there was nothing I could do, and Fritz knew it. If I said anything to anybody, I could go to jail or get deported.

I moved Fritz's arm off my shoulder. "Count me out," I said. "I don't want any money from this deal."

"Okay by me," he said. "More for the rest of us."

That was the last time I saw Fritz while I was living in Paris, and I never want to see him again.

Now, I'm going every few days to the Jewish agency, and one day when I'm over there, in walks an old friend of Mama's, by the name of Fred Strauss. Old-fashioned man, round head with a wide face, wavy white hair, and a white handlebar mustache with waxed tips. Looks like some aristocrat—like some junker from the old Weimar Republic. Very friendly guy, too. He has a big, deep laugh and a very big heart. At home, he was always a generous man, especially with the poor Polacks coming into Germany. See, his grandparents came from over there. Turns out, Strauss is in Paris on business. He inherited the family import and export business, which has an office in New York, and he travels back and forth. He's a rich man, but he's a good man too, a real mensch.

Anyhow, he comes up to me and pumps my hand up and down.

"Gottfried Kahn! For crying out loud! What the heck are you doing here? Where's Rudolf?"

So I tell him what has happened to Rudolf and me.

"Can you help us get out of here?" I ask. "Maybe lend us some money to bribe somebody?"

"I can write a letter for you and offer you work there and financial support. Maybe that will help you. But I'm talking to you like a Dutch uncle, Gottfried. Your chances aren't good."

"But why not? The agency says the German quota isn't close to full."

"There's a depression in the United States right now. Thousands of people without work. And a lot of people in business and in the government—powerful people—don't want to let in any more Jews."

In the United States? I'm shocked. All I can say is, "Huh? Why?"

"Do you think it's only Europe where people hate Jews? The whole world hates us. Big shots in the United States too—in the government, in business."

"Don't we have to try?" I ask.

"Absolutely," he says. "And I wish you very good luck."

So we have some coffee, and then he leaves. He tells me not to give up. With his help and some luck, maybe we can make it.

So I work like hell to get all the papers we need. I get our relatives in New York to promise to stand up for us, to give us free places to live. Fred Strauss sends a letter and his bank statements. Every paper has a notary. Rudolf and I will have homes, and we will have jobs. I put together our whole histories, letters from everybody I can find—including men we worked for. I get letters from my boss at the Opel garage in Giessen and one from Herr Leopold, who owns the shoe shop where Rudolf worked. Mama also sends me a few letters, which she saved—one from Bosch-Dienst and one from Josef Albersmann, a guy I worked for in Giessen. All this, so the Americans will let us in. So the officials will see we're not bums.

I fill out papers, papers, and more papers. Siegfried pays a lawyer to look over all of the papers in New York—to make sure they are in good shape. The Jewish agency people say we've got everything going for us. They say there's a German-Jewish quota of twenty-six thousand, but so far this year, the United States has let in very few German Jews, so there is plenty of room for us.

Finally, I get a letter from the American embassy. We have an appointment in August. As soon as I get the news, I write to Rudolf, and a couple of weeks later, he comes by train to Paris. I'm very happy to get my little brother back, and I arrange a big party for him to introduce him to all my friends.

On the day of our appointment, I go with Rudolph and a guy from the Jewish agency to the American embassy in Paris. We go into a room and see a guy sitting behind a big wooden desk. He doesn't even look up to say hello. When he hears us sitting down, he calls our names, which he sees on the top of a big folder filled with papers.

"Gottfried and Rudolf Kahn?" he says.

"Yes, sir," we both say.

"German Jews?"

"Yes," we answer.

The bastard still doesn't look up. He starts pretending he's looking at our papers. He licks his thumb and flips through the thick pile of papers. It takes him only a couple of seconds.

"You boys have any money? A bank account of your own?"

"No," I say, "but we have family and friends in New York who have money. They will help us, and we will work very hard. Since we were kids, we have always worked. Take a look at our papers there."

"You have no investments, no savings?"

"Only what's in our pockets," I say. "But we have always worked, even ince leaving Germany. And in New York, we have places to live and jobs guaranteed to us."

He keeps his head down and says to the desk, "I'm sorry, but we have no room for any more German Jews."

That's it. That's all he says.

We sit there.

Then the guy with us from the agency says, "Sir, we know you have thousands of openings under the German quota."

He doesn't answer. He's tapping his pen on the desk. He's in a big hurry to get rid of us.

"I'm afraid I can't help you," he says. "Good day."

And that's it. He shoves our papers to the side. All my hard work. All for nothing.

The guy from the agency says, "I can't believe this!"

But the bureaucrat only says, "Please leave the way you came in."

We leave.

Rudolf and I go back to my hotel room and get drunk on some cheap table wine. We don't even taste the stuff.

The next day, Fred Strauss comes by. He says the guy from the Jewish agency told him what happened. He shakes his head.

"Wish I could say I'm surprised."

Rudolf says, "The United States is just like every other goddamn country. Nobody wants us. Nobody gives a good goddamn."

"Palestine," Strauss says. "Think about it, boys."

Me, I'm thinking maybe the Zionists are right after all. Nobody can kick you out of your own country. So I tell Rudolf maybe we should go to Palestine. Rudolf, he doesn't say anything.

I'm thinking things can't get any worse now, but I'm wrong again. When I come back from the market the next day, Rudolf is sitting on the bed, looking sadder than I ever saw him before. He doesn't say anything. Just hands me a letter from Mama.

My Dear Boys,

I am very sorry to write you with such terrible news, which came to us from our cousin Herman Haas in Zwesten. My dear brother, your Uncle Josef, is dead. Some Nazis went over to his farm and told him to get out. They were going to take away his cattle and close up his farm. Take everything away from him. They gave him an hour to pack a suitcase. Instead, Josef called up Herman and told him what was going on. He told Herman he was going to pack up and go. But he didn't go. When the Nazis came back, he was still there. He shot at them with his hunting rifle. He missed them, but they shot him, and they killed him. Then they went in the house and shot Anke. When Herman went over there, he found them both dead. The Nazis also turned the house upside down and took whatever they wanted. Herman and some friends buried Josef and Anke there, on the farm. They didn't dare have any kind of public ceremony in case the Nazis came back for them too. Here, we are all brokenhearted. In a million years, I never would have thought such a thing could happen.

Martin has arrived and is with us now, thank God. But he is very nervous all the time. When he arrived in Mexico, they locked the poor boy up in some jail. I guess they didn't understand him, what he was trying to tell them. Luckily, Siegfried found out where he was and managed to get him out of there. My poor boy. He doesn't understand all the terrible things that have happened to him. He is afraid of everybody but us.

Thank God, Papa and I are well. Clare also. She now has a baby boy. She would like for Papa, Martin, and me to come and live nearby her. So we will soon be going to Ossining, which is also in New York. I pray to God every day you boys will come to us very soon. Keep well, my sons.

Love and kisses,

Mama

Rudolf
1936 Vilassar de Dalt, Spain

XII

RUDOLF

Carme Sabater. The love of my life. I meet her while I'm at the chicken farm in Vilassar de Dalt in Catalonia.

First time I meet her, I'm driving the truck out of the farm, going over to town to sell some eggs. The little dirt roads around here—they get holes after a lot of rain, and I hit a big one. A tire blows and the tailgate falls open. So I get out, and now, I'm cussing a blue streak trying to keep all the eggs from spilling out and rolling onto the road. A lot of them already fell out and broke, and it's a big mess.

A little way off in the meadow near the road, I hear a girl laughing. Sounds like little bells, the way she's laughing. I turn around to look, and I see this girl, like some kind of mirage. Beautiful girl—tall, slim, graceful. She's standing there in the field next to a big brown mare. So I call out to her.

"I'm pretty funny, huh?"

She walks over to me, and as she does, she takes off a little blue riding cap. She has bright blonde hair in a long braid that swings back and forth. She's leading her horse loosely by the reins. Maybe it's my imagination, but when I look this brown mare in the eyes, I think she's laughing at me too.

The girl smiles at me when she gets closer. "I'm not laughing at you. It's the whole silly thing. The truck, the tailgate, the tire, the eggs. It's like a funny movie! It's not you."

"Okay," I say.

"But I have to admit," she laughs, "you sound very funny when you curse with that accent!"

She's a few years younger than me—maybe sixteen, seventeen. She whispers something to her horse, drops the reins, and lets the mare graze.

"Would you like a little help?" she asks. She starts helping me pick up eggs that aren't broken. Puts a bunch of them in her little cap, then sets them back in their boxes in the bed of the truck. The brown mare stands there and waits, nibbles on some grass.

"Thanks," I say. I smile at her. "Pretty horse you've got there."

She smiles. "Paloma! She's the best! She keeps all my secrets…"

She bends down to get more eggs, and while we're both working, I can't help watching her out of the corner of my eye. She moves like a dancer—that's what I'm thinking. That long blonde braid swinging over her shoulder onto the front of her shirt. Beautiful. Beautiful body, right? I can't help but look. She's got on some fancy-shmancy riding pants and high leather boots like rich lady riders wear in the movies. The way she moves, my eyes start peeling those fancy clothes off her. But when she looks up at me to hand me her cap filled with eggs, I can't think straight anymore. She's got eyes like I never saw before, deep blue-green eyes. The same color as the Mediterranean Sea.

"I'm Rodolfo," I say. This is the name they call me here.

"I'm Carme," she says. "You like to ride horses?"

"Only did it a few times," I tell her. "I love them though."

"Me too," she says. "All animals, I love."

"Lions and tigers too?"

She laughs. Like I said the funniest thing in the world.

"*Especially* the big cats," she says. "Such power they have. Such beauty. I would love to see them in the wild. In Africa and India!"

"Me too..."

"You live near here?"

I nod. I manage to tell her I live over at the chicken farm.

She smiles again, then puts the cap back on her head.

"I better go. You know, I shouldn't be alone with you. If Papa finds out, he'll be furious." She laughs when she says this. "But he won't find out. My Paloma can keep a secret!"

I manage to thank her for her help and wave good-bye, and she hops back up on her horse. Smooth as silk, like she's been doing it all her life.

And that's it. She rides off. Just like that, she's gone, and I'm kicking myself. I forgot to ask her last name and where she lives. I'm so busy staring at her and dropping eggs all over the place that I completely forgot.

After this, I leave the truck and walk back to the farm. I tell Fritz and Pacher I blew out a tire and spilled eggs everywhere. They have a good laugh, and then they walk back to where the truck is, and they fix the tire. They both know I'm no good at this kind of stuff.

But I don't say a word to them about Carme. Why? I don't want any guy to know about her but me. If I tell my buddies about her, then maybe I've got competition, which I don't want. I already decided. If I can find her again, she's for me and only for me.

The next couple of weeks, I make trips every day with the truck. I take the same roads, hoping to see Carme again, but I never do. I'm starting to think I dreamed her up completely. Then one day, I meet her again.

What happens is, I'm sitting at the farm, taking it easy. I was driving around, going to little towns to sell eggs, and now I'm home. I'm doing the same thing I do every day after work—relaxing.

Now, like I said before, there is a long dirt road at the farm. It starts down at the entrance gate on the main road and runs straight up to the farmhouse. Close to sunset, I start to see a black dot way down there on the road. It's moving though, coming up closer to where I'm sitting. Finally, I can see what it is, and I'm a little surprised. Looks like a Catholic priest. Raising dust on the road, dragging himself along in a heavy, black cassock. He gets closer, and I see a plump little guy with a red face, glasses, and a little, round hat on top of his head.

Gustav, my puppy, starts to growl, but I tell him not to worry. A priest in a cassock isn't too dangerous. And Gustav is only a little pup, but he understands me.

So I'm watching the poor guy walking toward me, and I can see he's sweating like a pig. He's wiping his face off with the sleeve of his cassock, which doesn't look too good. I'm watching this, and I'm thinking, Poor guy. It's too goddamn hot to wear all those clothes.

Well, it seems like the priest—he's got the same idea. As soon as he comes up to me, he takes off his cassock. Then he plops down on the ground next to me. He's got on more clothes—a shirt and trousers—underneath the cassock. He pulls out a handkerchief from his shirt pocket, takes off his glasses, wipes them, wipes off his face, puts his glasses back on, shakes out the handkerchief, folds it into little squares, and puts it back in his shirt pocket.

"Hola!" He grins. "I'm Antoni Iglesias. Call me Antoni. Mind if I join you?"

"Why not?"

I offer him my wine jug, which he takes. He takes it and practically swallows the whole goddamn thing in one gulp. A priest, right?

"I'm Rodolfo," I say.

I leave him with my jug and go inside to get another one and some more wine. I tell Pacher, who is inside there, what's going on, and he says he's got to see this crazy priest for himself. Pretty soon, we're all three of us sitting there drinking, talking. Antoni, the priest, he's drinking like anybody else. Friendly guy, likes talking. Tells us how he grew up in the church and all of this. Says he got his last name, which means "church," because he was an orphan, and the Catholic church gives orphans a last name meaning "church" or a last name meaning "cross."

Pacher and me, we tell him our stories too, and he's nodding and drinking the wine. Nicest guy in the world. Says he's the priest for the Sabater family, which is a noble family living in the mansion on the hill behind the farm. We can see the place from down here at the farm, but we have no reason to go up there, and we don't.

After a while, we're all three drunk. Pacher brings out his guitar and starts singing and playing. Pretty soon, Antoni sings a couple of songs, and Pacher picks out the notes. Then we all try singing. After a little while, Fritz and Justus come outside, and we have a lot of fun together, all of us. Finally, a couple of hours later, Antoni smacks himself on the side of the head and starts cussing himself out.

"I got to go!" he says. "I got to get ready for Mass in the morning. Pray for me, boys!"

We're all laughing. He puts on his cassock and stumbles off down the road.

Next evening before sunset, here comes Antoni again. Sits down with me, drinks some muscatel, meets Eva. They talk chickens and eggs. He hangs around for a long time and stays for supper. After this, we talk again. Politics, politics, politics. We never cared too much in Germany, but now everybody's got to talk politics.

My friends and me, we're all revolutionaries. We want to see things change. Things are not fair for the little guys. I mean for people like us and other people working on farms and in factories. Which is what most people do, right? We, all of us, want more for the workers and less for the rich guys, who take and take and take. Why should they have so much—which they make from our hard work—and we have so little?

Antoni says he feels the same as us. He wants workers to have better lives too.

"But you're a Catholic priest, right?" says Pacher. "The church is against any change at all! They want to keep their money and their power!"

"My friends," he says, "The church is the conscience of Spain. How can we have a government without that?"

Justus says, "If the Catholic church is the conscience of Spain, I'm sorry for Spain."

"But who else educate the children, if not the church?" Antoni asks. "The peasants?"

"The church higher-ups are a bunch of fascists," Pacher mutters. "Bad as the goddamn Nazis."

"No, no, no," Antoni says. "The problem, my friends, is the government doesn't like my church. *This* is the problem. But we are not fascists! Merda!"

"I bet that rich family you work for supports the fascists," Fritz says.

Antoni shakes his head. "The Sabaters? No, my friends, not true."

Things start getting heated, so I go inside and come out with Pacher's guitar, some wine, and some cigarettes. Pacher takes his guitar and starts to play, and we all join in when he sings. Antoni sings the loudest. We pass around the wine, the cigarettes, and pretty soon, we're all happy.

"Can you play the *sardana*?" Antoni asks. "I'll teach you how to do it! The girls will love you!"

So he does. He can dance too! And we kid him plenty about the girls. But he's very good-natured and laughs at everything we say.

So we give up on politics. We drink and smoke and tell dirty jokes. We try to forget about the rest of the world. Why? We're happy. We've got work on this little farm, which is making money, and we've got each other. Nobody is bothering us here. We can enjoy our lives.

One night, Antoni and I go out for a little walk. We're walking, and I'm telling him the only thing I'm missing here is girls. Suddenly, he stops and smacks himself on the side of the head.

"Rodolfo, I'm a stupid man!"

Then he tells me he knows just the girl for me.

"She is a very nice girl. Smart too. And very pretty. Blonde, blue eyes."

He grins. With his hands, he draws an hourglass in the air. "Beautiful figure too, eh?"

"Antoni," I laugh, "shame on you. You're not supposed to notice those things."

"Says who?"

Then he tells me the girl's name is Carme, and she is the only child of the Sabaters, the rich people he works for in the mansion on the hill.

I'm shocked. My Carme? She lives up there?

He rambles on. "She is very pretty, very nice. The family is very nice too," he says. He puts his hand on his chest. "I promise. Not fascists!"

"They won't like me. I'm a Jew, you know."

"But that's stupid, Rodolofo. I tell you, they are very good people, Rodolfo. Very nice people."

I'm thinking, This priest is naive, and this is a stupid idea. This girl, Carme—she's Catholic, and she's rich. It can never work out for us. But all night long, I can't think of anything else. So the next day after work, I clean myself up, and I walk up the hill with Antoni. We go inside the Sabater mansion, and Antoni introduces me to Carme's parents. They smile, hold out their hands.

"Nice to meet you," they say.

Carme is quietly standing behind them. They step aside, and her father gestures for her to come forward.

"My beautiful daughter," he says proudly. "Carme."

Carme Sabater. She holds out her hand, and I take it.

She smiles and says, "Very nice to meet you, Rodolfo," like she never saw me before in her life. But those blue eyes of hers are dancing, and they have the whole ocean in them.

Turns out, Carme's family goes way back. Big landowners for hundreds of years. Sons and grandsons of a *caballero,* a lord by the name of Juan Bautista de Sabater. He was an aristocrat with a lot of land and serfs and a couple of big castles—all the way back in the 1500s. So now I know why Carme's parents have a mansion up here.

Carme's father says, "Young man, would you like to take a little tour?"

I smile at Carme, and she smiles back. Her father takes her arm, and her mother takes my arm. Then her mother and I walk behind Carme and her father. Antoni follows behind us, and they show me some of the mansion. It's too big to show me all of it.

It's a fancy-shmancy place, like a castle. I don't know how to act, what to say. Gottfried would laugh at me. He'd be asking all kinds of questions and taking pictures.

They have a chapel in the mansion too, which they show me. My buddy, Antoni, he's the priest in charge of this chapel.

After the tour, Carme's father asks me, "Rodolfo, would you like to sit down? Have a little drink with us?"

"Thank you," I say. "I would enjoy that." Naturally, I'm thinking, The longer I can look at Carme, the happier I'll be.

Sabater is a big man, athletic looking, with broad shoulders. He's blond with blue eyes like Carme's—but lighter, much lighter. Carme's mother is not as tall as Carme, but she moves like Carme, like a dancer. She is pale with very dark hair and wide brown eyes. But her eyes twinkle the same way as Carme's.

So we sit down on big, heavy chairs in the parlor. A servant brings us wine and little sweets on a tray. Then Sabater says, "I've been wanting to meet you. I've been hearing what a wonderful job you are doing at the farm."

Why he cares, I don't know. But then, I get another surprise.

It turns out Glauber's clients, the Jewish Dutchmen, are leasing the farmland from Sabater. The Dutchmen built the farm and the buildings on the land, and they own the chicken farm business, including the eqipment and the animals. Once a month, when Glauber comes to see me, he also comes up here to the mansion and pays Sabater rent for the land, and the amount he pays goes up when we make money on the business.

After this, I get more comfortable, because Sabater wants to talk about the farm, and I can talk about that all day. He knows I'm the manager, so he wants to ask me questions. I'm happy to answer them. I explain how we're making the farm grow, all we're doing there. Carme and her mother, they sit and listen while her father and I talk. He wants to know the whole story. I tell him. We have good cash flow. We've got steady customers and more coming. There are no payables, except for the line of credit from a Dutch bank, which we use for operations. That has to be paid down every month, but the bank is very happy with us now. They even refinanced the loan at a lower interest rate, and they gave us a bigger line of credit. So we are making investments, buying some equipment, some better feed. And now we're adding some goats and sheep, which we're raising. Why? I'm planning on selling goat cheese and wool soon.

"I don't want to put all our eggs in one basket," I joke.

"Or in one cap," says Carme.

We both laugh. Her parents don't understand our little joke, and they don't pay any attention.

After we talk, Carme's parents tell me to come over again soon. Her father enjoyed meeting me, and he wants to hear more about what's going on at the farm.

Later on, Antoni comes by the farm while I'm pitching some hay.

" Hey, Rodolfo," he says. "I just came by to tell you the Sabaters liked you very much. Carme's mother, especially. She thinks you are very good-looking." He winks at me and laughs. "So maybe she needs a pair of strong glasses, huh?"

I put down my pitchfork and stand up very straight. I stick out my chest. "Antoni, take a good look. I'm a regular Valentino." I start turning around very slowly. "Can you see me better now?"

He plops himself down on the ground. He laughs and slaps himself on the side of the head. Then he crosses himself. "Oh my God," he says, "it's true. It's true! You could be Valentino's brother. How did I not see it before?"

"Maybe you need a pair of strong glasses, huh?"

We both laugh, and then I dust myself off and go inside the farmhouse. I bring out a jug of muscatel. We sit and share it. Awful stuff.

"Sabater's wife, you know, is the brains of the outfit," Antoni says. "Whatever she wants, he does."

I get serious for a minute. "Yah, but do they know my background? Do they know I'm a Jew?"

He waves me off. "I tell you, my friend, this is not a problem."

Now to tell the truth, this confuses me. Why would Carme's parents let a poor immigrant like me come around, even if they don't know I'm a Jew?

But for some reason or other, Carme and her mother invite me to come over again, so I go. This time, Sabater isn't home. So Carme, her mother, and I sit around and have something to eat and drink. Then I show them some card tricks, and we have some laughs. We play some card games together. They ask me about my accent, where I'm from, and I tell them. But that's it. They don't ask me any more questions about how I got here. They don't ask me about my religion. I don't get it, but I don't tell them either. We talk, have some laughs, enjoy the time we're together.

After a few visits like this, Carme's mother starts to let me spend some time alone with Carme. This is what I want, naturally. So her mama says it's all right if we sit together at her house, eat some nuts, drink a little wine together, play some card games. But when we want to go out, it's a different story. Her parents, they're strict when it comes to Carme going outside the house with me. To do this, we always need a chaperone.

We have only two ways to be together without being watched. One way is by pretending to be somebody else at a *baile de más-caras*, a masquerade party. People wear costumes and masks and pretend they're somebody else. Very popular in Europe—here in Catalonia too. So Carme and I, we do what young people are allowed to do. We get together at these balls. Tell each other our disguises beforehand and find each other this way. It's kind of silly, but it's the only way we can dance and hold each other in public. A few times, when the room is crowded, we find a way to sneak away, a place to hide outside. To touch, to be by ourselves.

The second way we can be alone is when we go out to ride horses. She tells her parents she is teaching me how to ride, and once a week, on Saturdays, we go for a couple of hours. The Sabaters have beautiful horses, and I ride on a brown stallion that is the brother of Carme's mare. We have to have a chaperone, naturally, but Antoni agrees to do this. Who is a better chaperone than the family priest, huh?

But Antoni, he's a good guy. He doesn't follow us like he's supposed to. Just tells us to meet him at such and such a place after an hour or two. He gets off his horse, spreads out a blanket, eats something, takes a little nap in the meadow. He knows how to give us some time together, some privacy.

When we go out riding, Carme and I find out we have a lot in common. Both of us, we love the outdoors, hiking, kids, animals, dancing, having fun. We both want to travel around the world. We both like to joke, to laugh. She's got a good sense of humor. Knows how to laugh, how to relax, have a good time. And she's smart too. Keeps me on my toes.

One Saturday, we're out riding, and Carme says, "Let's do something different today."

She's acting all mysterious, which is fun for me, and naturally, I wonder what she's up to. She's got a lot of color in her pretty cheeks, and she's all dressed up in her fancy riding outfit. I'm right behind her, watching that bobbing bottom and that blonde braid jumping as our horses trot into town. We go to the center of Vilassar de Dalt, and there it is—her "something different." The whole town is outside there, getting ready for a big celebration tomorrow. Everybody is out in the streets. Lots of people mixing together, talking, and laughing. Where we stop, there are a bunch of guys practicing how to make high ladders out of their own bodies. They compete in teams of ladder-makers. Each team has its own costumes, and each team makes a tall pyramid by standing up on top of each other's shoulders. So there are more guys at the bottom and fewer guys as the ladder gets higher.

Carme is very excited, telling me all about the ladder-making, which is part of a big holiday. What we're seeing today is their dress rehearsal. Everybody is having a good time.

Then all of a sudden, a block from us, we see a guy coming out of a building. He's yelling and cussing and dragging a young boy behind him. Both of them, the guy and the kid, they're barefoot, filthy looking, wearing rags. But the man, naturally, is much bigger than this boy. He stops in front of the building and starts beating this poor kid with his hands, smacking the kid pretty damn hard—even punching him in the face with his fists.

Carme, she rides down the street, and I follow her. She jumps off Paloma, and she grabs a riding crop. Before this, I never saw her remove that thing. Paloma, she just stands there, and Carme starts walking fast, snapping her riding crop. She's heading over to this guy and this kid.

There's a young man about Carme's age who sees what's what, and he tries to stop her. Seems to know who she is.

"Don't go there, my sweet lady," he warns. He's very respectful of her. "Forget them. The whole family is nothing but dirt."

Carme, she acts like she doesn't even hear him. She looks straight through him. Gives her whip a hard pop in the air and keeps on walking. The young man, he shrinks back into a wall, then slips away.

Now, all of this happens so fast I'm not sure what to do. But I better do something, or Carme is going to get hurt. So I jump off my horse and run up to her. I'm figuring there's going to be a fight.

But when I catch up to her, she's standing in front of this bum and his kid, and I can see the bum is drunk. Can smell him too. He stinks of cheap wine. Up close, he's bigger than I thought. I give him a dirty look and get ready. But before anything can happen, Carme pops her whip again, and the bum looks up at her. He stands there and looks. He doesn't move. Carme stands there too. She stands in that fancy outfit, holding her riding crop, and she doesn't say a word either. She stares at the boy and then at the man. Drunk as the guy is, he looks embarrassed.

He lowers his head and mutters, "The boy was stealing food."

But Carme doesn't pay any attention. She turns to me.

"Rodolfo," she says. "I want to take this boy to Father Antoni."

This poor kid, he's bleeding, shaking, and crying—curled up on the street like a little worm. I pick the boy up and sit him on my horse in front of me so I can hold him. He looks like he's maybe six years old, and he weighs practically nothing. He doesn't talk—just sits slumped in front of me like a rag.

Carme puts away her riding crop and gets back up on Paloma. The father of the boy, he shuffles his feet. He never looks up from the street. We start to ride away.

"That bastard," she says. "He doesn't deserve a child. I'm taking this one away for good."

"Can you do that?"

She doesn't answer me.

So that's it. We ride off, back to where Antoni is waiting for us. Carme tells him the story, and he takes the kid away with him.

Later on, I find out from Antoni that Carme's father—he's got a lot of authority in these towns around here.

"You see," he says. "This is the way it has always been. The Sabaters are in charge. Most people know this. Nobody would try to go against them."

"Yah," I say, "but what about the family of the boy? Maybe his mama wants him. Or somebody else, like a grandmother or someone."

Antoni shrugs. "Then they can come and beg Sabater to get him back," he says.

"And can they get him back?"

"No, they won't ever get him back. He belongs to the church now."

Right or wrong, the Sabaters have the power to do pretty much whatever they want. But they do what's best, no? Like what Carme just did, for instance. She could have ignored the whole thing like everybody else, but she cared about this kid, and he is much better off now. Antoni says the kid is not six or seven years old like he looked. He's eleven years old. Must have been starving to death in that family of his. Some family.

All the time now, I think about Carme and how much I love her. She doesn't know I'm a Jew, and I'm afraid to tell her. I'm afraid her parents will say I'm not good enough for her if they know. But I've been putting it off and putting it off much too long. I decide I have to tell her the next time we go out riding.

When the day comes along, I'm down in the dumps. We go out and ride on our horses. Carme can tell something is wrong, but she knows me. Knows I'll talk when I'm ready. Finally, I tell myself, This is it. I stop my horse, and she stops hers. Antoni stops too, but he stays back—far away from us. I take a long look at her.

"I have to tell you something very important. Something I never told you about me. And if you can't see me after this again, I'll understand."

Her dark-blue eyes widen.

"I'm a Jew," I say.

She breaks out laughing. "Oh, Rodolfo! Don't you think I know that?"

I'm shocked. "You know?"

"Of course."

"But how…?"

"Oh, Rodolfo, of course I know. After I met you on the road, I asked Antoni to find out all about you. Why do you think he came to see you at the farm?"

"Your parents…?"

"Mama knows," she says.

"She doesn't care?"

"Rodolfo, my grandmother—Mama's mother—was a born a Jew, and her parents were Jews. When my grandmother married my grandfather, she had to become a Catholic. But she always felt Jewish, and sometimes, she would light candles on Jewish holidays. I didn't know my grandmother, but that's what Mama said. Anyhow, Mama knows, and she doesn't care. She likes you very much."

"But what about your father?"

"He wants to make Mama happy. And he wants to make me happy. But he doesn't know yet."

"Then you have to tell him. He might object."

"Papa?" she says. "Why would he? He isn't religious at all!"

"You have your own priest, your own chapel. You say Mass."

"Yes, of course, Rodolfo," she says. "We do it because we have to. It's expected. Nothing more. None of us believes in all that stuff."

She leans over to me and whispers, "You know, don't you, that I never, never, never confess?"

I ask her then and there if she will marry me.

And she says, "Oh, Rodolfo, of course I will. I love you."

And I love her too. Oh, how I love her.

But this is not the end of it, naturally. The next Saturday, when I come over to the mansion, Carme tells me we aren't going out riding. She says her father would like to talk to me.

"Don't worry," she says. "He likes you. Mama loves you. I love you."

So Carme's father and me, we sit down in his library, which is full of books. We talk about the farm. We drink a little wine. Not that dirty muscatel. Good wine.

Then he says, "Rodolfo, I understand you and my Carme would like to get married."

"Yes," I say. "If she'll have me."

"You come from a different background, a different country, a different religion. Do you think this is a good idea?"

"We're all different people, no? What does it matter? Carme and I, we love each other. I will take very good care of her, I promise."

He swirls the wine in his glass. Seems to be studying it. Says, "I like you, Rodolfo. You're a good man. You're not educated, but you have a good heart and a good head for business. You'll do well. But my daughter is still young. I would like her to wait until this summer, when she is at least eighteen, before she marries anyone."

"I understand," I say. "Of course I'll wait."

He nods. "Good. But her age is not my biggest worry. Because even if I like you, and even if I know you'll take good care of her, there is a much bigger problem. Carme can never marry a Jew."

My heart sinks. "Sir," I say, "I'm not a very good Jew."

He laughs. "And I'm not a very good Catholic."

I smile and raise my wine glass. "To every man's religion," I say.

He raises his glass. "But alas, it is still a problem, Rodolfo." He takes a drink. "You see, it matters what you *call* yourself. What people think you are. It matters very much."

"But I'm the same man, no?"

He shakes his head. "Rodolfo, do you believe you're welcome here—a Jew in Spain?"

"Probably not," I admit.

"No. And do you think you're safe here? You're not."

"Nobody has been bothering me. We mind our own business at the farm. Everybody has been good to us."

"Yes, but you must realize what is happening here in Spain?"

"I know there might be a civil war if things stay as they are..."

"Yes," he says. "Do you know Hitler is sending money here already? Also men and weapons? So is Italy. The Catholic church is against the Spanish government. We might have a dictator like Hitler here."

"But most people in Spain—the workers—support the government we have right now. Isn't that so?"

He laughs bitterly. "But sadly, my friend, that makes no difference at all. You see, the money wins. The money always wins. And it's not the workers who have the money. It's the church and the landowners and the fascists."

"Do you support them?"

"No, of course not. But I can't go against them, Rodolfo."

"So what are you saying?"

He sighs. "You must convert, Rodolfo. It's the only way."

I take a deep breath. "You want me to join a church that supports the Nazis? I can't do that, sir. I ran away from the Nazis. They tried to kill me."

"Let me put it to you this way. If you become a Catholic, you'll be safe here. My family will use our influence. Protect you."

"I am what I am."

He sighs and takes another drink. "Look, conversion? It's nothing. You say a few words, that's all. It's nothing to convert. You don't have to believe. Do it for Carme's sake, Rodolfo, and for your own safety."

For a few minutes, neither of us says anything. Then he says, "You're a good man, Rodolfo. Do we understand each other?"

"I understand you," I say.

"Good," he says. He stands up and I do too. He puts an arm around my shoulder. "Good," he says again, as he walks me out.

Well, it's a short distance down the hill to the farm, but it feels like a long way. I do understand Carme's father, as I told him. But I don't think he understands me. I'm never going to convert. Why? One, I have no use for religion—any religion. And two, if I ever converted to Catholicism—even if I don't believe in it—it would kill my family.

When I come to visit Carme the next day, we go out for a long walk. Antoni follows us at a distance. I tell Carme what her father said. I tell her I can't convert.

"Why should you?" she says. "It's ridiculous!"

"Well, your father says I can't marry you unless I do."

"He's not marrying you," she says. "*I* am. Besides, it's all superstition anyway. That's what he says himself!"

"But it's still important to him, Carme."

"Not to me! What difference would it make? You're the same man!"

"That's what I told your father," I say.

"I'll talk to him," she says. "He'll change his mind. I know he will." She laughs. "He always gives me what I want. And I want *you!*"

I shake my head. "I don't think your father is going to change his mind this time, my love."

"Oh, he will. Mama loves you too. Just give him a little time. You'll see."

A couple of weeks pass by, and nothing else happens. We go out riding as usual, and Carme says her father seems to be in a good mood. He's been saying nice things about me. So I'm thinking, Maybe I made a mistake. Maybe he thought it over, and he's okay with things the way they are. Then she tells me her parents are planning a big party for their twentieth wedding anniversary, and I'm invited. It's going to be a fancy-shmancy deal, which means I have to go to Barcelona and buy a suit, which I do.

When I walk into the party, Carme's wearing a long, blue silk gown—almost the color of her eyes—and her hair is twisted into a crown of golden braids. She looks like a princess—like something out of this world. To my eyes, there's no girl but her in that room. Naturally, every other man in the room is staring at her. But it's *my* hand she grabs. Right now, I'm the luckiest guy in the world.

We have to walk all around the room, here and there, so she can introduce me to cousins, aunts, uncles, family friends. Most times, I like parties. But I have nothing in common with these people, nothing to say to them. That doesn't matter, though, because Carme does all the talking. I smile and nod. Being with her—that's all I want.

At this party, they have a local band, a *cobia*, which starts to play the sardana. This is one of the dances Antoni taught me, so I grab Carme, and we dance. Makes me feel good to dance with her. When they start playing a rumba, everybody watches Carme, because she's such a beautiful dancer.

Now, I see another band coming in, and I'm surprised when I see Pacher with them. Pacher's got his guitar, and he and the guys with him are dressed up like Tyroleans from Bavaria. We keep dancing, but I'm wondering what's going on. Out of the corner of my eye, I see my other friends from the farm—Eva, Justus, Fritz. All of them are coming in here. What are they doing here?

I start to steer Carme across the dance floor toward my friends. But before I can get over there, Carme's father stops everything. He walks over to the German band, which is standing up on a little stage, and he claps his hands together to get everybody's attention. Then he starts talking.

"Tonight is a wonderful night. It's our anniversary, of course. But we have another surprise for everybody! A wonderful surprise!"

Everybody is listening. Everybody likes a surprise.

He says, "The next song is in honor of my beautiful daughter, Carme, and her fiancé, Rodolfo. They are getting married this summer!"

Carme and me, we're in shock. Nobody told us anything like this was going to happen. The crowd cheers, pushes us to the center of the room, makes a circle around us, and the German band starts playing "An Der Schönen Blauen Donau," which means "On the Beautiful Blue Danube." It's a famous waltz by Johann Strauss. Everybody in this room stands in a circle, and we're in the middle, dancing.

"Carme," I whisper, "what the heck is going on?"

She whispers back, "I don't know!"

We dance, and pretty soon, other people join in with the dancing. The band plays another song, and this time, Pacher is singing to us: "Dein ist mein ganzes herz! Wo du nicht bist, kann ich nicht sein." Which is a beautiful and very popular German love song. The words mean, "Yours is my heart alone! Where you are not, I cannot be."

When the song ends, Carme's father walks up to us. He pulls us aside.

"Children," he says, "I talked to Antoni, and tomorrow, he will start giving Rodolfo religious instructions. Your mama and I will make the wedding right here in August, on the day after your birthday, Carme."

"Papa, what are you talking about?" Carme says. "Rodolfo doesn't want to become a Catholic."

Her father frowns. "I explained all this to Rodolfo, and he told me he understood me." He looks at me. "Isn't that so, Rodolfo?"

"With respect, sir," I tell him, "I did say I understood you. But I never agreed to convert."

"Papa," Carme cries, "why should Rodolfo convert? None of us believes in all that mumbo-jumbo! Rudolf and I don't care about religion. You know that! What difference does it make?"

Well, this is a very big mistake. What Carme says makes him furious. His whole face gets swollen and red, and he glares at us. He stands there with his fists clenched at his sides, and then he quietly spits out his answer.

"*This is not a debate!*"

Carme and I are holding hands. She gives my hand a squeeze to let me know she's on my side. We don't say anything.

But Sabater isn't finished. He glares at Carme.

"After tonight," he growls, "you may not see him again. Not until he has become a Catholic in our church. You want to get married? Then he must do this. It is a small thing. No more discussion!"

He storms away and grabs his wife. They start to dance, and he doesn't look back at us. We can see he's telling Carme's mother what's happened, because when she looks our way, she has a worried expression. She's trying to talk to him, calm him down. But I know he's not going to change his mind.

Carme is crying. I lead her to the dance floor and hold her.

"Carme," I say, "let's leave. We can go to France. We'll cross the border and go find a way to get married."

But she's afraid. My little sweetheart, who took such a big chance on me. This time, she's afraid. And she's right to be afraid. She's right. Seventeen years old, and everybody knows her, knows who she is. Everybody knows the Sabaters. How can we get away with it? How can we run away?

After this, Sabater is true to his word. He doesn't let me come to the mansion to see her, and he doesn't let her go out. We sneak letters back and forth, back and forth. Antoni helps us out. But he tells me he can't marry us unless I convert.

"My friend," he says, "do this for your own sake. After you marry, you can leave here and believe as you wish."

We're getting nowhere.

Spring comes and goes—the longest spring of my life. Then one day in July, I get a letter from Gottfried. He says he has an appointment for us at the American embassy in Paris. I write a note to Carme. I tell her I'm going to Paris to try to get permission to go to the United States. I ask her to be patient, to wait for me. If I can go to the United States, I can save money and find a way for us to be together. She writes back and promises to wait for me—whatever it takes.

While I'm packing my suitcase for my trip to Paris, I find the handkerchiefs we bought in Switzerland for Clare and Mama. I'm thinking, I've got no ring, nothing to give to Carme. But this hand-kerchief is pretty, no? And it's got Carme's initials—"CS." Same as my sister Clare. At least, it's a little something for her. I put the handkerchief in a small box, and I give it to Antoni for her.

I slip a note inside. "Remember me. I love you."

Antoni brings a note back from her. It says, "I love you, Rodolfo. I'll wait for you. Carme."

And that's it. I leave. Fritz drives me to Port Bou, and I catch a train to Paris. But even as the train is leaving, I have hope. Carme and me, we're going to be together again, even if it takes a long time.

When Gottfried meets me at the train station in Paris, I'm very happy to see him. And he's excited to see me. To tell the truth, I didn't realize I missed him as much as I did. First thing we do, we go and grab some beers, listen to some music at a bistro. Then we go to his apartment.

The next few weeks pass by. Carme writes me, but she says not to write back. She tells her parents I went to Paris, so now her father is checking the mail. He wants this to be the end for us. That's not our plan, though, and her letters keep coming every few days. She says the boy she rescued in town—he's doing pretty good. He's liv-ing in a place like Antoni did as a kid, and she goes with Antoni to see him. She says people are talking about problems in Spain all the time now. There are big strikes, a lot of people getting killed. There are workers attacking churches and killing the priests. There are people who want to make Catalonia separate from the rest of Spain. There are even women wanting more say-so. Carme likes one group, by the name of *Mujeres Libres*—free women. She says she isn't allowed to join them, but she likes what they're doing.

Here in Paris, I try to keep busy. I go everywhere with Gottfried and his friends, but I'm always thinking of Carme. I don't talk
about her though. I don't want to get into any discussions with
Gottfried. I know what he would say anyhow, because he used to
say it all the time at home. Was the same stupid thing everyone
said—me too. "You play with the shikses, but you marry a Jewish
girl."

Once or twice, Gottfried asks me about the letters I'm getting
from Spain. I tell him I found a cute shikse to play with over there.
He laughs, and after this he doesn't ask questions.

In Paris, Gottfried throws a party for me. We get together with
some of his new friends. Fred Strauss is in town, working with the
Jewish relief agency, and he tells us he gave them a letter promising
to hire us in New York. The agency guys think this will be a big
help, because Fred has a lot of money, and they think that's what
it will take.

Gottfried and I, we spend the days walking around Paris, seeing the sights. But we don't want the gendarmes to pick us up, so
we have to be careful. We only take the subway when it's crowded,
and we go to places where there are a lot of people around, so we
can get lost if we have to. We don't want any attention.

One day, we see a bus and two or three police cars pass us
by. Inside the bus, there are some old-fashioned Polacks. The men
have skull caps on their heads, and they have beards. The women
are wearing head scarves. Little kids are looking out the windows
with their hands pressed against the glass.

Gottfried tells me he saw the same thing once before. He says
they passed a new law in France to get rid of Jews from the East.

There used to be a lot more of them here, mostly peddlers and other poor people from Poland. They settled here many years ago. Now, they're being deported. Where to? That's anybody's guess. We can't help feeling sorry for these people, but there's nothing we can do.

During the second week of August, I suddenly stop hearing from Carme, and I start to worry, because the newspapers say civil war has broken out in Spain. It's the fascists and the church against the government—exactly what Sabater expected. But I tell myself not to worry too much. Vilassar de Dalt is a farm area far from Madrid, which is where most of the fighting is. The odds are Carme's father found out about her letters, and he's watching her to make sure she doesn't write to me.

I'm thinking Gottfried and I will have our appointment at the American embassy in a few days. Maybe then, we can get to New York, and I can find a way to send for Carme. Finally, the day comes, and we go to the embassy. But we find out fast that we're out of luck.

Gottfried and I, we're not deadbeats. We have Siegfried, Hubert, Clare's husband, my aunts and uncles—all promising to give us money, places to stay, and jobs. We even have Fred Strauss, a rich American, guaranteeing us. But the guy in charge here, the vice consul, he says unless you have a lot of money in your own name, you can't go to America. So now what?

In Paris, we keep talking with Gottfried's buddies. Most of them are Jewish refugees like us. We see pictures in the papers of new Italian fighter planes. The Italian dictator, Mussolini, is sending them to Franco, the anti-government leader in Spain. And naturally, Hitler is sending Franco new airplanes, pilots, trained soldiers, tanks, guns—all the latest.

There are a lot of guys here, who say we have to stand up and fight in Spain, or else the Nazis are going to take over Europe. One man we talk to, by the name of Carl Einstein, he's a big shot here in Paris—a famous artist and all of this. Says he's Albert Einstein's nephew. Anyhow, he says he's going to Spain to fight. Fifty years old, and he's going over there to fight. He says we need to forget about leaving Europe. We have to stop Hitler in Spain. If Franco wins in Spain, he says Germany will feel free to start another war to get back all the land they lost in the last war. I think he's right.

How I'm seeing things now is like this: There are times you have to fold. You get a terrible hand. Bluffing doesn't work. You can't win, and there's nothing more you can do. This is the hand we have right now. My brother and I, we've been on the run for over three years already. We can't go back to Germany, we can't go to the United States, and no country in Europe wants us. To me, one place in Europe is as bad as the next one. So I decide. Except for my family, everyone I love and everything I ever worked for is in Spain. My girl, my friends, my work. I'm going to go back to Spain, and I'm going to fight for what I love.

So I tell my brother, "I'm going to Spain. At least in Spain, we can fight the bastards instead of sitting here and waiting for them to catch up with us. I'm sick and tired of running."

"We can stay here in Paris and fight them," Gottfried says. "We can join the underground right here. There's plenty we can do besides getting shot at."

We talk and talk and talk. He is against fighting in another country's war, but I don't change my mind. Finally, Gottfried says, "Okay, let's go."

He says he's coming with me, because otherwise, I'll probably shoot myself in the foot. What he really means, though, is he wants us to stay together. And that's what I want too. So I tell him I'm happy he's coming with me, and I can see it makes him feel good.

A couple of weeks later, we get on a train to Port Bou. This time, though, I don't have to jump off the train in the tunnel. Everything is different now. There are people on the Spanish border, who are standing around waiting around for guys like us. They're trying to get people to sign up to fight against Franco. There are a lot of different groups who want us to sign up with them—socialists, anarchists, Trotsky communists, worker's groups, and so on and so on.

All the groups here are against Franco. Gottfried and I, we decide to go with the biggest group, because we figure it's going to have the most support and the best equipment. This group has a banner that says, "Partido Obrero de Unificacion Marxista," which means "Workers Party of Marxist Unification"—a long name they shorten to POUM. It turns out POUM is a socialist bunch. They lean to the left, but they aren't communists. My brother and I, we're not communists either. We agree no man should lack for food and a roof over his head. But if a man works harder than another man, why shouldn't he earn more? So we sign up with POUM, and they give us government papers and Spanish names too. Now we're officially Rodolfo and Gottofredo Kahn, two Spanish brothers. And just like that, we're not illegal refugees. We're legal. We're soldiers fighting for the Republic of Spain, for the loyalists.

After a couple of hours, they put us in a little van with some other guys, and they drive all of us to Barcelona. We get some food to eat on the way. Guess what they give us? Chicken and eggs.

On and off, all the way to Barcelona, somebody is shooting at our van. We're a little surprised, because we didn't know there was shooting going on in Catalonia. We have no guns. So we sit there on the floor of the van and listen to the bullets hitting the sides. The shooting comes and goes, but luckily, nobody gets hurt. It takes hours and hours to get to Barcelona. How we all get there in one piece, I don't know.

When we do get there, the city is quiet. Crowded with people, right? But no shooting. The van stops and lets us out at the Hotel Colón on La Rambla, which is where we're going to sleep. And sitting out in front, we see an old farm truck with metal plates bolted on it. These plates cover the front, the back, the sides, the roof. Sticking out of the tailgate, through a hole, we see a long barrel from a rusty, old cannon. Gottfried and I are scratching our heads. This is an armored tank?

Up and down La Rambla, we see banners hanging from buildings. Very colorful too, like a big circus. The anarchists have banners in black and red, even shoeshine boxes painted black and red. There are signs for the socialists, the Trotsky communists, this one, that one, another one. There's scribbling all over the buildings too. To tell the truth, I don't recognize this street anymore.

We wait with the other guys outside the hotel, and there we meet some more POUM volunteers. They come from everywhere, so everybody is trying to translate what everybody else says. A regular Tower of Babel. There are women and kids here too. It's a party, no? Everybody wants to fight.

Loyalist volunteers and sympathizers
Fall 1936
Barcelona, Spain
POUM headquarters

After a while, they take some of us down to the hotel basement. This is where they give us what they call "training." How to use ammunition and all this. Mostly, though, what they say is, "Watch out you don't blow yourself up."

Which makes sense when we look at the antiques they give us for guns. All different old guns. I get a 1910 Modelo Mauser 7x57 mm from Mexico. Gottfried gets a single-shot M1871 Vetterli 10.4 mm from someplace—maybe Russia. After this, they show us some big buckets on the floor. They have all the cartridges mixed together in the buckets. Some fit this gun, some fit that gun, some fit no gun. Everybody picks through the buckets like kids looking for toys. If you find cartridges to fit your gun, you can have fifty of them. But I can't find fifty that fit. Neither can Gottfried.

Now they give us some more junk, which they call "supplies." There are used US Army rucksacks only a few of us get. But everybody gets a pitiful, little ditty bag. Yippee. They give some guys Sam Browne belts and pistols. I get one, and Gottfried doesn't. He gets a leather jacket and I don't. We both get brown shirts and khaki pants that don't fit. We both get little hats with pointy ends. Some guys get helmets and boots, but they don't give us any. Sorry, boys, we're all out.

After this, we go outside behind the hotel and play around with our guns. We try loading them, shooting at some targets on the wall. But there are so many different types of guns that everybody has to figure out what the hell to do with whichever one he has. Gottfried's rifle is old, but it works if you shoot one cartridge at a time. My rifle won't shoot at all. Keeps jamming up. I ask them for another one, but they've got nothing else, so they tell me I can get another one later on. Then they give us hand grenades. They tell us how to use them, but not to practice. They say they don't have enough to let us waste any by practicing. But it's a good thing nobody tries to practice, because these crazy grenades kill the guys who use them faster than they kill anybody else. What happens is this: before you can throw the grenade, you have to peel off a piece of tape, which holds down the lever. But when you peel off the tape, the grenade explodes in your face and blows you up.

So that's our training, the whole thing. We don't know—should we laugh or cry?

It's not long after our training when Gottfried hears about an airfield outside of town. Seems like our side has some Russian and German planes out there, but we don't have enough mechanics. So naturally, Gottfried volunteers, and they send him out there to work on the airplanes. But it turns out the airplanes are just like the guns and everything else—somebody else's old junk.

I get assigned to the infantry. Some infantry. Here's what I'm doing. I'm marching through the paths of a garden, which they call a drilling field. This goes on all morning, every morning. After this, there's nothing to do, so we play cards.

Every day, I do what they say. But every day, all I can think of is, When can I get away from here? When can I go to Vilassar de Dalt? Finally, I get a day off. I clean up, borrow an old truck, and go.

Vilassar de Dalt is not too far from Barcelona, but it's a long drive this time. This group and that group block up the roads, stop up the traffic. But it's a beautiful, bright day with a strong breeze. All I can think about is my Carme, seeing her again. I'm singing. I'm happy. Even if her parents don't want us to be together, we're going to be together. There's a way, and we'll find it. I'm sure we will.

Finally, I get to the entrance gate at the chicken farm. But when I get out of the truck, I see the gate is completely locked up with a big padlock. There's also a big sign tied onto the gateposts. In Catalan, it says, "Confiscated by the Republic of Spain, State of Catalonia." I look at it again to make sure. But that's exactly what it says.

My own side took over my farm? Huh?

I figure somebody probably made a mistake. So far, everything I've seen in this war is mixed up. That must be what happened here. I figure I can walk down there and talk to whoever is running things. I can help to get this thing straightened out.

So since the gate is locked, I have to climb over the top, which I do. I drop down onto the other side, which is the long dirt road to the farm, and I start walking. While I'm walking, I'm thinking about this again. Maybe what they did wasn't a mistake. Maybe they took over the farm so they could make sure they can feed us. Seems like there is always a shortage of food for our guys. So maybe that's it. Must be that they need to control the chickens and the eggs and the equipment we have here. Makes sense to me now.

But one thing I don't understand—why it's so quiet on the road. Where is everybody? Usually, somebody is coming or going. And where is Gustav? He always barks and comes running to greet me. Seems to know I'm at the gate even when he's all the way down at the farmhouse.

I'm still too far down the road to be able to see the farmhouse, but now I'm starting to get a bad feeling. This road is too quiet— much too quiet. By now, I should already be seeing and hearing activities at the farm. Animals, people, equipment moving around. And I should be smelling the farm—the hay, the chickens, the other animals, the smells of food cooking. But I'm not. What I'm smelling is something putrid, like rotten eggs. And when I come to the place the farmhouse should be, I understand. They didn't confiscate the farm to run it. They burned it down. All I'm seeing now is ashes. Piles and piles of ashes.

They took everything out of here and burned the buildings down to the ground. My farm is gone. The whole place is gone. No animals. No barns. No truck, no equipment. Nothing. Nothing but broken pieces of furniture, broken glass, stones, rotten eggs, spoiled food, and ashes. Ashes everywhere.

Everything I worked for is gone.

I can't believe it. Why?

I would have given them anything they wanted. Anything they asked for, anything they wanted, I would gladly have given to them. I would have helped them run this place too. They would have had a supply of good food all the time from this farm. Why did they have to destroy everything? And where are my buddies? Are they somewhere in these ashes too?

I start to look around on the ground, and in the piles of ashes, I find a few bones. I pick them up and look them over. They are dog bones. They killed Gustav? I guess he was trying to protect. I trained him to do that. But I still don't understand it. Why didn't Pacher or Justus stop them? They loved Gustav, and he listened to them. And what happened to them? And to Fritz? And Eva? I don't see any human bones in these ashes. So where is everybody?

The whole time I'm walking around the farm, I'm feeling sick. Like somebody poured poison down my throat, and I can't throw it up. I'm scared to death too. I can't pick up my head to look at the hilltop, because I'm scared of what I might see. Of what might have happened to the Sabaters. To my Carme. Did they burn down the Sabater mansion too? They probably did. They probably wanted to destroy all of the Sabaters' property. That's got to be the reason they burned down my farm. Makes complete sense now.

But thinking about this, I still have hope. See, there are no signs anybody got killed at the farm. Far as I can tell, only Gustav got killed. I don't see any human bones or dried blood—nothing like that. So I'm pretty sure my buddies left here alive.

I figure somebody around here knew what was coming. A peasant around here must have warned them. They must have had to leave in a big hurry. That's why they left everything here, including food to spoil. That's why Gustav is dead too. They couldn't take an animal with them.

So I figure if somebody warned my buddies, then the Sabaters definitely got warned. Either one of my buddies or one of the peasants around here. The peasants here know everything about everything. And they don't just work for the Sabaters. The Sabaters treat them like family. Pay them well, give them extra money when they need it, help their kids—all these things. Carme and her mother are always helping somebody who is having a baby or somebody who is sick.

And even if nobody told the Sabaters what was coming, I'm positive they would have told Antoni. Why? The peasants around here are very religious, and Antoni is their priest. So they would at least have warned Antoni, and he would have warned the family.

So now I'm not scared to look up at the hill. And when I do, I see what I expected. There's nothing up there anymore except the charred stone shell of the mansion. When I walk up there, everything seems the same as it did down below. Ashes and burned stuff. Rubble everywhere. Broken glass. Even broken stained glass from the chapel. Broken pieces of furniture, torn-up paintings, broken kitchen stuff. Nothing left. No mansion, no horse barn, no chapel. No people or animals. But I don't stop to look through the ashes.

Right now, I'm in a hurry to find somebody. Someone who can tell me where Carme is hiding.

I walk down the back of the hill, where the peasants live in their little houses. I don't see any kids playing outside right now, which seems very strange to me, because in the late afternoons, kids are always playing out here. Sometimes, I used to stop and play with them. They all know me.

I look around for somebody, but no one is outside. Then I notice a house with its front door wide open. I go up and yell inside there, but nobody answers. I walk through the open door, take a quick look. Nobody home. Just a few sticks of furniture and some junk on the floor. No people.

I walk back out and go to the house next door. I knock on the door, but nothing happens. I wait a little while and knock harder. Still nothing. I'm turning to leave, to go to another house, when the door finally opens. A bent, wrinkled old woman is standing there. I tell her hello, and she nods. I think she recognizes me. I've been around here a lot with Carme.

"What happened here, grandma?" I ask.

She shakes her head slowly and motions listlessly toward the inside of the house.

"You see?" she says shakily. "Nobody here. Gone. All gone."

"I didn't hear you too well, grandma, "I say. "Can you tell me more? Can you tell me what happened?"

She shakes her head again. "My children, my grandchildren, all gone. They leave me here to die."

She's looking right through me. I try to bring her back.

"Grandma," I say. "Who was here? What did they want?"

She shrugs. "Soldiers. I don't know."

I take her gently by the shoulders. "Tell me what happened."

"The men, the boys," she says, "they went with the soldiers. To fight. Now, in the village, only old ones and babies. Babies with mamas. My children, my grandchildren. Gone."

"And the Sabaters?" I ask. I point to the hilltop where the mansion stood. "What about the Sabaters? Do you know where they are?"

She looks at me, and now I'm sure she knows who I am. "I am so sorry," she says. Tears roll down her cheeks. She's wringing her hands.

"*Estan morts,*" she whispers. "*Estan morts.*"

She can't look me in the eye. She puts a shaky hand over her mouth and lowers her head. Then she turns away from me and closes the door.

I stand there. I stare at the wooden door. I can't move. Over and over, I hear her whisper—*Estan morts. Estan morts. Estan morts.*

Dead. They're all dead.

There's a gust of wind, and the open door of the neighbor's house slams shut. When I turn around, the impossible blue sky starts spinning in circles, and I throw up.

I wipe my mouth off and drag myself back to the hilltop. I start to kick at the rubble—I uncover pieces of furniture, broken ceramics, glass, and ashes under ashes. Piles and piles of ashes. I kick at the ashes, and in the breeze, they scatter everywhere. Some fly into my mouth. I spit them out.

I kick at the ashes, and now I see some fragments of bones in there. Human bones. I move away. I see a pile of broken ceramics and burned clothing. I get down on my hands and knees and rake through this pile with my fingers, looking for something of hers—anything. Anything I can hold onto. I find a scrap of a handkerchief. Maybe the one I gave her, maybe not. I leave it there.

It's no use. My Carme is dead. The girl I loved more than my own life—she's gone.

Now the sun starts going down. I walk down the hill and past the ashes of the farm. I don't stop to look back. I walk down the road to the front gate and climb over the top. When I get on the other side and see that sign on the gate, I rip it off. Rip it off and tear it to pieces. I pick up the torn pieces and tear them again and again.

I get back in my truck and watch the pieces blow around in the breeze. Some of them stick to the fence before they slide down to the ground. Some of the pieces flop up and down on the dirt like dying fish. But most of them scatter like ashes. I drive the truck back to Barcelona.

After this, I'm a man who doesn't give a damn. I don't give a damn, huh? After this, I don't give a damn anymore.

XIII
GOTTFRIED

Not long after we get to Barcelona, Rudolf goes off to see his chicken farm. When he comes back, he says it's gone. Says our guys closed it, took everything, and burned it down completely. Later on, we find out that his German friends who were there, they joined up with the loyalists.

When he gets back from the farm, Rudolf is very upset. I know he's mad. He worked hard on the chicken farm, and he says our own men burned it down. Guess he's mad at his buddies too, because after all the work they did, nobody let him know. I try to talk to him, but he doesn't want to talk to me.

When I get mad, I don't feel like talking either, so I leave him alone. Me, I stay mad for a long time. But Rudolf and I are different too. He's very easygoing. When he gets mad, he gets mad, and then he gets over it. Forgets all about it. But this time, he doesn't. Goes around moping for days. So of course, I start to worry. He's not Rudolf. Not joking, not laughing, not gambling, not anything.

"Look," I tell him, "it wasn't personal, Rudolf. Franco's guys are in the area up there. Our guys are burning down all the farms, so the fascists can't hide in them or take them over."

He doesn't answer me.

"What the hell's eating you up like this?"

"Leave me alone."

The only other thing he says is that he wants to fight. Fight Hitler, fight Franco, fight everybody.

He says, "I'm goddamn sick and tired of this. When the hell are we going to fight?"

Me, I'm not too anxious, especially after I get a good look at the weapons and everything else. The other side, they've got Spanish Mausers that fire 7x57 mm cartridges, and they've got new guns from Germany and Italy. We've got everybody else's trash. They've got one man in charge—Franco. We've got a bunch of different groups and nobody in charge. They've got German panzer units—highly trained soldiers—who are training their soldiers. Our guys, all they know how to do is march around, pretending like they know something. Which they don't.

If you ask me, the whole thing is completely nuts. This is why I'm happy to be working on airplanes and not fighting. The airplanes are old, but maybe we can fix them up, make them work.

Doing nothing—which is what the infantry guys are doing—that would drive me crazy.

Every day, here's what Rudolf does. Marches, cleans his rifle, smokes too much, drinks too much. He doesn't talk, doesn't laugh. He gambles, of course. But it's completely serious with him now. He doesn't enjoy himself like he used to, and he's a sore loser now. Gets into fights over cards, which he never used to do. But what makes me worry most is this: One time, we're at a bar, and a pretty girl wants him to dance with her. He walks away, ignores her altogether. I'm thinking, Who the hell is this guy?

In October, Rudolf finally gets his wish. They tell him he can go and fight. There's a lot of fighting around Sietamo, which is in Aragón, a few hours from Barcelona. Our guys have been trying to stop Franco from advancing into Catalonia, so we have been fighting in this area on and off since summer, and a lot of guys have already been killed there. Mostly our guys, which is no surprise. But if we don't hold onto this area, the other side is going to take it and move closer to Barcelona.

"Rudolf," I tell him, "we've got bad odds in this fight." Which we do. I tell him, "We're supposed to get new guns and supplies from France and Russia. Let's wait."

I'm going," he says. "I'm glad to be going. You do what you want."

It's not only our weapons that are a problem. Like I said, we've also got too damn many different little groups and too damn many guys who want to be in charge. The big shots can't get together—even with the majority of the whole country on our side. Each big shot wants an army of his own. They all act like a bunch of little kids. Matter of fact, POUM—the biggest group—might be the stupidest of all. They tell us we can decide for ourselves if we want to go and fight or not.

They ask us, "Who wants to sign up for this battle?"

Leaders of armies, they're supposed to *tell* their soldiers. What kind of army asks its soldiers to take a vote?

Every day now, Rudolf is out practicing shooting. I give up trying to talk sense into him. I can see his mind is closed. This is when I decide I have to go along with him. If I stay here and work on airplanes, I'm going to be worrying the whole time anyhow. So I might as well go.

Now, I start telling myself that I'm going, and the more I say it, the easier it's getting. Matter of fact, I'm starting to get myself excited. See, new rifles are showing up—good ones too. Rudolf and I get them and start to practice with them. Practicing with my new rifle, I'm getting to be a pretty good shot, which is a good thing, because Rudolf can't hit the side of a building. I figure I'm going to be covering for him.

I say to Rudolf, "You sure you definitely want to go?"

And he says, "I'm going."

So I say, "Not by yourself. With your aim, you'll shoot yourself in the head. I'm going with you."

I expect him to laugh, but he doesn't. All he says is, "Suit your-self."

We've got guys from POUM going with us, but we don't know if guys from any other groups are coming along or not. Everybody on our side goes running around like chickens with no heads. Meantime, Franco is not taking votes. He already has thousands of men in Sietamo, and I'm betting he's got new German airplanes up there too.

Soon enough, the day comes for us to leave, and they load us up in old trucks. We drive up into the hills. The altitude is getting higher as we go, so it's not exactly warm up here. I'm glad to have a leather jacket, but most guys don't. Rudolf, he's got a blanket from someplace. He's also got a skin bag instead of a plain old canteen like the rest of us. I never saw one like it before. It has goat hair on the inside. Says he won it gambling.

The roads going up into the hills are pretty bumpy. They're messed up completely, but that's something we expected. Most of the guys in our truck are like kids going to a party—drinking cheap muscatel, singing marching songs. But the truth is most of the guys in this truck *are* kids. A couple of them look like they might be only twelve or thirteen years old.

Rudolf and I don't sing. I'm too nervous, to tell the truth—nervous and excited both. Rudolf? He's just sitting there the whole time, looking at nothing and nobody, shining his rifle with a rag. For a second or two, I think I see Papa sitting there, shining his Iron Cross. I get a very strange feeling. I look away.

Outside the truck, there's nothing to see but rocky hills, brown fields, and poor little farmhouses. Most of the farms look abandoned. I can see some fields where the farmhouses got burned down. Everywhere, I see fields of crops drying out, dying, or already dead. Right now, it's harvest time, but nobody can harvest anything here. How can they, with everything that's going on? Far away in the distance, I can see the Pyrenees Mountains. I close my eyes and try to imagine Rudolf and me up there skiing. Gives me a little peace, a little break from what's really going on.

Finally, the truck stops, and everybody jumps out. We're at a town, but not much of a town. Most of the houses and buildings have been shot to pieces. There are piles of trash and broken junk all over the place. Shit too, some of it fresh and stinking. I'm thinking, These nincompoops! Don't they even know how to dig a latrine?

Right away, we hear some shooting. Our guys, they start running in all directions with nobody telling them where to go, what to do. Rudolf and I run over to some filthy guys, who are waving and yelling at us. These guys act like they know what to do, so that's where we go. They show us a trench, and we jump down there after them. Turns out these guys are happy as hell to see us, because we're replacing them. Tomorrow, they're going back to Barcelona.

The boys we came up here with—they're all POUM like us. But most of the boys we meet up with here—they're another group—anarchists, who live around here or near Barcelona. And quite a few of the anarchists are very young—fourteen, fifteen, sixteen years old. It's not easy for me to talk to these boys, because all they speak is Catalan or Spanish, and I don't speak either one yet. But Rudolf, he's been here long enough to speak pretty well. So for the first time in our lives, he's doing the translating for both of us. I feel like the whole damn world is upside down.

The boys who take us into the trench—the ones who have been here awhile—give us some tips. They say they're showing us how to kill lice, which are always in the trench. They light little fires with matches and hold the matches next to their trousers. At the same time, they laugh and tell us not to burn anything off, because we'll never get new balls. Then they laugh some more and tell us we'll never get rid of the lice either.

We don't have a lot of supplies, but at least we have matches, little candles, and cigarettes—even if they taste terrible. But this trench is damp and filthy. Nothing but mud, rocks, trash, broken pieces of junk, piss, and piles of shit. At first, we're careful to step over the shit, but after a while we give up. No way to avoid it.

When night comes, the kids in our trench find dugouts to crawl into. The dugouts are holes in the walls of the trench—like wormholes for men. The kids crawl inside them and sleep, but Rudolf and I don't sleep. All night, we're smoking and looking up at the stars. Now and then, we hear shooting.

I say, "Did you ever think we would be fighting a war in a trench like Papa?"

Rudolf, he just shrugs. Can't get a word out of him. He smokes, looks around, leans against the thick dirt wall, shuffles his deck of cards. Always has cards with him.

The next morning at dawn, we try to get a look around. Nobody's got maps, but everybody's flying flags. So if it's not our flag, I figure it's Franco's. But some of the guys straighten me out. They tell me that sometimes the fascists put up our flag to confuse us, and sometimes we do the same thing to them. So now, I'm starting start to learn more about what we're up against.

Like I thought, Franco's guys have new German rifles, so of course we want to take them away. But so far, our guys haven't been able to do it. See, we're camped pretty far away from the enemy positions. It's stupid, because most of the time, everybody is out of range and shooting at nothing.

Except at night. This is when small parties sneak out of the trenches and try to crawl up close enough to the other side to kill somebody. So right away, of course, Rudolf insists he's going out at night.

Like I said before, our guys, they act more like a democracy than an army. If a guy doesn't want to go someplace, he doesn't go. But there are always volunteers, and Rudolf is one of them. He acts completely crazy, like he *wants* to get killed. I remind him that even the best gambler can lose. He ignores me completely.

The first night when we go out with a party, Rudolf goes off by himself, and I follow a little behind him to keep an eye on him. Right away, somebody starts shooting in our direction. We both duck behind a big boulder. Then Rudolf looks out, sees some movement, and gets off a couple of shots. Now, it's completely quiet out there. We decide to go ahead and crawl out from behind the rock, but I make him keep down.

A few feet away, we see a body. He got one, all right. A kid too, maybe all of fifteen or sixteen years old. So Franco has kids fighting too? Why does an army with new German equipment, with help from German soldiers and everything else—why the hell do they need kids to fight for them?

Anyhow, this boy, he's lying on his back, staring up at us, trying to say something—"mama," I think. Then there's blood pouring out from his mouth and nose and eyes, and then his eyes look solid, like glass.

"Shit," I say, and I vomit. This is when Rudolf finally decides to say something.

"He would have killed you too," he says.

Then he makes a little joke. First joke I hear him make in a long time.

Says, "You've got to learn to say *merda*, Gottfried. Not *shit*. It's an easy language, Catalan. Can't you learn?"

Well, it sure as hell isn't funny.

I can't even look at Rudolf right now. My mind is racing. I can see my brother Hubert after he shot a neighbor kid with a pellet gun. That kid—he wasn't really hurt bad—but Mama beat Hubert hard with Papa's belt, and after that, she screamed at us, "Don't any of you ever shoot a gun at anyone! *Ever!*"

I vomit again, but Rudolf doesn't notice. He's busy searching the dead kid. He picks up the kid's rifle, pumps it up and down in the air.

"Yippee! A new German rifle!"

"You keep it," I say.

He looks at me like I'm nuts. "Don't worry. I will."

And he does. He also goes through all the dead kid's stuff, takes a flashlight, a watch, and a knife—all of which we don't have. Even takes the kid's shoes. I can tell he's happy with himself. But I'm sick. Who the hell is this guy? What the hell am I doing here with him? Do I know my brother at all?

Next night, they ask for volunteers again, this time to clean out an enemy nest in another part of Sietamo. Franco's guys, they keep coming in at night, shooting up our trenches. We know they have reinforcements, because more of them come every night. They're killing more and more of our guys.

To tell the truth, I'm thinking about not going out this time, but Rudolf says he's going. The way he's acting, I've got to take care of him, like it or not. So I volunteer to go too. This time in our party we have about twenty volunteers, and at least ten of them are kids.

But there are a few guys our age too, and we're surprised to see a guy we know—our old buddy, Fritz. Well, he's really Rudolf's old buddy, not mine anymore. Not since got me mixed up with that "mirabelle" business in Paris.

I can't believe my eyes when I see Fritz up here. He still looks tough, but he looks ten years older. His hair is almost completely gray, and his eyes sink back in his skull.

First thing he says is how sorry he is about the chicken farm.

"A whole bunch of POUM guys in old trucks showed up one day and said they were there to burn the place down. They wanted to kill all of us, because they thought we worked for the rich people who owned it."

"What did you tell them?" I asked.

" We had to convince them we were on their side. To prove it, we had to help them burn everything down. Then they took us with them to Barcelona and watched us sign up to fight for POUM."

Fritz shakes his head like there's something he wishes he could forget, but he can't.

"They burned everything down, Rudolf. Took away all the animals, except Gustav. Shot him."

"Yah, I know," Rudolf says. "Guess he must have run after them. Tried to chase them away. We trained him to protect…"

Fritz nods.

Rudolf asks, "Where are Pacher and Justus? And Eva?"

I see a couple of tears welling up. Fritz crying? This shocks me.

"Pacher and Justus got killed near here last week. That's why I'm here. To get some of the bastards who killed them."

"And Eva?"

"They sent her off to work with some farmers." He shrugs. "I guess they've got to try to figure out how to feed us."

"Stupid," says Rudolf. "They had our farm. It could have fed us."

Then Fritz says something to Rudolf that I don't get.

"They burned the big house on the hill, Rudolf. Killed everybody up there. Called them the "class enemy." From the farm, we could see some POUM guys going up there."

Fritz wipes away some more tears. Tough Fritz. I never could have imagined this. "I'm sorry, buddy," he says. "I couldn't stop them. I tried. I tried."

Rudolf and Fritz stare at each other, and then they both look down. They're both wiping tears off their faces.

I guess they've got some secret between the two of them. Me, I feel kind of hurt that Rudolf didn't tell me, but he didn't, and I'm not going to ask him.

Fritz says he's coming with us on our mission tonight. We're the oldest ones, so we try to lead the younger boys, make them slow down, keep their heads down. We all walk with our backs bent over, trying to keep as quiet as we can. We can't use flashlights in case somebody's out there; but in the dark, it's very hard to see all the broken rocks and gravel, so we do make some noise. There's no shooting yet, but we figure there will be. So we're waiting for it. Scared of it and waiting for it both. Maybe even wanting it. To get the waiting over with. But somehow or other, we manage to get into the area without seeing anybody. We think, Well, maybe they already left, went off to another area. Maybe we can leave here too.

But the kids with us want to fight, and since nobody is here to fight with, they decide to go and burn down the Catholic church in town. Me, I don't like this. I don't want them to do it, and I say so. But Fritz and Rudolf don't object. Matter of fact, Rudolf agrees with them.

"It's my birthday, right? I say burn the thing down."

This is the first time today when I realize it's his birthday. Not only that, he's twenty-one years old today. But I don't wish him a happy birthday.

Right after this, I see some kids next to the church. A kid takes out a grenade and pulls off the tape on the lever. He blows himself completely to pieces, because the grenade is a piece of junk, and he can't throw it away fast enough. The other kids look shocked, but they don't stop what they're doing. Another one throws a grenade, and they get a fire going. I want to leave, but we don't. Instead, like moths, we all stand around there, watching the flames jump into the sky, watching the church burn.

All of a sudden, we hear men coming our way, and they're shouting and shooting. A German bomber flies over us—very low—and it lets loose with machine gun fire. A couple of our boys get hit and drop. The rest of us start running as fast as we can, back the way we came.

At the edge of the town, we take cover inside a small house. Old place, made out of heavy stones with a big, heavy wood door, which we lock from inside. We push some furniture up against the door, but in minutes, we're surrounded. Don't know how many they are, but to us, it looks like hundreds. And it looks like a real army. They've got on uniforms—all the same kind of uniform. Except that some of the men there, they have a different look. Darker men, hard. Not kids. Turns out, these men come from Africa—Moors from North Africa.

Some of the young boys with us, when they see these men, they right away start blubbering. See, everybody says the Moors in this war are mercenaries. The kids with us, they say these guys will cut us up into little pieces and cut our balls off while we're alive. Fritz doesn't make things any easier for them. He tells them this is the truth.

Right away, they start shooting at us through the windows. Then Fritz cracks a joke. I guess it's a joke. Not very funny though.

Says, "You want to keep your balls, boys? Then you better shoot theirs off first!"

And now, I can't believe my eyes. These kids, they kneel down and take out rosaries from their pockets. The same kids who couldn't wait to burn down a Catholic church. Rosaries. This is something I can never forget, how all of a sudden, they've got religion and they're good Catholics again. Kneeling down, praying with their rosaries.

The shooting goes on awhile, and we have one boy in the house who is lying on the floor dead. Gets killed because he stands up near a window. We tell them to stay down, but maybe now they won't forget. Some of his friends are crying. He was a popular boy. So now, the others are crying that they want to go home.

"Shut up," Fritz says. "You want to go home? Then pay attention to what we tell you! You think this is a game?"

I start to look around, try to find something in this place to give the kids to eat. I find some olives, that's all, a few jars of olives. We took nothing with us, and the food is on the other side of town, where we bivouac. But most of us aren't hungry anyhow. I'm not; that's for damn sure. Finally, the shooting stops. So we have a little meeting. The majority decides to let a few guys sneak out, try to get some help for us. I say it's stupid. Stupid to give young kids the same power to vote that we've got, and stupid to try this right now.

Me, I'm not volunteering to go out there. I want to survive. Whoever goes out there is crazy. But three of the older kids—school friends—they say they want to go, and nobody else says no.

As soon as they get outside, we hear them start to scream. We hear men laughing and shouting, then more screaming. Finally, thank God, silence.

But what I don't understand is why Rudolf doesn't volunteer to go out there, the way he seems to want to kill himself. Finally, I ask him.

"Let them come and get us," he says.

"Yah," says Fritz. "We'll get more of them that way."

I guess they both figure there's no hope, so let's kill as many of them as possible when they finally break in.

Altogether, we're in the house about twenty-four hours. Longest day of my life. Seems like a year. Every time I take a chance to look outside, I see more of them. They're just playing with us like wild animals play with prey. Some of them are playing a game, shooting their machine guns up and down the front door. As thick and heavy as it is, the door is holding up. But for how much longer?

They manage to shoot five more of us while we're holed up during the daytime, and all but one are young boys. They are in terrible pain, screaming for their mamas. There is no way we can stop their pain, so Fritz decides to shoot them all dead. Maybe he's right. But I don't help him. For some reason or other, Rudolf doesn't help him either.

When it gets dark again, the shooting stops. We can hear them out there laughing at us. They're eating and drinking, having a good time. One of them comes up to the window to taunt us.

"Say your prayers, children. Tomorrow, you die."

Inside the house, we're sure this is our last night alive. Nobody talks, nobody sleeps. A few boys curl up like babies. A few sob and pray with their rosaries. Rudolf and Fritz smoke and play cards. I sit in a corner and watch them.

Then about 2:00 a.m., we suddenly hear a loud crack, and we all jump. But it's not a bomb—it's thunder! I can't believe our luck! It starts pouring cats and dogs with plenty of thunder, lightning, and wind. It takes me one minute to make a break for it. I don't want to sit and wait for them to kill me. I want to live! Maybe God is giving me a chance.

I climb outside through a shot-out window. I can see others behind me, following me out. It's raining and blowing so hard, I can't see more than a meter in front of me. But I'm not think-ing about that. And I'm not thinking about Rudolf or Fritz, what they're doing. Matter of fact, I'm not thinking of anything, except I want to live.

Lucky for us, the rain keeps coming down in buckets, and there's constant racket from the wind and thunder. I'm sure the fascists have soldiers looking for us, but I know the weather isn't helping them. Lightning scares the hell out of most men, and there's a lot of it. I keep low, and I hope I'm making progress, but I can't tell. I feel like a strong current pushing against me, keeping me from moving fast enough.

Suddenly, I can hear yelling and shooting behind me, coming closer. A grenade explodes, but I don't stop.

Then I think I hear somebody shout, "Where's Fritz? Where's Rodolfo?"

My heart stops.

Somebody starts yelling, "Rodolfo! Fritz!"

And then I see them. They're both lying face-down in the mud. Fritz is dead. The grenade blew off the back of his head. Rudolf's pants are full of blood, and he's unconscious, but I roll him over and put my head to his chest, and he's breathing.

Two guys are standing next to me, and they start dragging Fritz out of the mud. "Leave him," I shout. "He's dead! My brother is alive!"

One of the boys comes to help me, but the other one keeps dragging Fritz's body through the mud.

Then another grenade explodes. What's left of poor Fritz drops, and the guy dragging his body falls on top of him. Now they're both dead. The two of us who are left, we hold up Rudolf the best we can and drag him with us.

I thank God it's blowing and raining so hard, because I don't hear anybody coming after us, and we soon see a small building. It's what's left of a house, and it's not much. But it's dry, and we drag Rudolf inside. He's drenched in blood from the waist down. We pull off his pants. Blood pours out his backside.

The other guy and I, we take off our shirts and tear them in pieces as best we can. We know our shirts are filthy, but somehow we've got to wrap him up so he won't bleed to death. We make a wrapping like a tourniquet and wind it around his lower back, in and out between his legs. We know we're cutting off the blood to his legs, but we don't know what else to do. Then we drag him with us in the rain until we finally get back to our camp.

We've got a tent there with a medic and a couple of beds. The medic cleans Rudolf up and puts on new bandages, but he's bleeding so much they bandage him over and over again. He's the color of paste, and I'm afraid he's going to die.

I start yelling. "We've got to get going! He needs a hospital!"

"We can't go," the medic says. "We need to take at least three wounded men along when we go."

"But he's going to die!"

The medic says, "Maybe. But that's the rule. Three wounded before we go."

It's very hard for me to do nothing to help Rudolf. I walk back and forth so much the medic finally shouts at me, "Sit down, goddammit, or I'll shoot you myself!"

So I sit down by Rudolf, hold his hand, talk to him, tell him to hold on. But he can't hear me or anybody else. I actually pray for a couple more guys to get hurt. Hard to believe. But I'm relieved when they get two more wounded and put all three men in a truck, even they're lying on dirty blankets in the bed of an old coal truck. I get in with them so I can keep Rudolf's head on my lap.

This truck is in bad shape, like everything else. The ride is terrible with all the ruts and bumps in these roads, and the other poor guys are crying and screaming. Thank God, Rudolf is unconscious.

Me, I thought we were driving to Barcelona, but for some reason or other, the truck stops at a field hospital. A couple of medics carry Rudolf and the other guys inside, and the first thing they do is lie him down on his stomach and take off all the bandages. So, of course, the open wounds start bleeding again. This scares the hell out of me. He already lost so much blood. And besides, I always thought you washed out a wound and then kept it covered up to heal.

"Why are you doing that?" I ask.

The nurse, a chubby young woman with a tired face, says, "Shh, take it easy. We need to leave his wounds open to the air."

She takes out some kind of netting and lays it across the top of the wounds.

"What's this?"

"It's to keep out the flies," she says.

"But it will stick to the wounds!"

"Please," she says, "go outside and wait, so we can work in peace."

I feel sick to my stomach. I go outside, but after a few minutes, I go back in and find a medic. All I want is to get my brother out of this hellhole.

I ask the guy, "Can I please take him off your hands? Can I borrow a car and drive him to Barcelona?"

But the medic looks at me like I'm nuts. "Listen, buddy, I don't have time for this. I've got a man back there who lost both arms."

Me, I walk back and forth, trying to figure out what to do. I can't help thinking about a hospital I remembered in Germany. Was a Catholic hospital in Giessen. Very clean—nothing like this. I was in that hospital when I was six or seven years old. They operated on me and took out one of my ribs. Why, I don't remember. But I remember the place, and it was like day and night, that Catholic hospital and this stinking place here.

The way Rudolf looks—I can't leave things alone. So I go over to another medic.

"If you won't take Rudolf to Barcelona right now, I'm going to get a car any way I can and take him myself."

"No you're not," the guy says. "You want to kill him? We'll take him in the morning with the others. You can't do it alone."

I'm frustrated and upset, but he's right. He's right. There's nothing I can do by myself to help my brother. So finally, I give up. I sink down on the dirty tile floor with my back against the wall, and I try to close my eyes. I'm worn out, but I can't sleep. Over and over, I keep seeing and hearing the fighting in Sietamo. Over and over, and I can't make it stop.

Finally, thank God, morning comes. I look at Rudolf lying on the bed, and I can see his eyes are open. He's just staring. I go and squeeze his hand.

"Rudolf," I say. "It's me. You'll be okay. You'll be okay."

Maybe he hears me, but I don't know. He doesn't seem to. His hand is limp. He closes his eyes again. After another hour, two medics come to take him and the other wounded guys to a hospital train going to Barcelona. I tell them I'm going with them. Nobody stops me. Nobody says I can't go.

The train is already full of wounded boys and men, plus two nurses who are running around from one to the other. What they can do here, I don't know. Somehow or other, they squeeze us all in there. They line up the wounded guys in rows on blankets on the floor. It's hot and miserable, and all I hear are men and boys crying and moaning. It's a stew of rotten garbage, wounds, piss, shit, and sweat. They've got some windows open, but the train is going so slow you can't feel much outside air. It doesn't cool us off, and it doesn't make the stink any better.

It takes hours longer than it should to get to Barcelona. See, in every little town, the train has to stop. People are standing by the tracks at every train station, cheering and holding baskets with clothes and food. Some of them are holding up signs: "For our heroes from the front." Their kids, see? Their own kids, who are in pain—maybe dying—they are inside this stinking train, crying for their mamas, and their mamas are standing outside and waving signs. Heroes.

When the train stops, some of them come inside to look around for men or boys they might know. If they see somebody they know, they crowd in with the rest of us. If not, they leave something—a piece of fruit or a clean blanket or a jug of water. If a man or boy has died on the train, they get a couple of men to take off the body.

Finally, we get to Barcelona, and they take Rudolf and the others off the train and over to the General Hospital of Catalonia. By this time, though, Rudolf is wide awake and screaming with pain. I'm wishing he was unconscious again.

I ask the doctors, "Can't you give him something?"

"Sorry, we can't use morphine unless a man is dying. He's not dying."

So they take him away and make me sit in the hall and wait. I'm walking back and forth. When they come out again, they tell me they checked him over, and they took out all the shrapnel they could find. But his wounds are infected, and if they can't stop the infection, they might have to cut off his legs. The doctor says all they can do right now is try to clean out the infection so it won't get worse. But even if they do that, he can't guarantee anything.

They're going to clean it out, he says, by burning it out. They tell me it's going to be painful for Rudolf, but I can come with them and hold his hand while they burn it out.

So they put my little brother on a table. Then they take a piece of metal and heat it up to sterilize it. They stick a piece of cotton in his mouth, and a nurse says, "Rodolfo, bite down on this cotton. Bite down hard."

Me, I can't look, but I squeeze his hand. They take that piece of heated metal and stick it into the wounds to burn out the infection. They say they will have to do this to him three times every day.

I throw up again, just standing there. A piece of cotton in your mouth and hot metal burning you on the spots where you already hurt like hell. Torture. It's torture, plain and simple. That smell— oh my God—I can never forget it. Never.

Finally, they finish, and they take him to a big room, where a lot of other wounded guys are lying. I go with them. I want to stay with Rudolf, but they tell me I can't stay there. They send me to a hotel for POUM fighters in Barcelona. If he gets worse, they promise to come and get me over there.

Next day, I go over to POUM headquarters. I can't be sure anybody there knows what happened where we were fighting, because nothing works right on our side of this war. So I tell them what happened, and it turns out—naturally—they didn't know.

I say that I would like to work at the airfield to be near Rudolf, and since that's what they wanted me to do in the first place, they say yes. I probably didn't need to ask them anyhow. These idiots. They wouldn't know the difference, whatever I did.

They give me a room at the hotel in Barcelona, and I start working again at the airfield. After a few weeks, Rudolf seems to be getting a little stronger. His wounds are not healed, but the infection is going away little by little, and the doctor stops saying they might have to cut off his legs. I can see he's still weak, but at least he's starting to eat and act more like a human being.

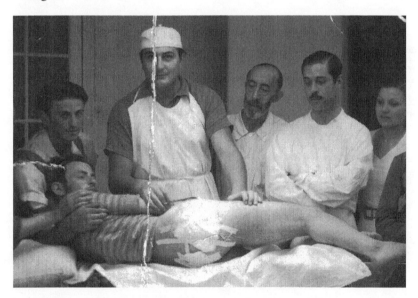

Rudolf (on stretcher), Gottfried, caregivers
Fall 1936
Barcelona, Spain

So every morning now, I stop at the hospital to see Rudolf, and every evening after work, I go to see him. But the rest of the time, I'm at the airfield. The boys there act very happy to get me back as a mechanic, and I'm happy to do something I like. But "mechanic" is not my official title. Officially, I'm a "machine gunner," because everybody's supposed to be some kind of fighter. But me, I'm no machine gunner.

We've got only one machine gun at this airport, and I never tried to shoot it. All I know about this gun is that it's old—like everything else we've got—and it's supposed to be a field gun, not a gun mounted in a plane. But one day, they ask me to mount it in the back of a plane. I tell them it's not made for that, but they say it's all we've got. So I rig it up somehow or other, but I tell them we can't count on it to work. They laugh and say it's my problem if it doesn't work, since I'm a machine gunner. I laugh too. Who the hell would even want to fly our planes?

Like everything else we've got, the planes here are obsolete. Mostly, I work on two CN Focke-Wulf FW 56s, which are German planes that replaced the even older Nieuport 52s.

I'm not too worried about the machine gun I stuck in one of these old planes. Even if the plane can fly, and even if that machine gun can shoot, I figure everybody knows we don't stand a chance against Franco in tha old plane. See, everybody knows Franco has new Fiat CR 32 biplanes with built-in machine guns that can do 350 rounds apiece. Matter of fact, since August, these planes have been shooting down our planes wherever and whenever they want to.

But it turns out I'm wrong. Not everybody understands that our old planes can't win against Franco's. And it's my bad luck that my superior officer, who is a hothead, doesn't understand anything at all.

Says, "Come on, Gottfried, let's go up. You man the machine gun."

I say, "You've got to be kidding!"

I try and explain to him, talk him out of it, but he keeps it up.

Finally, he says, "I'm your superior officer. Get in there!"

Now, I could have said no anyhow. Could have said, "I vote no." Could have talked to a higher-up and said I don't want to fly with him, and they probably would have let me out of it. But I didn't do that.

First of all, I'm officially supposed to man this machine gun and know how to use it. Also, I figure we can't fly very long in this old plane, so we'll have to come back down right away. Besides, we'll be in the area right around here, which is mostly our territory. And to tell the truth, I was embarrassed to tell a higher-up that we shouldn't fly a plane I had worked on, even if I didn't trust it.

So now I make a very stupid mistake. I go up in the plane with this pilot, and I sit in back with the damn machine gun I rigged up. And the minute we get up in the air, one of the new Italian Fiat biplanes comes out of nowhere and starts shooting. Like I said, I don't even know how to use this machine gun, but I never get the chance to try. Right away, our plane gets hit, and so do I. My little finger is hanging halfway off my right hand. Looks terrible, but for some reason or other, it doesn't hurt. Matter of fact, I've got no feeling in it at all. Makes me wonder whose hand I'm looking at.

The pilot—the lucky bastard—isn't even hurt. He dives and lands the plane in a field. That CR 32 should have blown us out of the sky. Was only dumb luck that it didn't.

So now, it's my turn to bite down on a hard piece of cotton. And then, they cut off my finger. But it's not too bad. See, from the time I stabbed my right hand with that fish bone, there wasn't much feeling left anyway. Now, though, there's no feeling in my hand at all.

Rudolf and I are both together in the hospital. They put me on another floor. When I walk over to Rudolf's area later on, he asks where I've been, why I haven't been there to see him lately. So I show him my bandaged hand, which is in a sling.

"I was busy getting wounded," I tell him. "I have to keep up with you, don't I?"

For some reason or other, we both start laughing. Don't know why, but the situation—it hits both of us the same way, and we laugh like crazy men.

My wound heals over pretty fast, but now my right hand is stuck in one position. I can't move my fingers, so everything takes me longer. I don't like people staring, feeling sorry for me either. So for a long time, I keep my right hand in my pocket when I can.

Rudolf's wounds don't heal up like mine. With him, the healing goes very slow, but at least he's alive, and he has his legs. The nurses like him, of course, and they take good care of him. I think one of them is in love with him. She even gets him a pass to leave the hospital for a few hours one Sunday, and she takes him to a bullfight. Naturally, he comes back with his pockets full of money.

Now, both of us finally start to enjoy some time with each other again. We play skat like we did when we were kids. We talk about the good times we remember, about our family, about Germany, about things we hope we can do someday. I write letters to our family with my left hand, and Rudolf tells me what he wants me to write for him.

Rudolf says, as soon as he can, he wants to go back and fight. But the truth is, he's in bad shape. He's got no strength. Can hardly walk, much less fight. He needs to go someplace quiet so he can get well. And me, I've had enough of this crazy war. Maybe if I thought we could win, I'd go back. But how can we win? All the big shots on our side are still fighting with each other, and we don't have the weapons or money Franco has. So all I want to do now is get out of here and try again to get us out of Europe. But I know how my brother thinks now. To get him to leave with me, it can't be my idea. So I make a plan.

As soon as I get out of the hospital, I go and see the big shots at POUM headquarters.

"Can I please take Rudolf to France to heal up?"

They say, "Sure, fine."

See, they're getting plenty of volunteers, so they're letting volunteers like us come and go with no problem. For once, I'm happy they don't know how to act like a real army.

They tell me we'll get our discharge papers in a week. I figure this means it will take a month, which turns out to be true.

Next thing I do, I have a little talk with Rudolf's main doctor. I tell him I'm very worried about Rudolf. Tell him how strange he started acting right after we joined up. Tell him I'm afraid he's going to end up like our father if he keeps fighting, but he insists he wants to go back.

"We've got friends in Lyon," I say. "I think they'll give Rudolf a place to stay, so he can get his strength back. But he won't listen to me. Can you help me out?"

The doctor has no problem with my idea. Matter of fact, he likes it. He tells Rudolf he is not going to allow him to go back to fighting for at least one year.

"Is there someplace you can go to get you strength back, Rodolfo? Maybe someplace where the climate is good?"

Naturally, Rudolf thinks of Lyon.

By this time, it is already December of 1936, and Rudolf has been in the hospital for about two months. When the doctor is having his little talk with Rudolf, Franco is bombing Barcelona. Rudolf now knows he won't be allowed to fight for a year, and he doesn't want to sit around the hospital. This is when I say something.

"Maybe we should ask if they'll let us go to France, Rudolf. What do you think?"

"Yah," he says. "Ask them. If I can't fight for a year, at least I can try to get well as soon as possible."

Naturally, I don't tell him I already got permission a few weeks ago.

At the end of December, when they give me our papers, I tell Rudolf we have permission to go.

Turns out to be a good time for us to leave Spain, and not just because of the bombing in Barcelona. We're packing up to go when we hear that thousands of new Italian soldiers are now coming to

Spain to fight for Franco. To me, this means the end. No way our side can win this war.

I've got to admit POUM treats us very well when we leave Spain. They give us government identification papers and a letter introducing us to the Spanish consul in Bordeaux, asking him to help us find work. They even give us a little money for volunteering to fight—money we never asked for.

When we're finally on the train, on our way out of Spain, I tell Rudolf I have a little surprise for him.

"How would you like to take a little side trip to Monte Carlo? I hear they've got a lot of nice casinos."

He grins. It's good to see. "You mean it?" he says.

"I already made reservations," I tell him. "We can stay there a few days, see the area. Have a little fun. Then we'll go to Bordeaux. What do you say?"

Well, he's very happy, of course, and for once, everything works out right. We stop in Monte Carlo and see the area for a few days. I get us the best hotel rooms I can find too. Why not?

It's beautiful around Monte Carlo. Warm, sunny, and—best of all—peaceful. They have cannon in the parks, but they are only decorations, thank God. I see guns differently than I used to, and loud noises make me jumpy. I understand much better now what happened to our father. If I had seen much more killing, I would probably be crazy myself.

Right now, I'm just happy to be alive, to see Rudolf alive, to be having a good time together. And the best part? He wins enough money to pay for everything in Monte Carlo and for the rest of our trip to Bordeaux on top of that. That's my little brother.

Gottfried (front), Rudolf
December 1936
Near Monte Carlo, Monaco

XIV

RUDOLF

On the train out of Barcelona, I'm sleeping off and on. I'm still hurting pretty bad. Can't get comfortable.

But then Gottfried says, "How about taking a little detour? We can spend a couple of days around Monte Carlo. Do a little gambling."

"We've got money?"

"Don't worry," he says.

Surprise!

It's been a long time since Gottfried and I went somewhere for a good time. Except, I guess, to see the Graf Zeppelin after we left home—which wasn't my idea of fun. But Monte Carlo? Now, that's a different story. Beautiful, sunny, and great casinos.

So we go there and enjoy ourselves. We stay in a fancy hotel room. The whole time, I'm looking at Gottfried. It's hard for me to believe this is my brother.

"Uh, Gottfried, isn't this too much to spend for a room?"

He laughs. "You can win it back, right?"

We drink and gamble at the casinos, and I have a good time. Gottfried even gambles with me, plays some blackjack. But he's not too good, and he gets mad when he loses. So most of the time, he watches me play, and when I win, he keeps most of the money and gives me a little to play with. It doesn't matter to me. I keep winning anyhow.

We stay in Monte Carlo a couple of days, and we drive around the area. Already, I'm feeling stronger. Poker does me good, right? Gottfried says there's something wrong with my brain, not just my backside. But he's happy to see me smiling, and I have to admit I'm smiling when I'm gambling.

But even so, it's taking me a long time to get well, and there are plenty of times when I don't care if I get well or not. Nights mostly—that's when it's hardest for me. That's when my brain goes to town, and I can't stop thinking about everything. Carme, what we lost. What I lost. The war. Even my dog. All of it comes back and back and back.

Gottfried, he doesn't know about Carme. But he can see I don't bounce back so fast. He keeps telling me I'm alive, so I have to live, be happy. Here's to life, right?

Wish I could be like Gottfried sometimes. He shows me his right hand that's missing a finger and how the other four fingers don't move anymore. Then he grins and shows me how well he's doing. And he is, too. He can write with his left hand, and he can fix things almost as well as when he had two good hands. Maybe it takes him longer, but he keeps going. He doesn't give up.

After we're in Monte Carlo a couple of days, I hit it big. This is when Gottfried remembers to start worrying about money again. So now, we leave and take a train to Bordeaux.

We check into a little hotel. I need to rest, so Gottfried leaves me there and goes to see a guy by the name of Rafael Ramos, who is the Spanish consul in Bordeaux. Gottfried shows him the letter POUM gave us, which asks Ramos to help us find work.

Ramos says the French have a new premier—a Jewish guy by the name of Blum.

"He supports more rights for refugees," Ramos says, "so I won't have trouble finding you a job, Gottfried."

We're very surprised about this. Why? One, a Jewish socialist is charge of Catholic France, which is hard to believe. And two, the French government hated refugees when we left a few months ago. First, they loved us, then they hated us, and now they love us again?

Ramos also tells Gottfried the new premier supports the Spanish government in the civil war against Franco. "But," he adds, "not openly."

Ridiculous, no? The democracies are afraid to help the people fighting for democracy, but the dictators aren't afraid to help the people fighting for dictatorship.

The Spanish consul, Señor Ramos, contacts a friend, by the name of Professor René Ross, and this professor gets Gottfried a job as a *traçeur*—kind of like a mechanical job working with blueprints and carpenters. It's at a big ship-building outfit in Paris, by the name of Société Anonyme des Ateliers et Chantiers de la Loire.

"Get to know Proessor Ross," Ramos says. "He's a big shot in the Popular Front, so maybe he can help you get to the States."

From Bordeaux, we go to Nice. The Fregonaras, who helped me in Lyon before the war, have relatives in Nice. They want me to stay with their relatives, which will be safer for me than staying with them again in Lyon. We never figured out who reported me in Lyon, and if I go back there, maybe I'll get caught again.

When we get to Nice, Madame Fregonara and Francine are waiting for us with their family. They jump up and down and hug me and don't let me go. Finally, they take us over to their relatives' house, and everybody there makes a big fuss over us. They've been cooking and cleaning, and they invite over some other people— more relatives and friends, and all this. It's a big house they've got here, and they have nice rooms for Gottfried and me.

After a week, Gottfried leaves me in Nice and goes to work as a traçeur in Paris. I'm very happy to let the Fregonaras' cousins play nursemaids. They take me out to relax on the beautiful beaches, and we go on little picnics. They try to introduce me to girls, and I try to be polite and go out with them, but it's hard for me. When I see a pretty girl, what I think of is Carme. A girl laughs, and I want to cry.

But if I'm going to go back to Spain to fight, I've got to get well. So I keep trying to go out, to get better. We are hearing how a lot of new volunteers are going to Spain to fight for the government now—guys from Italy, the United States, Russia, and other places. They say Russia is actually sending over good weapons and supplies for a change. So I still have hope. I only wish I could help somehow.

And then one day—like somebody up there heard me—my old buddy from Lyon, Ernest Moos, shows up. He's still selling junk at flea markets. He looked me up, because he thought I might want to help smuggle guns to the loyalists in Spain.

"It's pretty dangerous," Ernest says. "If you get caught this time, they'll send you back to Germany for sure."

"I don't care," I say. "Let me help. At least, I can do that."

So Ernest gives me the facts.

" There are a French companies which are secretly manufacturing guns and ammunition for the Spanish loyalists. New Mannlicher Berthier M 07/15s and Hotchkiss machine guns. Lebel rifles too—good rifles, not crap."

"Does the French government know?"

"Not officially. If we get caught, they won't help us."

So what we're doing is sneaking this stuff out a little at a time. Ernest works out the details with the manufacturers and a local outfit, which buys and sells farm machinery. The local outfit owns trucks that haul stuff from here to Bordeaux and other places. On these trucks, our guys load up the weapons. We put them in boxes made for tools and equipment. Then, on top of the gun boxes, we stack boxes actually filled with tools and equipment.

The trucks we load up—they go to Bordeaux. The actual tools and equipment go wherever they're supposed to go, and the gun boxes go to a warehouse. When they get enough boxes in the warehouse, loyalist sympathizers come to Bordeaux and take the weapons to Spain.

Helping with this work makes me feel good. Maybe I can't fight, but I can do a little something, right? I'm not strong enough to move the heavy stuff, so the other guys have to do all this. But I can help with organizing and keeping track of what's what, and I can watch over the loading of the trucks, which we do at night when nobody sees us.

One night when we're loading, I notice a skinny guy acting kind of twitchy, like a squirrel. Don't remember seeing him before. So I watch him awhile, and I can see he's got a little notebook. He writes something down, sticks the notebook and pencil in his pants. He walks around, smokes. Looks around. Takes out the notebook again, writes something, sticks it back in his pants pocket. Then he goes and helps load up a few things on the truck. He repeats all this a few times. I don't like it. I go up to him.

"What's in that notebook of yours?"

First, he freezes, and then he decides to punch me in the face and take off. Stupid man. I yell, so of course he doesn't get too far. Some guys grab him and take a look at his notebook. Turns out he's writing down the names of the men we have working here, what's going on, all of this.

Now, it's me who catches him, but it's not me who does anything about it. A couple other guys shoot the bastard and stick his body in the trunk of somebody's car. They dump him someplace, I guess. Where, I don't ask. But after this, we don't get too many other spies sneaking around.

So I'm passing my time here in Nice, feeling better, working to smuggle weapons into Spain. Meantime, Gottfried's working in Paris, but he comes here on weekends. He's doing okay, but there are guys he's working with who won't talk to him. There are a lot of people like this in Paris now. They're scared Jewish refugees are taking their jobs. Naturally, this doesn't make sense, but it's nothing new. There are the usual strikes and signs saying, "Jews get out!" The same old things. Just more than there was before.

But Gottfried says there's something going on in Paris, which is keeping things from getting worse right now. A lot of men have construction jobs, because they're working on a big exposition, which is coming in May near the Trocadero. Supposed to be about world peace. Pretty funny, huh? Anyhow, they're clearing acres and acres for buildings and exhibits.

Now, I don't say anything about my smuggling work, but I'm happy Gottfried is doing something to help the loyalists too. He tells me he's trying to get people in Paris to give money to them. It's not easy though. People who once had money don't have much left. But Gottfried goes to meetings almost every evening after work. Meets people, makes new friends.

One weekend, he talks to me about Professor Ross, who is the man the French consul knew—the one who helped Gottfried get his job in Paris. Seems like Gottfried and the professor get together pretty often. The professor knows all about us, and one day he asks Gottfried to bring me to Paris to meet him.

So this is how I get to know Professor Ross. He's a very good man, a mensch. Like the father I wish I'd had. Looks like a professor too. Mostly bald with a fringe of gray hair, thick glasses, a bushy beard. He is a strong socialist, and he teaches the Russian Revolution. He's very worried that the communist Stalinists won't help the Spanish loyalists enough. He thinks Stalin doesn't really care about Spain.

Professor Ross is kind of lonely, because his wife died, and his only son is fighting in Spain. Naturally, he's interested in what we saw and did there. He loves to talk to Gottfried and me, and when I come to Paris to meet him, he takes us out every day. We spend a lot of time with him—talking, playing cards, going places together. He treats us like we're his kids.

One day, he invites us to come with him to a matinee. It's a popular musical by an Austrian, name of Franz Lehar. In French, it's called *Le Pays Du Sourire*. In English, it's or *The Land of Smiles*.

From the name, I'm thinking it's a happy show, and when we sit down in our seats, I tell Professor Ross, "Land of Smiles, huh? I can use some!"

"Well," he says, "I hate to disappoint you, but it's a love story about a man and a woman from different countries and backgrounds. The music is beautiful, but I'm afraid the story is sad."

When I hear this, I can't help myself. I wish like hell I was someplace else. But I'm not.

So I'm watching. And I'm trying not to think about Carme. But when the hero starts to sing a love song to his girl, I can't take it. This is the same song they played for Carme and me that night at her parents' party. The same goddamn song. I have to take out my handkerchief. I blow my nose. Then I get up.

"Excuse me," I say. "I have to go outside."

I go out and walk around in the fresh air.

After some time, I go back inside the theater, but I stand in the lobby and wait for Gottfried and Ross to come out.

The professor screws up his face like Mama used to do when she got worried about me. "Are you all right?"

"I'm fine."

"Are you sure?"

"I must have had something for lunch that didn't agree with me," I say. "I'm okay now. Matter of fact, I'm hungry."

I should have been an actor, no?

"Okay, I'll take you boys out to eat. But first," he says, "stand over there. I want a picture of you."

We stand there, but I can't say he took a very good picture.

Rudolf, Gottfried
Spring 1937 Paris, France
Outside theater after *Le Pays du Sourire*

Professor Ross, he's very interested in politics. Seems like he knows everyone in the Popular Front, the party in charge of France.

He knows the premier, who has put him in charge of some government work. Most of it is in Saint Nazaire, a town on the ocean. They build ships there.

Professor Ross has a suggestion. "What about you boys moving to St. Nazaire? I can get you jobs at the shipyard. They need workers, and the pay is good. Besides, I think maybe it's safer than Paris right now."

Gottfried and I discuss his idea. We can use the money, and I would like to have a job now. I'm tired of sitting around. But I'm not so sure about jobs at a shipyard. Why? One, I don't know a submarine from a sailboat. And two, I'm a klutz. I remind Gottfried of this.

"You of all people, you should know this is a bad idea. I have two left thumbs."

Gottfried laughs. "Yah, but we have one good left thumb and fourteen good fingers between the two of us. Should be enough."

We talk it over with the Fregonaras and our other friends, and they agree with the professor.

So in April, we move to Saint Nazaire, and they make us both traçeurs at the shipyard. Gottfried tells them I have experience, which I don't. But he shows me what to do. I get a blueprint, and I get a hammer. I knock out the blueprint on a piece of metal. But like I already said, I'm not mechanical. My fingernails get full of blood, and they stay bloody all the time.

We're traçeurs, but we also have to help with the ship-building work. The main thing we help with is riveting, which everybody hates—for very good reasons. They make a rivet by heating up a piece of iron, like a short rod. They heat it in a furnace until it's red-hot. Then a guy called "the tosser" takes it out of the furnace with some tongs, and he throws it over to a guy they call "the catcher." Looks like a blob of fire flying through the air. The catcher holds up a cup and catches the hot rivet in that. Catch it, don't catch it, catch it, don't catch it. If you miss, maybe you get burned. Maybe you start a fire. If you do catch it, then another guy takes the hot iron rod out of your cup with some tongs. He sticks it into a round hole in the hull, which they've already cut out with a drill. Then another guy takes a fast hammer and slams the hot iron rod all the way into the drilled-out hole. When he gets done, you have your rivet in the hull.

Tossing a hot rivet or catching it in a cup, you better be fast and exact. I'm not a good man for this job. I'm no good at being a traçeur, and I'm no good at rivets either. But they don't have enough help, so I have to keep doing it—even though my aim is bad. One time, I even start a little fire when I don't catch the hot iron rod, but nobody much cares. They just put out the fire and toss me another one.

It's dumb luck that I never get hurt, but poor Gottfried, who always catches and throws perfect, does get hurt. He happens to be working with some guys, who are doing welding. These guys are on top of ladders leaning high up against the hull. Gottfried is standing on the floor next to one of these ladders, and he's looking up. He's watching the guy on top of the ladder to see how he does the welding. But it's dark way up there, so it's not easy to see what's going on. This is when my brother makes a big mistake. He takes off his safety glasses. And while he's looking up, steel splinters start falling down, and one of them lands in his right eye.

At the time, I'm doing riveting work, so somebody comes to get me, and I go with him to the hospital. They operate on him right away. They take out his eyeball to remove the steel splinter. Then they put his eyeball back in the socket. The best thing that can happen, if he gets lucky, is he will see again but not too well.

So they operate on him, and he comes out of there with a big bandage. Says it doesn't hurt too bad, but he's mad at himself for taking off his safety goggles. A week or so after this, they take off the bandage, and now he can't see too well out of this eye anymore. But he's Gottfried, right? Smiles and says he's happy he can see at all.

After we've been in Saint Nazaire for a couple of months, Gottfried's birthday rolls around. It's May 6, 1937, which is exactly four years since we ran away. So we invite Professor Ross, Ernest Moos, the Fregonaras, and some other friends to come into town for a little birthday party for Gottfried. We're sitting in a café, talking about what happened in Guernica last month—how the Germans bombed the whole town for no reason except to test out bombers and bombs.

Then Professor Ross tells us he's changing the subject. He's got some good news for us on Gottfried's birthday.

"Premier Blum is coming to Saint Nazaire to see the ship you are working on," he says. "And I want you boys to make sure you are there to meet him."

Why this is good news, we don't understand. But we don't have time to ask, because suddenly, a guy comes running into the café, shouting.

"The *Hindenburg*! The *Hindenburg* blew up! The *Hindenburg* blew up!"

The whole place goes crazy. Women start screaming and people jump up and run out.

Professor Ross, he shakes his head.

"End of an era," he says. "End of an era, boys."

The *Hindenburg* was Germany's newest and biggest zeppelin. It was supposed to be the perfect airship.

Later on, we listen to the radio. A reporter who watched the crash iss practically crying.

"Oh, the humanity!" he says.

He makes it sound like this is the worst thing that ever happened in the world, right?

Gottfried, he's very upset about the *Hindenburg*. He's in love with zeppelins, so this crash makes him feel bad. Makes him feel bad it happened on his birthday too.

Now, I'm sorry it happened, naturally. But give me a break, huh? So a fancy balloon pops and kills a few rich people. Big deal. It's not the goddamn end of the world.

Gottfried 1937
St. Nazaire, France

XV

GOTTFRIED

When Léon Blum comes to visit the shipyard, Professor Ross is in the group with him and all the other big shots. They walk around, look at this and that, ask questions, shake hands. People with cameras—reporters, I guess—they're taking pictures the whole time. Then Premier Blum stops near us, takes a look at the ship we're working on, and makes a little speech about the way France needs to build more new and modern ships. Afterwards, all the workers stand in a long line to shake his hand. Rudolf and I stand in the line too, and when he comes closer to us, we see that Professor Ross is one of the men walking with him.

The professor gets himself next to Blum and says, "Léon, I want to introduce you to Gottfried and Rudolf Kahn. These are the two German brothers I told you about."

Blum smiles, shakes our hands, looks us over.

"Very happy to meet you boys," he says. "France appreciates your help here in Saint Nazaire."

And that's it. They all keep walking, and a few minutes later, the whole bunch is gone.

But a week later, Professor Ross calls me on the telephone.

"Gottfried," he says, "there are thosands of Spanish children whose families are sending them away because of the fighting over there. Some of them are orphans. The Spanish government is sending these kids to other countries, including France. But the French government can't take care of all of them."

"So," I say, "do you think we should we start a children's home in Saint Nazaire?"

"No," he laughs. "We found other countries to take some of them. Mexico is going to take up to five hundred, and I thought you and Rudolf might like to go on the ship with them. We can use a few more adults on their ship—people who can speak Spanish or Catalan."

It's like manna from heaven! Maybe, finally, we're going to get to the United States. Mexico is not far from there. From Mexico, I'm sure we can find a way.

But when I tell Rudolf, he says, "Gottfried, you go. I want to go back to Spain. I'm strong enough to fight again."

I yell at him. "Are you nuts? For crying out loud, Rudolf! What for? We can't win over there!"

"Why not?" he says calmly. "We've got new soldiers and good weapons now, and we're getting more all the time. Look, I want to be there when we stop Franco. When we stop him, we stop Hitler."

"Listen," I say, "you aren't going anywhere without me again! But Spain? You've got half an ass, and I've got one good hand and one good eye. Not only that, but look at what Hitler did last month in Guernica. We can never win this goddamn war."

He says he's surprised at me, because I'm usually the one who is hopeful. But this time, how can I hope? The news from Spain is mostly terrible. How can our side win the war? Franco has the big money, the united army, German weapons, tanks, planes, and panzers. He's got planes and fighters from Mussolini and mercenaries from Morocco on top of that. What have we got? Too little money, fighting among our leaders, and kids playing soldier. Even if our guys have more men and better weapons now, they don't have enough, and they don't have outside help. It's too late for us.

But Rudolf doesn't listen to me. He insists he's going back to fight. So I stop arguing. I know better than to do that anymore.

What I have to do now is go around him. Get him to listen to somebody else. Just like I had to get in cahoots with the doctor in Spain.

So the next day, I call up Professor Ross. Rudolf likes him and respects him. Maybe he can say something to convince my stubborn brother to take the ship to Mexico.

But before I can say anything to Professor Ross, he gives me very sad news. His only son, the one who has been fighting in

Spain, has been killed. I feel terrible. Me, I didn't know the professor's son, but he talked about him so much I feel like I did know him. What can I say? I tell him how sorry I am. I decide not to say anything else to him. He doesn't need to hear about our problems.

But the professor knows me. And he knows if I called him, I must have a reason.

"Is there something you were calling about?" he asks.

I decide to tell him. What if there's no other chance?

"I don't know what to do," I say. "Rudolf wants to go back to Spain and fight. But this chance to leave—thanks to you—it might be our only chance. It's the first chance anybody has given us in four years."

He's quiet. Then he says, "Rudolf isn't thinking straight. Let me handle it, Gottfried. Don't tell him we talked." I hear a long pause, then a sigh, and the professor says, "And don't say anything about my boy. That is important."

I get choked up. "Thank you so much."

The next few days, I say nothing to Rudolf about the ship or leaving or Spain. A few days after that, Rudolf tells me he's going to see Professor Ross. He goes, and when he comes back, he doesn't say anything about what happened. I don't say anything either.

Finally, when we're having lunch the next week, Rudolf says, "Okay, Gottfried, I decided I'm coming with you."

I know better than to ask any questions. I can guess what Professor Ross had to say to him anyhow. But the first chance I get, I call the professor and thank him for his help.

"Of course, Gottfried," he says. "I want you boys to get out of here. I want you to be with your family again and to live long and happy lives."

I say, "It's the most wonderful thing anybody ever did for us. We can never pay you back."

"Well," he says, "Pay me back by living good lives, getting married, having children, and writing me long letters."

Finally, the big day comes—May 24, 1937. Professor Ross comes to say goodbye, and so do the Fregonaras, Ernest Moos, and our other friends. It takes all morning to load up, but finally it's done, and our ship, by the name of *Mexique*, pulls out from the harbor in Nantes and moves into the Atlantic Ocean. Everybody on the deck stands at the rail and watches as everybody on the shore gets smaller and smaller, then disappears. Then the land disappears too, and that's it. France is gone. Europe is gone. Whatever happens next, only God knows. But now, I have hope!

We're traveling across the ocean on the *Mexique*, which is an old steamship, which was built during World War I to transport soldiers. It's a big ship, but it's not exactly the *Queen Mary*. It was never meant to carry hundreds of children, and there are almost five hundred of them on board. The kids go from the age of three or four to about fourteen years old, and they are mostly from the Basque region of Spain, where Franco has been bombing lately. Some of the kids are orphans from Guernica, but a lot of them still have parents. Their parents wanted to fight without worrying about the kids' getting hurt or killed. So they sent the kids away.

Spanish refugee children
May 1937
Aboard the *Mexique*

The younger ones don't really understand. They're lonely for their parents, and they cry a lot. Some of the older ones understand much more than children should have to understand. They almost never smile.

Our ride across the ocean is not too easy, especially at first. The water is choppy, and this old ship creaks and pitches. A lot of us vomit, but the poor kids have it hardest. The older ones walk around, trying to act brave. They raise their fists like we did when we were soldiers, and we greet them the same way.

There are all kinds of children here, naturally. Some of the boys like to talk about fighting for the republic when they get older. But some are war orphans, all alone in the world. Rudolf and I try to play with the quieter kids. Rudolf make faces and says silly things to them to cheer them up. Maybe they saw some terrible things. Maybe their mama or papa got killed. Takes a long time before a kid can get over something like that.

Nights are hardest for some children. Every night the first week, one little girl starts screaming and crying out in her sleep, "I can't swim! I can't swim!" She's scared to death of the ocean, and we have a terrible time waking her up and convincing her she's okay.

On this boat, when the kids get sick, there's trouble with diarrhea. Almost everybody gets it, and the whole place stinks. Nights, when it stinks too much, Rudolf and I sneak out and sleep on the deck. It's not allowed, but we really don't give a damn. What's the captain going to do to us anyhow? Throw us overboard?

Me, I'm sick sometimes too, but I'm grateful. Rudolf and I are alive. We're not running away or hiding or getting shot at. And we're getting closer to America every day.

I'm not sure how Rudolf feels though. There are days when he stands at the rail and stares at the ocean for a long, long time. I walk over and put my arm around him. I don't say anything. I just stand there with him, and after a while, he usually suggests we get a beer or something.

On the ship, I've got a few pieces of clothing and two special things. One is the little camera Herr Schuster gave me in Austria. The other a ivory chess set I bought in Paris. Took me a long time to save up for it.

Rudolf and I both love chess, which is something all the boys learned in Germany. As soon as we can, we take out my chess set and play. Pretty soon, we get people watching us. There are other men on board who like to play the game, and they can play pretty well, especially one of the crewmen. Matter of fact, he's always admiring my chess set. A couple of boys want to learn the game too, so we try and teach them when we can. At night, I keep my chess set with me. But one night, we're up late, and wego inside to sleep. I forget and leave my chess set on deck. Next morning, we come out, and it's gone. I go to the captain.

"Somebody stole my chess set last night."

"Where?"

"I left it on the deck."

"Sorry, but I can't search hundreds of people."

I think it was that crewman who took it, but I can't prove it. I'm mad, but there's nothing I can do.

The second week on the ship passes slowly. Rudolf and I try to play some games with the kids, entertain them. Rudolf tells them stories, which they love. But every day, we're spending hours doing nothing but mopping up, washing kids, or cleaning clothes. So we're very happy to see the island of Cuba when we get to it, and we're even happier when the ship stops there to refuel. We want to go ashore and walk around Havana with the kids. But the captain says no—it's against the rules. And anyhow, we won't be here long. Nobody can leave the ship.

So Rudolf and I decide to relax on the deck and watch the activity on shore. We're relaxing, leaning against the hull, talking about what we're going to do when we get to Mexico, when we see a man in a sharp white suit and hat walking up the gangway. Rudolf sees him first. He jumps up and shouts.

"Fred Strauss? What the hell?"

Now I jump up too. Strauss comes on deck, laughs, pumps our hands.

Says, "I never expected to see you boys again after I saw you in Paris last summer. But here we are! I'll tell you why I'm here, but right now, you boys go and pack up. We're leaving. I've got to go and see the captain."

Which he does. Tells him he's a friend of ours here on business, and he wants to take us out to lunch in Havana. Says he'll bring us back in a couple hours before the ship leaves. Maybe he bribes the captain—I don't know—but he pulls it off.

So we come back on the deck with our suitcases, and we wave goodbye to the kids. They don't know what's going on, but neither do we. We wave to them, and they wave back, and that's the last we ever see of them.

We follow Fred to the dock and then to a car parked nearby. It's an American car, a brand-new 1937 Plymouth with a driver inside. He tells us to get in, so we get in, and we start to drive. Where we're going, we don't know. But pretty soon, Fred tells us the whole story.

"I was in New York a few weeks ago on business, so I called your mother to say hello. She said you boys were on your way to Mexico by boat, and Siegfried had all the details. So I called him up, and here I am!"

He says he's taking us to a hotel by the name of the Hotel Naçional de Cuba. "And I want you to stay there until your family sends you a lawyer, who will get you into the United States."

To me, this feels like a dream. I'm sure any minute I'm going to wake up again on the ship with the children from Spain. But that doesn't happen, and it's not too long before we come to a beautiful building with a million different kinds of architecture. Me, I can't wait to get out my camera. We get out of the car with Fred, take a little walk around. It's like some kind of modern palace. We never saw anything like this before.

Fred says, "You boys like this place? It's only a couple of years old. Has all the latest."

Rudolf and I just stare at him. Like it? Huh? What can we say?

Fred smiles. Says, "Good."

He marches us up to the front desk of this fancy hotel and settles us in a fancy room. He tells us he wants us to stay here.

"No arguments," he says.

Naturally, Rudolf and I say no at the same time. This is too much. But he insists. "For me, it's a pleasure, boys. I'm glad you got the hell out. Europe is going to go up in flames."

He walks us over to the bar in the lobby there, orders us some rum. Says, "Best rum in the world, boys."

We drink it. We need it!

Then we go and have lunch at the hotel restaurant, order some tamales, which are pork with salsa wrapped up in corn husks. First time we ever ate these things. We also try out a new beer here, name of Cristal, but Rudolf and I don't order it again. Matter of fact, we don't much care for Cuban beer altogether.

Rudolf says, "This beer doesn't taste so hot. Must be all the stinging nettle in it."

He tells Strauss about our little lunch with the Bremen boys and their big shot Nazi uncle. Fred laughs, shakes his head, and tells us we're very lucky—something we already know. Then he says he's flying back to New York tomorrow. Wishes he could take us along, but he can't. We've got to have legal papers first.

Gottfried and Rudolf
June 1937
Havana, Cuba

After lunch, Fred buys us some new clothes. We protest, but he insists again. He buys us white summer suits and hats to go with them. Then he takes some pictures of us for our family.

Rudolf and I can't believe any of this—Fred Strauss, this place, this hotel. I think we must be in heaven. How can this be our world, the world we know? Warm air, blue sky, palm trees, flowers, beautiful beaches. People walking around happy, working, smiling, relaxing, laughing, eating, drinking, whistling. Music everywhere. No sick kids, nobody crying. No shooting, no war, no bodies blowing apart. No terrible news, no strikes, no hate signs. No Nazis.

It's impossible. But if it's a dream, I sure as hell don't want to wake up.

XVI

RUDOLF

Gottfried and I, we're trying to get used to our new lives here in Havana, but it's not so easy. Why? One, we never had fancy lives like this before, and we're not used to it. And two, we're still watching our backs, waiting for somebody to pick a fight, pass a law, tell us to get the hell out of here.

But as soon as I find out they have legal gambling everywhere in Havana, I start feeling better. There's even a nice casino right here in our hotel. So I'm passing my time like this—making new buddies, playing poker, blackjack, roulette. Anyhow, pretty soon we have some extra spending money.

Naturally, we buy a new chess set. And Gottfried right away starts meeting girls and wanting us to take them out. I have no excuse, so I go along. Beautiful, these Cuban girls. Can't help but see that. We take them to the beaches, buy them drinks, little gifts, take them dancing—all this. Look, I'm a man. I don't need to love them, and I don't. But I'm not a monk, right? I have the same needs as every other guy.

Anyhow, after a couple of weeks like this, we start to feel more normal. Which means my brother is worrying again. What if this? What if that? What if we run out of money?

"Look," I tell him, "we'll get money. Stop worrying."

It doesn't stop him, of course. But there's plenty to do here, and this helps take his mind off money. Like I said, there's the gambling. There's terrific music here too. Anything you want—conga, rumba, mambo. And always the girls. One time, we take a couple of them out to hear a famous singer by the name of Miguelito Valdez. Very smooth. Afterward, the girls feel romantic, want to hit the beds. Maybe they're with us, but they're not exactly thinking of us. They're thinking of Valdez. That's okay by me. I'm not exactly thinking of them either.

After a couple of weeks, a lawyer shows up. My aunts hired the guy and sent him down here. This lawyer, he's a small guy, by the name of Lentz. Pale, squinting all the time like he's been in a dark room. Skinny, bald, with thick, heavy glasses. Every ten minutes, he takes them off, wipes them with a white handkerchief, puts them back on. The only clothes he wears are a tan suit, tan shirt, tan tie, tan straw hat.

First thing he does, he gets himself a typewriter. Then he goes and sits up in a room in our hotel and bangs on the typewriter.

Bang bang bang, day and night. He makes up a hell of a story. To tell us all we're supposed to say when we go see the American consul.

Gottfried reads me Lentz's story after he finishes it, and the whole goddamn thing is full of lies. What's not a lie is only partly true. The story says we're two nice, clean-cut, young German boys who never did a single thing wrong. We got beaten up by some Nazis, so we ran away. Then we worked here and there to save money to come to the States. It says we worked in Spain, but we left when the civil war started and went straight to France. It says we volunteered to help out on a ship with some orphans from the Spanish war, so we could go from France to America.

This is it, Lawyer Lentz's story. He tells us to learn it by heart. After this, he throws questions at us like we're in school. If we don't figure out what he's getting at, he tells us the answers he wants. At least he doesn't hit us like our old teachers did, huh?

Now, Gottfried and I, we're not in the habit of lying. Mama didn't bring us up to lie. There are times we have to lie, sure. There are times everybody has to lie. Lentz says this is one of those times. He says we have to do it, because the United States hates communists. Won't let in anybody who was fighting on the same side with communists.

Lawyer Lentz, he gets us an appointment on a Friday afternoon with the American vice consul, a guy by the name of Parsons. When we get there, the secretary sends us to a room with an American doctor. He asks us both a lot of questions, and he examines us. Looks us over real good. Says he'll write up his report. After this, we wait in the lobby for a couple of hours. We talk to the secretary.

Gottfried asks her to go out with him, but she smiles and says her boyfriend would kill her.

Finally, they call us in. Parsons is sitting there with another secretary, a translator. Parsons, he's a good-looking man. He's got a strong face, but it's not a hard face. He's sitting there, and on his desk, he's got the story about us that Lentz wrote on his typewriter. And he's got the doctor's report, which he's looking at right now. He reads over everything. Takes his time too. Gottfried is jumpy. Picks at his hands, squirms around in his chair. I lean back and watch the ceiling fan go round and round. Nothing else to do. Finally, Parsons gets finished. He looks up at us over his glasses, which sit halfway down on his nose. Talks to us through the translator.

"Boys," he says, "I'm very interested in what you have to say in this story. I'm also interested in what our doctor has to say in his report."

He doesn't ask us any questions. Just takes off his glasses, sets them down on his desk, then raises his head and looks at us.

"Boys," he says, "you can take this story and stick with it, or you can tell me the truth."

This is exactly what he says. Then he says, "I'm sending you to that little room over there. You two talk it over. See which way you want to go. But if I were you, I would stick to the truth."

He's no fool, Parsons. He doesn't buy Lentz's story. The doctor looked us over very carefully, no? He talked to us, and he saw the wounds we have. He could see what's what, and he must have put it in his report.

But we're not sure what to do. Lentz is supposed to know, isn't he? And he says the Americans won't let us in if they think we're connected to communists. Communists are undesirable characters in America.

Gottfried says, "Maybe we spoiled our chances. You think Lentz knows what he's talking about?"

"Who knows?" I say. "All we know is our family hired him to help us."

"Yah, but maybe they don't know if he's got experience with this."

"I don't trust Lentz," I say. "The doctor here, he saw our wounds, and Parsons is no dummy."

"But what if this is how Parsons makes sure we don't get in? Gets us to tell the truth and then tells us to get lost?"

Which worries me too. So we go back and forth. We're not too smart, but we didn't do anything wrong by fighting against Franco. POUM was a socialist group, anyhow. It wasn't a communist group. But even if it *had* been a communist group, we aren't sorry we fought against that bastard, Franco.

So we come to a decision. Forget about Lentz. Tell the facts the way they were. Worst thing that can happen is we get stuck in Cuba. It wouldn't be the end of the world.

So we get up and tell the secretary we're ready to go back inside. We sit down and start telling them our story, our true story. And they're listening. We take a long time to tell them the whole thing. Parsons and his secretary, they ask questions and take a lot of notes.

One question Parsons asks is where the typed story on his desk comes from. We tell him about Lentz, about the way he made up this story and why he said he did it. Parsons shakes his head.

When we finally finish, Parsons says, "Okay boys. You come back on Monday at ten o'clock, and I'll give you my decision."

We leave there and go back to the hotel. Lentz is having a drink, which is what we want to do ourselves, so we walk over to the bar.

And Gottfried says, "Mr. Lentz, you might not like this, but we told the truth in there."

Lentz, he says, "Huh? What do you mean?"

We tell him. He bangs both hands on the bar counter. His glass jumps, and some of his rum spills out. He's furious.

"No no no!" he shouts. "With all the trouble your relatives went to? You've ruined everything! It cost them a fortune. And all for nothing."

The next day, Siegfried calls us up. He says Lentz called our aunts. Siegfried doesn't say we did wrong, telling the truth. But he says our aunts and Mama are worried, because Lentz told them to expect the worst.

Gottfried and I, we're miserable the whole weekend.

On Monday morning at ten o'clock, we drag ourselves over to the consulate. We're sitting and waiting. The secretary in the waiting area is not talking.

Gottfried whispers, "She acts like we're criminals."

I shrug. "Nah. She had a fight with her boyfriend."

So we're sitting there like bad boys, maybe thirty minutes. Then in comes Parsons. He's late. He motions to us to come into his office.

He starts looking over all the papers. Then he looks up at us. Says, "Well, boys, I went through your story, and I believe your story. But not your lawyer's lies. *Your* story. What you did was right." He pushes the papers aside, looks up at us, and says, "Everything looks okay to me."

He takes out a different folder from his drawer. Then he stands up, reaches across the desk, and hands it over to us.

"Here are your papers, boys. Congratulations! You're in."

Gottfried jumps up, almost shouts, "Thank you, Mr. Parsons. Thank you!"

Then Parsons says, "Only thing is this. I want to warn you boys. When you go to the United States, if you ever get involved in any communist activities—even if you go to the library and get communist books—you will never become American citizens."

The secretary smiles at us and shows us the way out, and we leave the place with our new papers. Gottfried's holding onto them. He's holding them good and tight against his chest.

It was cool and dark inside that building. Outside, the sun is shining so bright, it hurts our eyes, and it's hot out, steamy. I put on my hat and look around. I see the blue sky, the palm trees. I'm hearing music playing nearby. A pretty girl walks by, winks at us. Gottfried winks back. He's smiling from one ear to the other.

"Rudolf!" he laughs. "We're free! We're dancing!"

I'm smiling. I miss my family, and I want to see them, and I'm happy we'll get to see them again soon. But right now, I have a little score to settle.

I tell Gottfried, "Let's go over and give Lentz the good news."

So we go back to the hotel and find Lentz, and Gottfried tells him what's what. Lentz can't believe it.

"You must be kidding! That's unheard of! Just your dumb luck, that's all. They never before let in anybody with communist connections. Never."

"We're not communists," I say.

"You fought on the same side, didn't you?"

"We fought against Franco."

Gottfried chimes in. "Rudolf is right. Thank God, Mr. Parsons understood."

"Dumb luck," says Lentz. "That's why you got in. Dumb luck, plain and simple."

Makes me even madder. I look at Lentz in his lying eyes. I want to punch him, but I don't. Why? One, it's not kosher to punch a guy wearing glasses. And two, if I punch a lawyer, I'm going to need a lawyer. Last thing I need right now is another lawyer.

So what I do is, I grab his collar and pull him up to me, up to my face.

"Pay attention, Lentz," I tell him. "If you ever try to get money out of my family, I'm going to come after you. You hear me?"

He's shaking, nodding. I let him loose, give him a light, little shove.

"Okay, okay," he says. "Take it easy."

And that's it. He brushes off his tan pants, straightens out his tan shirt and tie, and walks away. We never see him again. And he never does send a bill. Never charges our family a penny.

Later on, Gottfried and I go down to the beach and watch the girls. Gottfried brings along his little camera, takes some pictures. Gets one of the girls to take a picture of us. Gottfried says, "Maybe we'll get lucky tonight."

We don't get lucky, but Gottfried gets a roll of pictures. He takes the film out of the camera so he can get the pictures developed. This turns out to be a good thing.

All we need to do for the next week is relax and get ready to go to Miami. So every day, we go to the beach after lunch and hang around there, looking for girls. One day, Gottfried lies down and says he's going to take a little siesta, so I go off for a walk. I need some peace and quiet, and it does me good.

When I get back, Gottfried says he's been looking for me. He's very upset.

Says, "My camera—it's gone! Only thing left we had from Europe. Somebody stole it."

I laugh. "You let some broad distract you, huh?"

"No!" he shouts. "It's not my fault. I was lying down, taking a little nap, but I had it right here. Right under my hat. Had my arm on top of my hat. Somebody sneaked up and took it."

"Forget it," I say. "You can get another one. Anyhow, we've already got plenty of pictures."

What I'm thinking about is how I've got no picture of Carme. Not even one.

"Yeah," he whines. "But that camera was the only thing I had left from Europe."

I blow up. "Goddamn it, Gottfried! It's nothing, just a goddamn camera. You have your life, don't you? It's just a camera. It's not your goddamn life!"

I should have known better. Now I hurt his feelings, and it's going to take him hours and hours to get over it. So I go out and buy him a new camera, a good one.

A week later, we're on a plane from Havana to Miami. Strange, but it happens to be July 4, 1937—Independence Day in the United States. It's our independence day too, in a way. It also happens to be my first ride in an airplane. On the plane, I'm looking out the window at the tops of the clouds and feeling like a little kid.

Like he's reading my mind, Gottfried says, "Makes you want to jump up and down on the clouds, doesn't it?"

My brother, he's been in plenty of airplanes, so this is nothing new for him. But he loves to fly, and naturally, he remembers the first time. He knows how I'm feeling.

Says, "Want to hear a good joke, Rudolf?"

"Sure," I say.

He tells me some dirty joke. It's kind of dumb, like most of his dirty jokes. But he gets so excited telling them that he always makes me laugh. Why? He's my brother. Drives me crazy sometimes, but what would I do without Gottfried, huh?

We land in Miami, smooth and easy. Right on time, too. But when we get out of the plane, we can see storm clouds rolling in from the ocean. Guess they must have been behind us, following our plane.

Gottfried gets himself busy taking pictures again. He takes pictures of the airplane we came on and the sign that says, "Miami Airport."

For some reason or other, the whole time Gottfried is busy taking pictures, I'm staring at the clouds rolling in, and I'm trying to remember the words to that old song about angels—the one Clare used to sing to us when we were kids.

While I'm thinking about this, trying to remember the words, Gottfried all of a sudden stops taking pictures.

Says, "Let's go, Rudolf. You know what they say. 'When angels travel, the sky cries!'"

Now, this old song never made much sense to me, so why both of us happen to think of it now, I can't tell you. But Gottfried and I, we're not deep thinkers. We're just a couple of guys passing through.

—The End—

Gottfried and Rudolf
July 1937

EPILOGUE

Gottfried and Rudolf made their way to New York, where they were reunited with their parents and siblings.

Front, left to right: Hubert,
Ernestine holding Clare's son, Abraham (Adolf)
Rear, left to right: Rudolf, Gottfried, Clare, Martin, Siegfried
1937 New York

Both brothers married around the time the United States entered World War II, and both proudly served their new country during the war. Gottfried enlisted in the US Army Air Corps and spent time in Australia as an airplane mechanic. He earned a citation for inventing a tool to prevent burn injuries. Rudolf joined the US Army as an infantryman in the Ninth Army, 29th Division, 116th infantry. During the summer of the D-Day invasion, his company made its way through France and entered Berlin, Germany immediately after the Russians.

Rudolf remained in Berlin while the US Army hired Germans for cleanup and construction. Rudolf's task was to interview and screen German job applicants in order to reject former SS men as workers. He took particular pleasure in discovering former SS officers, looking them in the eye, and telling them he was a Jew. When Rudolf told me this story, he quipped, "Naturally, *nobody* in 1945 Berlin had ever been a Nazi or had ever known a Nazi."

During the war, Gottfried's already-damaged right hand further stiffened and contracted, and he was sent home. He underwent a number of surgeries at William Beaumont Hospital in El Paso, Texas. When the war ended in 1945, the Army offered Gottfried a temporary job as a translator for Wernher von Braun and his coterie of German rocket scientists, who were quartered near El Paso. Years later, Gottfried told me, "If I'd known what those guys had been doing for Hitler, I never would have taken that job."

Gottfried stayed in El Paso and started an appliance repair business. In 1950, he started a sewing machine sales company and began establishing sewing machine distributorships. He, his wife, and their four children often piled into in Gottfried's small airplane and flew with him to various places. Within a few years,

Rudolf also moved to El Paso with wife and three children. Rudolf also went into business, buying out stores and reselling stocks of clothing. As soon as he arrived in El Paso, Rudolf also began a lifelong love affair with Las Vegas.

The brothers lived and worked near each other, and their children grew up together. Gottfried and Rudolf remained close and continued to drive each other crazy for the rest of their lives.

ACKNOWLEDGEMENTS

—To my husband, Paul, for your encouragement, patience, and understanding

—To my sons, Daniel and David, for critically reading the early drafts of this manuscript and offering so many helpful ideas

—To my sister, Marian Daross, for the many hours she spent editing this book and reviewing her suggestions with me

—To my talented nephews: Carson Kahn, for his unique, creative cover design, and Ely Kahn for his help building my website

—To Professor Richard Gunther for his input concerning the history of Spain and the Spanish Civil War

—To my brothers, Ronald (Arlo) and Gary Kahn, and to my cousins, Linda Gunther, Sandra Dillon, and John Simon for enouraging me to write this book, for adding to my research, and for sending me photographs I wouldn't otherwise have had

—To my friends and fellow authors for your moral support and your critical input along the way: Karen Berger, Amy Glaser Gage, Donald Herzberg, Victoria Herzberg, Carol Kaplan-Lyss, Peggy Hapke Lewis, Constance McIntyre— and especially, to Roland Merullo.

NOTES

Chapter I

4 *"German war prisoners had to work for us."* Of the 1.45 million prisoners of war held in World War I Germany, 750,000 worked in agriculture, and 330,000 worked in industry. Jochen Ottmer, *Kriegsgefangene im Europa des ersten weltkriegs* (Paderborn: Schöningh, 2006), 71.

5 *"He got very nervous, sick in the head. Shellshock, they called it."* German psychiatrists considered shellshock (post-traumatic stress disorder) to be a form of contagious "hysteria" in "weak-willed" men. They set up "neurosis stations" near farms and factories to treat patients in isolation from "soft-hearted" families. Treatment could consist of one or more therapies, such as hard labor, electroshock, fake injections, or "boring to death" (forced inactivity). Paul Lerner, *Hysterical Men: War, Psychiatry, and the Politics of Trauma in Germany, 1890–1930* (Ithaca: Cornell University Press, 2006), 151.

7 *"We needed a suitcase full of money to buy a loaf of bread."* Under the Versailles Treaty ending World War I, the victorious allies appropriated the German navy, 20 percent of the German coal, iron, and steel industries, and 13 percent of German territory (instantly costing at least 6 million people their German citizenship). The allies also imposed hefty reparations, which demoralized the German population and destabilized the German economy. In 1914, when World War I began, four German marks equaled one US

dollar. By 1923, 18,000 marks equaled one US dollar, and a loaf of bread cost 140 million marks. During this terrible economy, anti-semitic right-wingers falsely claimed that government unemployment subsidies were mainly going to Jews. Other right-wing anti-semitic propaganda also inflamed people. A mob of about 30,000 descended on a Jewish area of Berlin, which was populated mainly by eastern European immigrants. The mob relentlessly beat people and looted shops for about two days until the government regained control. By the end of 1923, the economy was in shambles. There were hundreds of soup kitchens throughout the country, including nineteen for Jews who were living in Berlin. Donald L. Niewyk, *The Jews in Weimar Germany* (Baton Rouge: LSU Press, 1980), 48–51.

7 *"Losing the war was hard on everybody. But for us—for Jews—it was even worse."* When Germany lost the war, antisemitic right-wingers falsely blamed Jewish army officers and civilians. Throughout the 1930s and into the 1940s, Hitler capitalized on this slander to foment antisemitism. Richard S. Levy, *Antisemitism, A Historical Encyclopedia of Prejudice and Persecution,* vol. 1(Santa Barbara: ABC–CLIO 2005), 623–24. Nor was this the first war-related antisemitic libel. In the middle of World War I, after 3,000 Jewish soldiers had already died and 7,000 had been decorated, German officials accused Jewish soldiers of shirking front line duty. They ordered a "Jew census" on the front lines. The census showed that 80 percent of Jewish soldiers—a disproportionately *large* number—had served on the front lines. The government quickly buried these results. Elon, *Pity of It All,* 338; *Leo Baeck Institute Yearbook,* vol. 19, Oxford Journals (New York: Oxford University Press,1974),143.

Despite endemic antisemitism in its armed forces, German Jews were devoted to their homeland. Amos Elon, *Pity of It All*(New York: Picador, 2003), 338. Jews fought and died for Germany in the same proportions as Christians. During World War I, over 100,000 German Jews (one in six) served in the armed forces; 12,000 lost their lives; and from 30,000–35,000 were decorated for bravery. Claudia Koonz, *Nazi Conscience*, (Cambridge, MA: The Belknap Press of Harvard University Press, 2003), 9; Michael Berenbaum, *The World Must Know: The History of the Holocaust as Told in the United States Holocaust Museum* (Boston, MA: Little Brown, 1993),19.

7 "*Siegfried... went to hear Hitler talk.*" In November 1923, Hitler tried to overthrow the government. He was convicted of high treason and sentenced to five years in prison. But Hitler had powerful supporters in industry, who arranged for him to have a comfortable confinement and a quick release (He served thirteen months). Lucy Dawidowicz, *The War against the Jews 1933–1945* (New York: Bantam Books, 1986), 5; Koonz, *Nazi Conscience*, 21–26.

While in prison, Hitler wrote *Mein Kampf,* which often quoted his idol, Henry Ford of Ford Motor Company. Ford had begun underwriting the Nazi Party in 1922 and continued to do so until forced to stop during World War II. Anthony C. Sutton, *Wall Street and the Rise of Hitler,* (Cutchogue, NY: Buccaneer Books, 2004), HTML version 2000 http://reformed—theology.org/html/books/wall_street/, 93.

Over the next few years after Hitler's release from prison, the Nazi Party organized a state within a state. It even had its own paramilitary force, the *Sturmabteilung* or SA. William L. Shirer, *The Rise and Fall of the Third Reich* (New York: Simon & Schuster,1990),169–71. When Hitler began speaking in public again, he deliberately curbed his antisemitic vitriol. But "*the racist planks of the 25-point Nazi Party program were clear to anyone who cared to read them... Leaving coarse antisemitism to his deputies, Hitler's politics of virtue elevated him above the party machine he controlled.*" Koonz, *Nazi Conscience*, 27—28.

7 "*When the American stock market crashed in 1929, things went from worse to terrible.*" As Germany's economy improved during the mid-1920s, the Nazis' fortunes declined. Laurence Rees, *The Nazis: A Warning from History* (New York: MJF Books, 1997), 31, 38. In fact, as of 1928, the Nazi Party had only twelve members in its 491-member *Reichstag* (parliament). "*One scarcely heard of Hitler or the Nazis except as the butts of jokes.*" Shirer, *Rise and Fall,* 168. But in October 1929, the US stock market crashed, US banks and businesses began calling in loans, and Germany's economy spiraled downward. The government tried to stop the bleeding by raising taxes, lowering family assistance and unemployment benefits, and excluding women from unemployment benefits—all to no avail. Rees, *Nazis: A Warning,* 38.

By the end of 1933 in Berlin, about 16 percent of the general population was unemployed. Because of new Nazi laws, 50 percent of Jewish workers were unemployed. Marion A. Kaplan, *Between Dignity and Despair, Jewish Life in Nazi Germany* (New York: Oxford University Press,1999), 28.

9 "*There were...very few Jews in our hometown and very few Jews in all of Germany.*" Despite an influx of 100,000 impoverished eastern European Jews into Germany, the total number of German Jews actually *declined* between 1900 and 1933.

The German census counted 503,000 Jews (0.7 percent of the German population) in 1933. Some sources put this number at closer to 525,000. Saul Friedlander, *Nazi Germany and the Jews: The Years of Persecution, 1933–1939,* vol. I (New York: Harper Perennial, 1998),12. About about 30 percent of the total number lived in Berlin. Larson, Erik, *In the Garden of Beasts: Love, Terror, and an American Family in Hitler's Berlin* (New York: Broadway Paperbacks, 2011), 57. There were only 855 Jews in Gottfried and Rudolf's hometown, Giessen. They amounted to about 2 percent of the total population. Erwin Knaus, *Die Jüdesiche bevolkerung Giessen 1933–1945* (Giessen, Germany: Gorich & Weiershaüsr 1982), 34.

22 *"Why should we move to some faraway desert? We were Germans. Germany was our home."* About 90 percent of German Jews did not support Zionism. But from 1933 to 1938, the Nazis enthusiastically supported Zionism as the best way to get rid of German Jews. SA men gave Jews mock one-way tickets to Jerusalem and held up posters saying, "Get ready for Palestine." Niewyk, *Jews in Weimar Germany,* 140–41. In August of 1933, the Nazi government formalized its relationship with the Zionist movement.

Under the Nazi-Zionist transfer agreement, Hitler moved about 60,000 German Jews plus $100 million of their money from Germany to Palestine. Edwin Black, *The Transfer Agreement* (New York: Carroll & Graf, 2001), 382. The Nazi government also helped German Zionists organize camps and agricultural centers throughout Germany in order to train prospective settlers for their new lives in Palestine. (Oddly, these camps flew the flag that Israel eventually adopted.) In 1935, when the Nazis banned all other Jewish groups from meeting, they expressly exempted Zionist groups. Max Nussbaum, "Zionism Under Hitler," *Congress Weekly,* (New York: American Jewish Congress, September 11, 1942); Francis R. Nicosia, *The Third Reich & the Palestine Question* (Piscataway, NJ: Transaction Publishers, 2000), 57–60.

11 *"Then all of a sudden—just like that!—there were no more freedoms."* As soon as he became chancellor, Hitler began arresting political opponents and opening concentration camps in which to confine and punish them with hard labor.

In late March 1933, the Nazi Party prevented its political opponents (eighty-one communist members and twenty-six social democrats) from attending a Reichstag meeting. At this meeting, the parliament gave Hitler dictatorial power. Berenbaum, *World Must Know*, 16.

By August 1933, all sources of opposition had been eliminated. The Nazi government had abolished parliamentary democracy; banned all non-Nazi trade unions; shuttered all anti-Nazi publications; assumed control of the press; replaced most civil servants—including judges—with Nazis; banned all other political parties; severely restricted the employment, property, and marital rights of Jews; and started a systematic program to sterilize all disabled people. Koonz, *Nazi Conscience*, 29–46,170–78; Dawidowicz, *War against the Jews*, 58–61.

14 "*We even exchanged Easter eggs and matzos with him.*" Antisemitism existed for hundreds of years in Germany, but for the most part, the 1800s and the 1900s (before the economy collapsed following World War I) were not bad times for most German Jews. Jewish-Christian relationships were generally peaceful, although antisemitic violence did break out periodically. Some violent demonstrations stemmed from difficult economic periods and/or from fears that Jews were obtaining too many rights and privileges. Christhard Hoffman, *et al*, eds. Werner Bergmann and Helmut Walser Smith, eds., *Exclusionary Violence: Antisemtic Riots in Modern German History* (Ann Arbor: University of Michigan Press, 2002), 40–50.

Nevertheless, by 1914, most German Jews were more secular than their counterparts in most of Europe, and they were far more assimilated in Germany than in most other places. Jews married non-Jews on a regular basis, held public office, attended public schools, participated in athletic and social organizations, had careers in the military, and contributed as fully as non-Jews to the welfare of their country. Jonathan Friedman, *The Lion and the Star: Gentile-Jewish Relations in Three Hessian Communities, 1919–1945* (Lexington: University Press of Kentucky, 1998), 80–89.

Even in rural areas, where Jews and non-Jews rarely intermarried, *"there were edges where the boundaries between gentile and Jewish communities blurred and local customs overtook religious beliefs."* For instance, rural Jews baked Christmas honey cakes for their Christian neighbors and gave them matzos at Passover "to ward off lightning." Ruth Gay, *The Jews of Germany: A Historical Portrait* (New Haven: Yale University Press), 226. Non-Jewish farmers and Jewish cattle traders also exchanged Easter eggs and matzos. Friedman, *Lion and the Star,* 80–91.

Chapter II

27 *"Clare always liked boys, but she fell for the wrong one when she got older... Nice guy too, but not Jewish."* By 1927, many Jews had converted to Christianity and had raised Christian children. At least one in three German Jews living in Germany was married to a Christian. Niewyk, *Jews in Weimar Germany,* 98–105.

As of 1930, about 60,000 German Jews were *"either apostates, children raised without Jewish identity by a mixed marriage, or Jews who had simply drifted away."* Edwin Black, *IBM and the Holocaust: The Strategic Alliance between Nazi Germany and America's Most Powerful Corporation* (Washington, DC: Dialog Press, 2008), 55.

In 1933, the Nazis decided that any person with one Jewish grandparent was a Jew—regardless of that person's professed faith or beliefs. Koonz, *Nazi Conscience,* 9, 14, 25.
Hitler called Christian-Jewish marriages "racial treason" or "bastardization." In 1935, the Nazis banned all intermarriage between Jews and non-Jews.

38 *"He says he's a higher-up in the... SA."* After World War I, the German army had a surplus of new brown shirts. Hitler bought them and outfitted his followers with them; hence, the SA's nick-

name became the "Brownshirts." John Toland, *Adolf Hitler* (New York: Doubleday & Company, 1976), 220.

As Hitler rose to power, the SA reinforced his rise with bullying and brutality. They disrupted gatherings of communists and others opposed to National Socialism and brutalized people to suppress opposition and generate fear. The SA appealed to unemployed and angry young men. Within a few months after the Nazis took power, the SA grew from 400,000 to 1.2 million. But the SA's street violence in the spring of 1933 backfired. Too many people in Germany and abroad publicly denounced SA thuggery. Hitler therefore created another paramilitary force, the *Schutzstaffel* (SS or "Blackshirts"), which recruited more educated men and used more sophisticated police tactics. As the SS's influence grew, the SA became "culturally and politically marginal." In 1934, the SS killed the SA's top leaders. Although the SA continued to exist after this, law enforcement control moved to the SS and its various arms, including its secret police force (the *Gestapo*). Koonz, *Nazi Conscience*, 81–84, 96–97.

39 "*Everybody who is not Aryan... can't be part of the volk.*" The Nazis believed physically and mentally disabled people "polluted" German society and siphoned off resources needed to build a healthy, pureblood Aryan nation. In 1933, the government made sterilization compulsory for anyone with a physical or mental disability. In 1935, the government prohibited anyone with a hereditary or infectious disease from marrying and reproducing.

In 1936, the Nazis established clinics to create "pure" German children. Unmarried pregnant women with racially-approved traits gave birth to between 6,000 and 8,000 children—many with SS fathers. Mark Landler, "Results of Secret Nazi Breeding Program: Normal Folks," *New York Times*, November 7, 2006.

Between 1939 and 1945, the government murdered from 200,000 to 270,000 physically and/or mentally disabled men, women, and children. Many were first subjected to horrific medical experiments, so the government could learn how to most efficiently kill groups of people. Disabled children were the first victims of Zyklon B, the insecticide later used in Nazi gas chambers. Michael Berenbaum, "T4 Program," *Encyclopedia Britannica Online*, s.v., accessed November 11, 2012. topic/714411/ /T4—Program; Berenbaum, *World Must Know*, 61.

39 "Hitler's going to put the German people... back to work. He's going to give the volk more living space. He's going to build up the best army in the world." Hitler built a sophisticated, modern military. But he could never have done so without phenomenal support from major American businesses. Moreover, corporate decision-makers knew that they were helping Germany rebuild its military and rearm, which violated the Versailles Treaty. Sutton, *Wall Street*, 21–23.

In 1936, the US ambassador to Germany, William Dodd, wrote to President Roosevelt:

> *"At the present moment, more than a hundred American corporations have subsidiaries here or cooperative understandings. The Du Ponts have three allies in Germany that are aiding in the armaments business. Their chief ally is the IG Farben Company, a part of the Government which gives 200,000 marks a year to one propaganda organization operating on American opinion. Standard Oil Company (New York sub company) sent $2,000,000 here in December 1933 and has made $500,000 a year helping Germans make Ersatz gas for war purposes; but Standard Oil cannot take any of its earnings out of the country except in goods. They do little of this, report the facts at home, but do not explain the facts. The International Harvester Company presi-*

dent told me their business here rose 33% a year (arms manufacture, I believe), but they could take nothing out. Even our airplane people have secret arrangements with Krupps. General Motors Company and Ford do enormous businesses here through their subsidiaries and take no profits out. I mention these facts because they complicate things and add to war dangers." (William E. Dodd, *Ambassador Dodd's Diary, 1933–1938* [New York: Harcourt, Brace & Co., 1941],197–98).

A few of the many disturbing facts about corporate America's entanglement with the Nazi regime follow:

- In the early 1920s, Henry Ford began underwriting the Nazi Party and continued doing so even after World War II began. Ford's money helped pay for Nazi uniforms, offices, employees, automobiles, factories, and weaponry. Hitler called Henry Ford "a great man" and "my inspiration." He put Ford's framed portrait above his desk and awarded him Germany's highest civilian honor. Sutton, *Wall Street*, 90–92; Andrew Nagorski, *Hitlerland: American Eyewitnesses to the Nazi Rise to Power* (New York: Simon & Schuster, 2012), 60.

- Beginning in 1933 when Hitler took power, New York-based IBM and its CEO, Thomas Watson, leveraged their Nazi connections in Germany and did millions of dollars in business with the Nazi party for the next twelve years. Through its German subsidiary (Dehomag), IBM leased and regularly serviced its high-speed sorting equipment to the government. IBM also regularly provided *custom-made* punch cards to enable the Nazis to research generations of records in order to identify and classify people as Jews. IBM punch cards and equipment not only enabled and facilitated the roundups of Jews, but they enabled the Nazis to systematically track and manage everything from assets to slave labor pools to selections at ghettos to train schedules for transporting Jews to death camps. Black, *IBM and the Holocaust*, 9-11.

- US banks made "a flood" of loans to Germany under Congress's 1924 Dawes Plan and its 1929 Young Plan. Nagorski, *Hitlerland*, 50. By 1933, the year the Nazis took over, Germany already owed American creditors a total of $1.2 billion. National City Bank and Chase Manhattan Bank alone held over $100 million in German bonds. Larson, *In the Garden*, 19, 37.

- Among those involved in making and servicing multimillion-dollar loans to German industries directly or indirectly engaged in rearming the country were Owen Young (president of General Electric Company), Charles Dawes (author of the Dawes Plan), and JP Morgan. "Without the capital supplied by Wall Street, there would have been no IG Farben in the first place and almost certainly no Adolf Hitler and no World War II." Sutton, *Wall Street*, 33–44.

- John D. Rockefeller's Standard Oil Company spent millions of dollars on oil exploration in Germany in the 1930s. In 1934, Germany could produce only 300,000 tons of synthetic gasoline from coal—not enough to sustain even a small army. But Standard Oil transferred critical technology to the Nazi's largest company, conglomerate IG Farben. This technology enabled IG Farben to fulfill 85 percent of Germany's synthetic gasoline needs, as well as almost all other war matériel requirements necessary to wage World War II. Sutton, *Wall Street*, 67–75.

- The following American corporations and/or their subsidiaries also had major contracts with IG Farben and thereby helped finance the Nazi war machine: Alcoa, Dow Chemical, DuPont, Ethyl Export, Ford, General Electric, General Motors, ITT, and Texaco. Among the products IG Farben developed as a result of American investment was Zyklon B, which the Nazis used to murder millions of people in gas chambers during World War II. Sutton, *Wall Street*, 15, 21–22, 49–61, 89–94.

- Averell and Roland Harriman, American financiers, politicians, and heirs to the Union Pacific and Southern Pacific Railroad fortunes, established the Union Banking Corporation (UBC), a New York bank, which served as a front for United Steelworks, a German mining and steelmaking dynasty, which controlled over 75 percent of Germany's iron ore reserves. Shirer, *Rise and Fall*, 144–45. Bankers Prescott Bush and George Herbert Walker were directors of UBC. George Herbert Walker and Averell Harriman set up a German branch of UBC to funnel money to the Nazis. The Bushes and the Harrimans facilitated the shipping of gold, coal, steel, and even US Treasury and war bonds to Germany. They continued doing business with the Nazis until 1942. At that time, under the Trading with the Enemy Act, the US Congress liquidated UBC and compensated the Bushes and Harrimans for the loss of their interests in the bank. Ben Aris and Duncan Campbell, "How Bush's Grandfather Helped Hitler's Rise to Power," *The Guardian*, September 20, 2004. Accessed November 15, 2012. http://www.guardian.co.uk/world/ 2004/sep/25/usa.secondworldwar.

44 "*The Nazis can't take them in fast enough.*" In 1933, the Nazis were overwhelmed by the number of people trying to join the party. The party closed its membership rolls in June, and "although a steady stream of individuals were invited to join the Nazi party, the general rolls did not officially reopen until 1937." Koonz, *Nazi Conscience*, 81–82.

44 *"The university... fired all their Jewish professors."* A think tank for the "final solution," the University of Tübingen was the first "Jew-free" university in Germany in 1933. That year, the school fired junior faculty member Hans Bethe, who later became a Nobel Prize-winning theoretical physicist. (Jewish teachers—even Christian converts—rarely became full professors.) Bethe was Protestant, but the Nazis considered him Jewish because his mother was Jewish. J. Horgan, "Profile: Hans A. Bethe–Illuminator of the Stars," *Scientific American* 267(4) (Stuttgart, Germany: Holzbrinck,1992), 32–40. Video of Bethe telling his story, accessed November 15, 2012. http:// www.webofstories.com/play/4503?o=R.

In 1933, only 4 percent of German university students and under 3 percent of teachers were Jewish, but antisemitism was endemic to faculty and student life.

Antisemitic student violence was commonplace. Fourteen of Germany's twenty-three universities witnessed student violence against Jewish students in 1919 and 1920. Sanford L. Segal, *Mathematicians under the Nazis* (Princeton, NJ: Princeton University Press, 2003), 69–79; Jonathan Friedman, *Lion and the Star*, 43.

"Most professors and intellectuals, like most lawyers and judges, in an unparalleled abdication of mind and honor, submitted to the National Socialist state and enhanced it with their prestige." Dawidowicz, *War against the Jews*, 61.The Nazis established over thirty research centers, four research divisions, eighteen university professorships, and numerous university courses in "racial science." Berenbaum, *World Must Know*, 28.

Non-Jewish physics professors mocked Einstein's relativity theories as "Jewish physics." Many professors enthusiastically offered the Nazis "scientific" rationales for their antisemitic agenda; they also published and promoted antisemitic textbooks, popular books, and news articles. Koonz, *Nazi Conscience*, 46–68, 202–03, 215–20.

Chapter III

48 "*[Polish Jews] started coming to Germany when we were kids. This made the regular German people nervous, even some of the German Jews.*" By 1932, about 100,000 Jews from eastern Europe (mainly Russia and Poland) had immigrated to Germany. Berlin was 4 percent Jewish in 1933, while the entire country's Jewish population was 0.7 percent. The Jewish "centers of life in Munich and Berlin loomed disproportionately large, however, in creating the public image of the east European Jew in Germany." Although people saw the immigrants as "different," they "*quickly took on German speech and culture, often reluctant to reveal their place of birth so as to blend all the more seamlessly into the local scene.*" Ruth Gay, *Jews of Germany: A Historical Portrait*, 239.

51 "*Let's go and see your Graf Zeppelin.*" The LZ-127 was a remarkable feat of engineering. Completed in 1928, the first transatlantic airship was almost eight hundred feet long. It was fueled by two types of fuel: a form of propane gas and hydrogen. It usually cruised at about seventy-three miles per hour, and when using both fuel types, it could cruise for up to one hundred eighteen hours. Within its single gondola, it contained a flight deck, a map room, all operational spaces, passenger cabins for up to twenty-four people, common areas, crews' quarters, a galley, and restrooms. Between 1932 and 1937, it made sixty-four uneventful round trips between Germany and Brazil; but it was grounded in 1937 after the *Hindenburg* exploded. Gillaume de Syon, *Zeppelin! Germany and the Airship, 1900-1939* (Baltimore, MD: Johns Hopkins University Press), 2005.

53 *"A Jew and a communist, both... What's the difference?"* Several well-known communist leaders were Jews, but the vast majority of Jews rejected communism because of its atheism and its opposition to capitalism. Niewyk, *Jews in Weimar Germany,* 196–97. Moreover, German communist leaders were vitriolic antisemites. In 1923, the German communist party leader, Ruth Fischer, exhorted students to "hang Jewish capitalists from the street lamps." In 1933, communist broadsides read, *"SA and SS! You have shot enough workers. When will you hang the first Jew?"* Niewyk, *Jews in Weimar Germany,* 69.

54 *"Is smoking illegal now?"* The German cigarette industry capitalized on Nazism with ads and collectible trading cards glorifying Hitler and Nazi beliefs. Koonz, *Nazi Conscience,* 69. The Nazis wanted healthy young people to breed future warriors. They thought smoking was unhealthy and tried to discourage it, but they never banned it. R.N. Proctor, "The anti-tobacco campaign of the Nazis: a little known aspect of public health in Germany, 1933–45," *British Medical Journal,* December 7,1996. Accessed November 15, 2012. http://www.ncbi.nlm.nih.gov/pmc/articles/PMC2352989/.

60 *"They beat Martin very bad."* The Nazis randomly assaulted individuals from the beginning to the end of the Nazi regime, but they attacked a great many people during the first few months of 1933—especially people they thought were Jews, communists, or gypsies. They beat people with fists, cattle prods, whips, knives, chains, and belts; and they forced people to cut grass with their teeth, drink castor oil, walk on all fours, and denounce themselves as pigs. In Nazi strongholds throughout Germany, the SA assaulted pedestrians, invaded and looted stores, destroyed homes, and tore up offices. Rees, *Nazis: A Warning,* 73; Koonz, *Nazi Conscience,* 35–39. Dorothy Thompson, an American journalist in Berlin,

wrote that the "*SA boys simply... take people into so-called Braune Etgen* [brown rooms], *where they are tortured. Italian fascism was a kindergarten compared to it.*" Andrew Nagorski, *Hitlerland*, 106. Berlin alone had fifty torture stations where at least five hundred to seven hundred fifty died, and many endured mock hangings and near-drownings. Larson, *In the Garden*, 17. The SA assailants were rarely prosecuted. Koonz, *Nazi Conscience*, 38–9, 287.

In March of 1933, the SA staged its first government-sanctioned attacks, in which they targeted Jewish lawyers and judges and destroyed their offices and courtrooms. In April, they staged a countrywide boycott of Jewish-owned shops, pharmacies, and professional offices. But the German people revered law and order, and the general public neither rallied behind the boycott nor approved of the SA's thuggery. The international press also reacted angrily and negatively. So Hitler quickly decided to change his tactics. He denounced the very violence he had previously approved and chose to use the law as his new weapon of choice. Between April and December of 1933, the Nazis peacefully passed one law after another designed to isolate Jews from society. New laws and regulations barred most Jews from public office; banned the employment of most Jews as government workers and as state-employed doctors, lawyers, and teachers; restricted Jewish participation in schools, trade organizations, and social organizations; forbade Jewish medical students from dissecting non-Jewish cadavers; denied Jewish doctors reimbursement from government health insurance plans; forbade Jewish conductors from finishing concert seasons; outlawed all Jewish organizations (except Zionist organizations); made the "Heil Hitler" salute a mandatory greeting (instead of the traditional "good day"); and revoked the citizenship of all Jews who had entered Germany after 1918. Vicki Caron, *Uneasy Asylum: France and the Jewish Refugee Crisis* (Palo Alto, CA: Stanford University Press, 1999),14–15; Koonz, *Nazi Conscience*, 42.

Because of SA brutality, the relentless antisemitic propaganda, and the plethora of new antisemitic Nazi laws, about 40,000 Jews left Germany in 1933. Some of these people returned to Germany, believing that they could live under Nazi rule as long as orderly conditions existed—even if their rights were greatly restricted. However, between 1933 and 1939, from 40 to 50 percent of German Jews (up to 360,000 people) left the country for good. Koonz, *Nazi Conscience*, 28–44, 38–39, 246; Berenbaum, *World Must Know*, 32.

Chapter IV

64 *"The Nazis... burned up a lot of books."* On May 10,1933, university students and professors across Germany held theatrically-staged bonfires. They burned books by such authors as Helen Keller, Ernest Hemingway, Berthold Brecht, Albert Einstein, Jack London, Sigmund Freud, Thomas Mann, Sinclair Lewis, Theodore Dreiser, Margaret Sanger, Karl Marx, and Erich Maria Remarque. The Nazis burned books by all Jewish authors and some by non-Jewish authors as well. (For instance, they considered Helen Keller "decadent" because she had socialist leanings.) In Berlin, the Nazi propaganda minister told 40,000 cheering people that the students were rightfully cleaning up "the debris of the past." Andrew Nagorski, *Hitlerland*, 106–7; Louis Leo Snyder, *National Socialist Germany: Twelve Years That Shook the World* (Melbourne, FL: Krieger Publishing, 1984),101–4. In the US, *Newsweek* called the book-burnings a "holocaust," thus coining the first use of that term in connection with the Nazi regime. Berenbaum, *World Must Know*, 19–21.

In 1888, Heinrich Heine, a writer and a convert to Christianity, witnessed a similar frenzied, nationalistic book-burning at the University of Bonn. It inspired him to prophesy the coming of a regime like Hitler's and to write a play in which a character famously said that when people burn books, they eventually burn people. Koonz, *The Nazi Conscience*, 70. The Nazis burned Heine's books in 1933, and when the German army entered France in 1941, they destroyed Heine's grave at the Montmartre Cemetery in Paris. Phillip Kossoff, *Valiant Heart: A Biography of Heinrich Heine* (Cranbury, NJ: Cornwall Books,1983), 209.

64 *"Our son in Berlin was... a lawyer. Last week, the Nazis fired him and all the other Jewish men."* About 67 percent of German Jews were working-class employees with jobs in small Jewish-owned companies. In the spring of 1933, the general unemployment rate was 16 percent, but more than 50 percent of German Jews were unemployed. Kaplan, *Between Dignity and Despair*, 28.

Although most German Jews were working-class people, there were wealthy Berlin Jews, who lived as ostentatiously as some wealthy Christians. Their lifestyles provided fodder to fuel Nazi propaganda, which caricatured all Jewish men as homely, fat, and greedy. Jacob Katz, "Anti-Semitism through the Ages," in *The Holocaust*, ed. Donald L. Niewyk (Boston: Houghton Mifflin, 2003),12–24.

69 *"Not Jewish, but they treat us like we're their own kids."* An uncounted number of European Christians helped Jewish refugees throughout the 1930s by protesting Nazi brutality, by employing Jews illegally, by hiding them illegally, and by helping them financially and in many other ways. Koonz, *Nazi Conscience*, 178–82, 264; Victoria J. Barnett, *Bystanders: Conscience and Complicity during the Holocaust* (Santa Barbara: Praeger ABC–CLIO,1999), 118–31.

During the war years, in some occupied countries, the Nazis killed people who helped Jews. They also killed the neighbors, friends, and families of people caught helping Jews. The Nazis also offered money to people to provided information concerning the whereabouts of Jews. Only 1 percent of European Christians risked their lives to save Jews during the war; but interestingly, among those who did risk their lives were over 60,000 Polish Christians. In fact, more Christians in Poland tried to save Jews than did Christians in any other country. David P. Gushee, *The Righteous Gentiles of the Holocaust: A Christian Interpretation* (Minneapolis: Fortress Press,1994); Samuel P. and Pearl M. Oliner, *The Altruistic Personality: Rescuers of Jews in Nazi Europe* (NY: The Free Press, 1992), 1–3.

Chapter VI

84 "*You can't get asylum here. You can't work here, and you can't stay here.*" In 1933, only 0.5 percent of the Swiss population was Jewish; but within two months after Hitler took power, the Swiss government passed a law allowing only "documented" German-Jewish refugees to enter. The law further provided that such refugees could stay only long enough to find someplace else to go. Switzerland's policy was to offer asylum only to famous German Jews.

Between April and September of 1933, some 10,000 Germans—mostly Jews—fled to Switzerland. Like Gottfried and Rudolf, most were unaware of Swiss antisemitism. German Jews who fled to Switzerland usually ended up returning to Germany or fleeing to another country. Carl Ludwig, "*Die flüchtlingspolitik der schweiz seit 1933 bis zur gegenwart. Bericht an den Bundesrat,*" in Yehuda Bauer, *My Brother's Keeper, A History of the American Jewish Joint Distribution Committee 1929–1939* (Philadelphia: The Jewish Publication Society of America,1974), notes 86–87.

84 "*There are Nazis everywhere here too.*" The German Nazi Party banked in Zurich; German Nazi officers frequently vacationed

in Davos and elsewhere; and holiday houses for German youth existed throughout Switzerland. The former army chief of staff led the main Swiss Nazi political organization, the National Front. The National Front won a number of municipal and cantonal elections in 1933, trained teenagers as Nazis, and even selected sites for anticipated concentration camps. The Front also widely disseminated antisemitic propaganda, including *Protocols of the Elders of Zion*, a book claiming that an organized Jewish conspiracy planned to take over the world. In 1921, the *New York Times* exposed this book as a fraud; the Tsar's secret police had created the book by plagiarizing an old Russian pulp novel. Despite this fact, Henry Ford not only published it in one of his newspapers, but he also printed 500,000 copies and spread this libel throughout the world. Phillip Graves, "Jewish World Plot: The Source of *The Protocols of Zion*. Truth At Last," *New York Times*, August 16–18, 1921, 1; Herman Bernstein, *The History of a Lie, A Study* (New York: J.S. Ogilvie, 1921).

Chapter VII

95 "*They put the handicapped children into a van...*" In July of 1933, the Nazis began legally sterilizing people with mental or physical disabilities. Between 1933 and 1939, at least 350,000 disabled people were sterilized. Richard J. Evans, *The Third Reich in Power, 1933–1939* (New York: The Penguin Press, 2005), 507–8. Germany not only sterilized disabled people, but it developed a policy of murdering them. Nazis and sympathetic medical personnel also experimented on the disabled in order to determine the most efficient ways to kill people. Koonz, *Nazi Conscience*, 113; Henry Friedlander, "The Opening Act of Nazi Genocide," in *The Holocaust*, edited by Donald L. Niewyk, 39–53; Berenbaum, *World Must Know*, 61.

96 *"The German Zionists have made deals with the Nazis."* About 60,000 German Jews and 4.4 million Palestinian pounds moved from Germany to Palestine under the terms of a 1933 transfer agreement between the German government and the Jewish Agency for Palestine. Under the agreement, a Jewish immigrant would deposit a sum of money in a special account in a German bank. When the emigrant arrived in Palestine, he would open an account at a particular Palestinian bank. The German bank would then deposit half of the emigrant's money into his account at the Palestinian bank. The rest of the emigrant's money would be used to buy German finished goods, which would be exported to Palestine. See Bauer, *My Brother's Keeper*, notes 86, 87; Abraham Foxman, "Afterword," in Edwin Black, *The Transfer Agreement: The Dramatic Story of the Pact between the Third Reich and Jewish Palestine* (NY: Caroll & Graf, 2001); and Dawidowicz, *War against the Jews*, 82.

108 *"The Nazis keep trying to get people to stop trading with Jews, but... they're still doing it. Things are definitely getting better."* Despite the many restrictive antisemitic laws in 1933, and despite the German government's constant antisemitic propaganda, many Jews believed that life was stabilizing after the failure of Hitler's April boycott. *"A fateful pattern was established: after devastating physical violence against Jews, the regime curbed unsanctioned racial attacks and in their place enacted antisemitic laws. Many victims and bystanders failed to appreciate the threat of these bureaucratic strategies that in the long run proved far more lethal than sporadic attacks."* Koonz, *The Nazi Conscience*, 44.

108 *"The Zionist... got passage on a ship to Palestine."* Ships crewed by Nazis and flying swastika banners regularly transported Jewish passengers to Haifa during the 1930s. *"A leading German shipping line began direct passenger service from Hamburg to Haifa in 1933.*

It offered strictly kosher food on its ships, under the supervision of the Hamburg rabbinate." Lenni Brenner, *Zionism in the Age of the Dictators* (Westport, CT: Lawrence Hill & Co.,1983), 83. Many years later a traveler aboard one such ship recalled this strange combination as a "metaphysical absurdity." W. Martini, "Hebrisch unterm hakenkreuz," *Die Welt* (Hamburg, Germany: January 10,1975), cited in C. Polken, "The Secret Contacts: Zionism and Nazi Germany, 1933–1941," *Journal of Palestine Studies, Spring–Summer 1976* (Washington, DC: Institute for Palestine Studies and the University of California Press), 65.

The Nazis promoted Jewish emigration to Palestine, but not to other countries. The transfer agreement was simply an expedient, profitable way to purge Germany of its Jews—the Nazis' immediate goal from 1933–1938. However, the Nazis did not want the Jews to have their own viable country. Moving as many German Jews as possible to a single country served a different purpose: It would facilitate rounding them up in order to murder them later. Dawidowicz, *War against the Jews*, 85–86.

Chapter VIII

111-12 "*And the French government, they're not too different from the Swiss government. Nobody is exactly welcoming us with open arms.*" In 1933, France accepted 25,000 German refugees—more than any other country. The majority of German Jews fleeing Germany went to France for several reasons: (1) France and Germany shared a long border, so France was convenient; (2) Alsace and Lorraine had belonged to Germany from 1871–1918, so the language and culture there were as much German as they were French; (3) because of a labor shortage after World War I, France had been encouraging immigration; and (4) the French government believed that the Nazis would not have been in power, and there would have been no refugees if only the allies had taken a hard line against Germany's treaty violations; instead, the allies ignored France on this issue, thereby enabling Germany to rearm and rebuild.

By the end of 1933, however, the French government began changing its tune. As was true everywhere, the depression in France was getting worse. As more people lost jobs, France was shaken by government instability and a right-wing backlash against the flood of immigrants. The French government soon announced it would accept no more German refugees, and France—like Switzerland— would serve only as a transit country. Caron, *Uneasy Asylum,* 14–15.

120 *"Most French people don't care for Hitler either, and they don't like to make it hard for people who have to run from the Nazis."* In 1933, many French people warmly welcomed German-Jewish refugees like Gottfried and Rudolf. Jewish groups enthusiastically banded together and raised money to help refugees resettle in France. The French government provided free food and lodging in vacant military barracks and hospitals and encouraged officials to help refugees obtain work permits. But as the economy worsened, and more refugees flooded into France, pro-refugee sentiments became anti-refugee sentiments. By the end of 1933, the French government began adopting anti-refugee, antisemitic measures. Caron, *Uneasy Asylum,* 14–19, 98–99.

120 *"There's too much trouble in Paris, in the streets."* As middle-class unemployment rose in France, the right-wing government feared that German-Jewish immigrants would compete with French citizens for the remaining jobs. Some Frenchmen disagreed with this assessment, but most agreed with it. French Jews feared an antisemitic backlash if they didn't agree with the government too. Funding for refugees quickly began to dry up, and Jewish relief agencies began closing their doors. Without much opposition, the right-wing French government began passing

laws to keep new refugees out of France and to force German-Jewish refugees already in France to leave. For example, new laws barred foreign doctors and provided that foreigners must live in France for ten years in order to practice law or hold public office. These laws specifically targeted German Jews. Caron, *Uneasy Asylum*, 34–37. Even Jews who were long-settled in France were now barred from working in their usual occupations. Without work permits, job prospects, or alternative places to live, many Jewish people lived in squalor. Near the end of 1933, a full-scale riot erupted over the refugees' substandard living conditions in Paris. Caron, *Uneasy Asylum*, 40–42.

Chapter IX

125 "*The guy who wrote those operas was Richard Wagner, a big antisemite.*" The Nazis' eugenics-based policy of genocide did not "spring from Richard Wagner's head," but his antisemitic writings and his music heavily influenced Hitler. The Nazis staged theatrical, torch lit rallies and used Wagner's music and ideas to stir and reinforce German nationalism and devotion to the Nazis' ideals of German purity, virtue, and heroism. Milton E. Brener, *Richard Wagner and the Jews* (Jefferson, North Carolina: McFarland, 2005),1–3.

130 "*The government places are old army barracks. They're filthy with rats and lice.*" Many German-Jewish refugees in Paris had nowhere to live other than in substandard government-provided housing. There were frequent protests and food riots. By 1935, from 15,000 to 17,000 German refugees—mostly Jews—were living in poverty and in constant fear of arrest, deportation, or imprisonment. Caron, *Uneasy Asylum*, 97–100, 113–114.

131 "*If anybody else finds out that I am not legal, I can lose my job and maybe my life.*" In the fall of 1934, the Paris police conducted

raids for four consecutive nights and arrested four hundred undocumented immigrants. By 1935, France officially viewed all Germans who were living in France as temporary residents who needed to be resettled. The government issued deportation orders by the thousands. German Jews who were caught and failed to leave were incarcerated or escorted to the German border. Caron, *Uneasy Asylum,* 46–48, 100, 110.

Chapter X

146 "*Jews can't be German citizens.*" In 1935, the Nuremberg Laws deprived German Jews of their German citizenship and consigned them "to civil oblivion." But Jews were—after all—a tiny sliver of the population, and most Christian Germans had grown accustomed to the government's antisemitic agenda. Many Germans also bought into the Nazi propaganda against Jews, and those who didn't agree rarely spoke up. After all, vocal opposition could mean imprisonment or worse. No one could deny that the average person's standard of living had improved dramatically since Hitler took power, and the 1935 Nuremberg laws made some Christian Germans even more prosperous, because now, they could also cheaply acquire assets belonging to Jews. Under the new laws, Jews were no longer allowed to own businesses. Thus, the Nazis confiscated from 75,000 to 80,000 Jewish businesses and either liquidated them or turned them over to non-Jews. "... *the perception took hold that Jews were strangers in their own homeland.*" Koonz, *Nazi Conscience,* 181–89, 191–192.

160 "*They're helping get people out of German concentration camps.*" After 1935 and before World War II, the Nazis made a concerted effort to deprive Jews of their property. To get desirable property, they sometimes imprisoned a Jewish property-owner on trumped-up charges (such as "racial defilement", i.e. sexual intercourse with a

non-Jew). In some of these cases, Jews could get out of concentration camps by agreeing to forfeit their property and/or by paying bribes and promising to leave Germany. Koonz, *Nazi Conscience*, 191.

Chapter XI

166 "*Hitler and Mussolini are helping the rich people and the Catholic Church... put in a dictatorship.*" Spain became a dictatorship in 1939, because Italy and Germany supported an anti-democratic coalition (the military, the Church, and wealthy property owners), and because the world's democracies looked the other way. The coalition's uprising against the elected government began in July 1936. By the end of the month, German Junkers 52 and Savoia-Marchetti 81 transport aircraft had already carried 15,000 foreign legion soldiers and native regulars across the Strait of Gibraltar to fight against the elected government. Paul Preston, *We Saw Spain Die*, (London: Constable & Robinson, 2009), 6. Between 1936 and the war's end in 1939, Italy had sent Franco 70,000 soldiers and 759 aircraft, and Germany had sent 14,000 soldiers and 840 aircraft. Both countries also provided enormous amounts of matériel, including state-of-the-art weapons, ammunition, tanks, and other vehicles. Michael Alpert, *A New International History of the Spanish Civil War* (New York: Palgrave Macmillan–3PL, 2004),196.

173 "*You have no investments, no savings, no money of your own.*" Between 1933 and 1945, the US filled its German quota only twice—in 1938 and 1939—"*even though from 1932 to 1938 more people emigrated from the United States than came in as immigrants— the first time in all of American history that this had happened.*" In 1936, when the US denied Gottfried and Rudolf's applications, the German quota was close to 27,000, and half of these open slots were never filled. The economic depression in the US played a role in the government's opposition to less restrictive immigration policies. Antisemitism also played a part: In almost every poll,

Americans perceived Jews as "a major threat to the country." Nevertheless, between 1933 and 1945, the US received from 130,000 to 160,000 Jewish refugees from Europe—a greater number than any other country. Berenbaum, *The World Must Know*, 51, 53, 54.

Chapter XII

183 "*If the Catholic church is the conscience of Spain, I'm sorry for Spain.*" In 1933, Pope Pius XI signed a formal agreement with Hitler. It provided that the Catholic church would assist the Nazis in combatting communism, and that the German government would not interfere with the German Catholic church. In September 1936, Pius XI publicly endorsed overthrowing the elected democratic government of Spain. He extended a "*blessing in a special manner to all those who have taken [on] the difficult and dangerous task to defend and reinstate the honor of God and Religion.*" Franco relished the pope's endorsement, which gave theological and moral gravitas to his effort to install a dictatorship. Throughout the Spanish Civil War, Franco and his allies in the Catholic church cast their fight as a religious crusade against the evil forces of secularism. When Pius XI died, Pope Pius XII followed his predecessor's lead. He profusely praised Franco's victory in 1939, declaring "*immense joy*" for the "*victory which God has deigned to crown the Christian heroism of your faith…*" Arvo Manhattan, *The Vatican in World Politics* (New York: Gaer Associates, 1949), 97–98; Guenter Lewy, *The Catholic Church and Nazi Germany* (Cambridge, MA: Da Capo Press, 2000), 312.

During World War II, when Pius XII knew Germany was killing thousands of people in death camps, the pope never told his followers to oppose the Nazis or to help the victims; never told Germany's bishops about the death camps; never promulgated any policy against the Nazis; and never acknowledged the work of many courageous Catholic resistance groups. John Michael Phayer, "The Silence of Pope Pius XII," in *The Holocaust*, ed. Donald L. Niewyk, 248–49. The pope did, however, permit some Italian Jews to hide in Vatican buildings after the Nazis occupied Rome. Niewyk, "Possibilities of Rescue," *The Holocaust*, 235.

190 "*Carme is very excited... about the ladder-making, which is part of a big holiday.*" Since 1926, people in Catalonia have competed in teams to create multi-level, complex human towers or *castells* (castles). For a brief history of this colorful tradition, see http://en.wikipedia.org/wiki/Castell. Accessed November 10, 2012. For a video showing castle–building, see http://www.bbc.co.uk/news/world—europe—11742399. Accessed November 10, 2012.

194 "*My grandmother...had to become a Catholic... But she always felt Jewish.*" Due to centuries of persecution and expulsions throughout Europe, many Jews converted to Christianity. Some did so willingly, but unwilling converts and their descendants sometimes practiced Judaism secretly. Modern descendants of these "Crypto-Jews" may still follow some Jewish customs without necessarily knowing what they mean or where they came from. There are Crypto-Jews living in various places in the world today, including in the state of New Mexico. See Stanley M. Hordes, *To the End of the Earth: A History of the Crypto-Jews of New Mexico* (New York: Columbia University Press, 2008).

202 "*There are workers attacking churches and killing the priests.*" Spain's elected republic had been in difficult economic straits for several years before the Spanish Civil War began. As was the case everywhere, there was a depression, high unemployment, and labor unrest. Additionally, factions in Catalonia and in the Basque regions were agitating for autonomy. Thousands of peasants were also moving from rural areas to cities, and their migration precipitated social unrest. Political groups supported everything from a

return of the old monarchy to democracy to moderate socialism to Stalinist-style communism.

Most Spaniards wanted to keep an elected government, which supported land reform and greater rights for workers. Many Spaniards also supported greater separation of church and state, but the Vatican, the landowners and the military opposed this. The landed gentry and the church, with the help of the military, had always controlled the power and the purse strings and wanted to keep both. For two excellent analyses of the complex factors that led to the Spanish Civil War, see Paul Preston, *The Coming of the Spanish Civil War*, 2nd ed. (London: Routledge,1994) and Stanley Payne, *Franco and Hitler: Spain, Germany, and the World* (New Haven, CT: Yale University Press), 2008. For an interesting video of people involved on both sides of the war from beginning to end, see "Guerra Civil Española," http://www.youtube.com/watch?v=lgfP4fBJNMU&feature=related. Accessed November 10, 2012.

203 *"They passed a new law in France to get rid of Jews from the East."* As German Jews poured into France, the conservative French government decided to expel the "less desirable" Jews, who were mostly from Poland. Many were artisans and peddlers, who had lived in France a long time and had no place else to go. When they refused to leave, France rounded them up and imprisoned them. Caron, *Uneasy Asylum*, 35. In the fall of 1935, the government decided not to deport people who were "stateless" (in other words, who had nowhere else to go); however, the French police refused to recognize Polish Jews as stateless. They continued to round up them up and jail them. Caron, *Uneasy Asylum*, 62, 110.

204 *"Hitler is sending new airplanes, pilots, trained soldiers, tanks, guns—all the latest."* Helping Franco was a no-brainer for Hitler. Having Spain as an ally would threaten France; impede Britain's access to the Suez; provide more routes for German U-boats; divert

world attention from Germany's preparations for war in Europe; and offer a testing ground for new military weapons and strategies. By November of 1936, Hitler had already sent Franco twenty new Junkers 52s, six Henkel 51 fighter bombers (plus spare parts and personnel), Luftwaffe pilots, military advisors, Panzer Mark 1s, new 20 millimeter anti-aircraft batteries, the enormous German 88 millimeter gun, and men from Germany's highly-trained Condor Legions. Italy's dictator, Mussolini, who also had delusions of power, felt threatened by Britain's navy and liked the idea of making Spain indebted to him. Mussolini believed a victory for Franco would give Italy access to the Strait of Gibraltar and possible bases for expansion. Anthony Beevor, *The Battle for Spain: The Spanish Civil War 1936–1939,* (New York: Penguin Group, 2006),137–41.

205 *"At least in Spain, we can fight them instead of sitting and waiting for them to catch up with us."* From 5,000 to 10,000 foreign Jews fought for the Spanish republic against Franco in the Spanish Civil War. G.E. Sichon, "Les volontaires juifs dans la guerre civile en Espagne: chiffres et enjeux," *Les Temps Modernes,* vol. 44 (Paris: Gallimard,1988), 46–62. Most of the German Jews who fought in Spain, like Rudolf and Gottfried, were refugees who entered Spain from a country other than Germany. Gerben Zaagma, "Jewish Volunteers in the Spanish Civil War: A Case Study of the Botwin Company," (PhD diss, University of London, 2001). http://knaw. academia.edu/GerbenZaagsma/Papers._

206 *"We decide to join POUM because we figure the biggest group is going to have the most support and the best equipment."* POUM was the principal party of the workers in Catalonia. It controlled a 50,000 member trade group. Two of its leaders, Andreu Nin and Joaquin Maurín, were prominent Marxists, but POUM was a not a communist organization; it was a socialist organization. http:// en.wikipedia.org/wiki/ Accessed November 10, 2012.

In December of 1936, when Gottfried and Rudolf were leaving Spain, author George Orwell was just arriving there. He fought with POUM until June of 1937, and he wrote a famous memoir based on his experiences. Orwell's experiences as a POUM fighter were similar to those of Gottfried and Rudolf. For instance, Orwell described the problems with training and weaponry as follows: "*To my dismay, we were taught nothing about the use of weapons. The so-called instruction was simply parade-ground drill of the most antiquated, stupid kind... Yet this mob of eager children, who were going to be thrown into the front line in a few days' time, were not even taught how to fire a rifle or pull the pin out of a bomb.*" George Orwell, *Homage to Catalonia*, reprinted ed. (IndoEuropean Publishing. com, 2011), 5–6. http://www.amazon.com:/Homage–Catalonia–Library–Edition. Accessed November 10, 2012.

209 "*These crazy grenades kill the guys who use them faster than anybody else.*" The hand grenade (the so-called "FAI bomb"), which the men used for the first eight months, was said to be "impartial," because it killed both the man who threw it and the man it was thrown at. Men fighting for the republic had rifles that were mostly "scrap-iron." They had a few machine guns, which were fairly accurate at a few hundred yards (if they didn't jam), but they had very few pistols, revolvers, or bayonets. Most of the ammunition was "exceedingly bad," as well as scarce. Orwell, *Homage to Catalonia*, 23–24, 31.

210 "*The airplanes are just like the guns and everything else—somebody else's old junk.*" André Malraux, the French writer and adventurer, helped organize aid to the republic's air force despite the French government's official neutrality. André Cate, *Malraux: A Biography* (New York: Fromm International Publishing, 1997), 228–42. Malraux's efforts didn't do much good. The republic's air force consisted of obsolete planes and equipment as well as poorly trained, undisciplined personnel.

Russia was the only foreign government that openly helped the Spanish republic. It sent several hundred pilots in 1936. But they were inconsistently trained, and their equipment was inferior to that of the Germans, who tested all important Luftwaffe equipment, which they used in World War II, on the Spanish people. Beevor, *The Battle for Spain,*146, 218–282.

Chapter XIII

218 "*They've got... new guns from Germany and Italy. We've got everybody else's trash. Our guys, all they know how to do is march around, pretending like they know something.*" Orwell expressed similar sentiments. His unit was on the front lines for three days before any rifles arrived. "*I got a shock of dismay when I saw the thing they gave me! It was a German Mauser dated 1896... corroded and past praying for. Most of the rifles were equally bad and some of them even worse... It seemed dreadful that the defenders of the republic should be this mob of ragged children carrying worn-out rifles which they did not know how to use.*" Orwell, *Homage to Catalonia,*12–13. See also Beevor, *Battle for Spain*, 152–4.

219-20 "*Each big shot wants an army of his own. They all act like a bunch of little kids.*" Again, Orwell described the situation succinctly: "*As for the kaleidoscope of political parties and trade unions, with their tiresome names—PSUC, POUM, FAI, CNT, UGT, JCI, JSU, AIT—they merely exasperated me. It looked at first sight as through Spain were suffering from a plague of initials.*" Orwell, *Homage to Catalonia*, 34. See Beevor, *Battle for Spain*, 251–73 for a detailed analysis of the complicated political struggles among the leaders of various factions for control over the militias fighting for the republic.

220 *"Leaders of armies, they're supposed to* tell *their soldiers. What kind of army asks the soldiers to take a vote?"* Unlike Gottfried, Orwell admired this egalitarianism. *"The essential point of the system was social equality between officers and men. Everyone from general to private drew the same pay, ate the same food, wore the same clothes, and mingled on terms of complete equality. If you wanted to slap the general on the back and ask him for a cigarette, you could do so, and no one thought it curious. In theory at any rate, each militia was a democracy and not a hierarchy."* Orwell, *Homage to Catalonia*, 19.

224 *"Why does an army with new German equipment, with help from German soldiers and everything else—why the hell do they need kids to fight for them?"* In Gottfried and Rudolf's unit, as in Orwell's, *"The recruits were mostly boys of sixteen or seventeen... It was impossible even to get them to stand in line... Half of them were children of sixteen or under."* Orwell, *Homage to Catalonia*, 5,12–13. *"Here and there in the militia you came across children as young as eleven or twelve, usually refugees from Fascist territory who had been enlisted as the easiest way of providing for them..."* Orwell, *Homage to Catalonia*, 18.

228 *"They decide to go and burn down the Catholic church in town."* When Catholic peasants migrated into cities to work, many of them joined political parties, trade unions, and organizations that supported rights and privileges for ordinary people. Many deeply resented the efforts of the nobility, the church, and the military to oppose worker's rights and land reform. Resentment boiled over when Franco and the church presented their uprising as a religious crusade against atheistic communism. Many workers viewed the uprising not as a religious war, but as a way to keep most people poor and powerless. Angry workers viciously attacked and murdered clergy and burned down churches throughout Spain. Mary Vincent, *Catholicism in the Second Republic*, (London: Oxford University Press, 1996), 257–304.

229 *"Turns out, these men come from Africa—Moors from North Africa."* An oddity of the Spanish Civil War was Franco's reliance on more than 60,000 Islamic fighters from Morocco (the "Moors"). The Moors respected General Franco and believed he was fighting a holy war against communist atheism. The Moors had reputations as fearless and ferocious fighters, and Franco used them as "shock troops" in every major engagement. George R. Esenwein, *The Spanish Civil War: A Modern Tragedy*, (New York: Routledge, 2005), 88,153.

Chapter XIV

249 *"The French premier right now is a Jewish guy by the name of Blum, who supports more rights for refugees."* Despite France's anti-refugee stance in 1934 and 1935, and despite the ever-growing antisemitism, the French government didn't deport most of their German-Jewish refugees. But imprisoning them, then releasing them into poverty, then imprisoning them again was both burdensome and expensive. Strangely, after years of right-wing governments, a socialist Jew became the premier of France in 1936. Léon Blum's "Popular Front" survived only for a year, but during that time the government promoted legislation to regularize the legal status of refugees and to treat them more humanely. Joel Colton, *Léon Blum Humanist in Politics*, (New York: Alfred A. Knopf, 1966); Caron, *Uneasy Asylum*, 60–63. As was the case in Germany and Switzerland, the Jewish population of France before 1940 was less than 1 percent. As of 1940, there were only 350,000 Jews in France—including the approximately 75,000 refugees from other countries. Dawidowicz, *War against the Jews*, 360.

250 *"A lot of new volunteers are going to Spain to fight for the government now—guys from Italy, the United States, Russia, and other places."* About 40,000 volunteers from fifty-two countries, includ-

ing 2,800 Americans, joined the anti-Franco forces. The International Brigades served in medical, transportation, and combat units. See "Abraham Lincoln Brigade Archives," http://www.alba—valb. org. Accessed November 10, 2012. In addition to those who joined the International Brigades, another 5,000 foreigners also volunteered to fight against Franco. Beevor, *Battle for Spain*, 124.

253 "*A lot of men are working on a big exposition that's coming in May... Supposed to be about world peace.*" The 1937 International Exhibition with its ironic theme ("The Rights of Man") took place while fascism rapidly continued to gain ground. The imposing German and Russian pavilions faced each other as if to foreshadow the coming war. The unimposing Spanish pavilion attracted little interest. It centered on Pablo Picasso's painting *Guernica*, which portrayed the horror of Germany's bombardment and destruction of a civilian population for the sole purpose of testing weapons.

Within a few years, *Guernica* became famous worldwide. After the Nazis occupied France, a Nazi officer happened to notice a photo of the famous painting in Picasso's Paris apartment. "Did you do that?" he asked. And Picasso replied, "No, you did." Matthew Rose, "Alan Riding: On Cultural Life in Nazi-Occupied Paris," The Art Blog, http://www.org/2011/01/alan-riding-on-cultural-life-in-nazi-occupied-paris. Accessed November 11, 2012. In Rose's interview of Alan Riding, Mr. Riding stated that Françoise Gilot, Picasso's Paris mistress, confirmed this story.

256 "*Then a guy called 'the tosser' takes it out of the furnace with some tongs, and he throws it over to a guy called 'the catcher'.*" The dangerous riveting process Rudolf described was widely used in ship-building before World War II and sometimes afterward— even though safer and more effective metals and methods had been developed before the war. For a video showing riveting similar to what Rudolf described, see "Riveting Squad at Work at John

Brown's Shipyard, Glasgow in 1949," http://www.youtube.com/watch?v=CVjS1DsqYvo. Accessed November 10, 2012.

259 *"End of an era. End of an era, boys."* For a dirigible pilot's photographs and a first-hand account of the construction of the Hindenburg and its political ramifications, see Douglas Robinson and Harold Dick, *The Golden Age of the Great Passenger Airships* (Washington, DC: Smithsonian Books,1992).

Chapter XV

262 *"The French government can't take care of all of them."* By the end of the Spanish Civil War, up to 34,000 Spanish children had been moved from Spain to other counties. The US accepted none of them. France took 9,000; Britain, 4,000; Belgium, 3,500; and the USSR, 2,895. Enrique Zafra, Rosalía Crego and Carmen Heredia, *Los niños españoles evacuados a la URSS 1937,* (Madrid: Ediciones de la Torre, 1989), 35. Mexico took five hundred children, and Gottfried and Rudolf accompanied them on the *Mexique*, a 12,000-ton steamship built in 1915 for transporting French troops. In 1940, the *Mexique* sank when it hit a mine off Le Verdun, France.

269 *"We all think we can go ashore... But the Captain says no—it's against the rules."* The Cuban government refused permission for the children on the *Mexique* to disembark and visit Havana. The children traveled on to Morelia, Mexico. Many never returned to Spain. Much has been written about these children, including a play and a documentary film, *Los Niños de Morelia—Llegada a la ciudad de Mexico de 1937.* "Niños Morelia, Testimonios del exilio de niños de Morelia uploaded by betomixipillxi, 2/23/10,http://www.youtube.com/watch?v=WdfPLgTprmw&feature=autoplay&list=PL595BA82CE24CB885&playnext=1. Accessed November 9, 2012.

Chapter XVI

274 *"We take a couple of girls out to hear a famous singer, name of Miguelito Valdez."* The original "babalu" singer, Valdez became well known worldwide. Max Salazar and Al Angelero, *Mambo Kingdom: Latin Music in New York* (New York Schirmer Trade Books, 2002), 37–50.

275 *"Lawyer Lentz, he gets us an appointment on a Friday afternoon with the American vice consul, a guy by the name of Parsons."* James Graham Parsons (1907-1991) was a career diplomat. After his training in Asia, Parsons's first appointment was as American vice consul in Havana in 1936. For fifteen months, he decided which foreign applicants could enter the United States. J. Graham Parsons, interview by Richard D. McKinzie, Stockbridge, Massachusetts, July 1, 1974. http://www.trumanlibrary.org/oralhist/parsons.html#transcriptWagner. Accessed November 9, 2012.

277 *"What if this is how he makes sure we don't get in?"* Based on Parson's own words, he generally allowed only German Jews with status and wealth to emigrate to the United States from Cuba:

> *"The numbers were limited by the quota, which was fairly large for Germany. But we had just been going through the depression and financial qualifications for would-be immigrants were very stringent. I think this probably resulted in an overall selection of those who were more prudent in the protection of their money or more successful in earning money or status in life in Germany. The result was that we probably got a good proportion of the elite, and a good many others were*

> *disappointed. This is just a subjective opinion over these years, but that was the principle focus of my work in Havana."*

Gottfried and Rudolf had neither status nor wealth. They were exceptionally lucky that Mr. Parsons allowed them to emigrate to the US.

277 *"Worst thing that can happen is we get stuck in Cuba. Wouldn't be the end of the world."* Cuba *proportionally* accepted more Jews fleeing Nazi Germany than any other country, including the United States. Robert M. Levine, *Tropical Diaspora, The Jewish Experience in Cuba* (Gainesville: University of Florida Press,1993), 285. But Cuba also experienced economic turmoil and antisemitism in the 1930s. In 1939, Cuba refused to let several refugee ships dock. These included the *St. Louis,* a large ship carrying 933 Germans—mostly Jews. But the US also refused the *St. Louis* permission to dock in Miami, even though the US had already approved most of the passengers as emigrants, and even though these approved emigrants lacked only an official notice of their precise entry dates. The *St. Louis* was forced to return to Europe. Most passengers found homes in western Europe. However, two hundred fifty-four passengers (28 percent) ultimately died during the Holocaust. "Voyage of the St. Louis." last modified May 11, 2012. www.ushmm.org/wlc/en/article.php?Moduleid=100005267. Accessed November 11, 2012.

BIBLIOGRAPHY

—Alpert, Michael. *A New International History of the Spanish Civil War*. New York: Palgrave Macmillan–3PL, 2004.

—Angolia, John R. *For Führer and Fatherland: Military Awards of the Third Reich*. San Jose, CA: R. James Bender, 1976.

—Barnett, Victoria J. *Bystanders: Conscience and Complicity during the Holocaust*. Santa Barbara, CA: Praeger ABC–CLIO, 1999.

—Bauer, Yehuda. *My Brother's Keeper, A History of the American Jewish Joint Distribution Committee, 1929–1939*. Philadelphia: The Jewish Publication Society of America, 1974.

—Beevor, Anthony. *The Battle for Spain: The Spanish Civil War 1936–1939*. New York: Penguin Group, 2006.

—Berenbaum, Michael. *The World Must Know: The History of the Holocaust as Told in the United States Holocaust War Memorial Museum*. Boston: Little, Brown, 1993, 2006.

—Bernstein, Herman. *The History of a Lie: A Study*. New York: J.S. Ogilvie, 1921.

—Black, Edwin. *IBM and the Holocaust: The Strategic Alliance between Nazi Germany and America's Most Powerful Corporation.* Washington, DC: Dialog Press, 2008.

—Black, Edwin. *The Transfer Agreement.* New York: Carroll & Graf, 2001.

—Brener, Milton E. *Richard Wagner and the Jews.* Jefferson, NC: McFarland, 2005.

—Brenner, Lenni. *Zionism in the Age of the Dictators.* Westport, CT: Lawrence Hill & Co., 1983.

—Caron, Vicki. *Uneasy Asylum: France and the Jewish Refugee Crisis.* Palo Alto: Stanford University Press, 1999.

—Cate, Andrew. *Malraux: A Biography.* New York: Fromm International Publishing, 1997.

—Colton, Joel. *Léon Blum Humanist in Politics.* New York: Alfred A. Knopf, 1966.

—Daniels, Rogers. *Guarding the Golden Door: American Immigration Policy and Immigrants since 1882.* New York: Hill and Wang, 1984.

—Dawidowicz, Lucy. *The War against the Jews: 1933–1945.* New York: Bantam Books, 1986.

—Dodd, William E. *Ambassador Dodd's Diary, 1933–1938.* New York: Harcourt, Brace, 1941.

—Elon, Amos. *The Pity of It All.* New York: Picador, 2003.

—Esenwein, George R. *Spanish Civil War: A Modern Tragedy.* New York: Routledge, 2005.

—Evans, Richard J. *The Third Reich in Power,* 1933–1939. New York: The Penguin Press, 2005.

—Foxman, Abraham, "Afterword." In Black, Edwin, *The Transfer Agreement: The Dramatic Story of the Pact between the Third Reich and Jewish Palestine.* New York: Caroll & Graf, 2001.

—Friedlander, Henry. "The Opening Act of Nazi Genocide." In *The Holocaust,* edited by Donald L. Niewyk. Boston: Houghton Mifflin Company, 2003.

—Friedlander, Saul. vol. 1, *Nazi Germany and the Jews: The Years of Persecution, 1933–1939.* New York: Harper Perennial,1998.

—Friedman, Jonathan. *The Lion and the Star: Gentile-Jewish Relations in Three Hessian Communities, 1919–1945.* Lexington: University Press of Kentucky, 1998.

—Gay, Ruth. *The Jews of Germany: A Historical Portrait.* New Haven: Yale University Press, 1994.

—Gushee, David P. *The Righteous Gentiles of the Holocaust: A Christian Interpretation.* Minneapolis, MN: Fortress Press, 1994.

—Hoffman, Christhard, Werner Bergmann, and Helmut Walser Smith, eds. *Exclusionary Violence: Antisemitic Riots in Modern German History*. Ann Arbor: University of Michigan Press, 2002.

—Hordes, Stanley M. *To The End of the Earth: A History of the Crypto-Jews of New Mexico*. New York: Columbia University Press, 2008.

—Kaplan, Marion A. *Between Dignity and Despair: Jewish Life in Nazi Germany*. New York: Oxford University Press, 1999.

—Katz, Jacob. "Anti-Semitism Through the Ages." In *The Holocaust*, edited by Donald L. Niewyk. Boston: Houghton Mifflin, 2003.

—Knauss, Erwin. *Die Jüdesiche Bevolkerung Giessen 1933–1945*. Marburg, Germany: Gorich & Weiershaüsr, 1982.

—Koonz, Claudia. *The Nazi Conscience*. Cambridge: The Belknap Press of Harvard University Press, 2003.

—Kossoff, Phillip. *Valiant Heart: A Biography of Heinrich Heine*. Cranbury, NJ: Cornwall Books, 1983.

—Larson, Erik. *In the Garden of Beasts: Love, Terror, and an American Family in Hitler's Berlin*. New York: Broadway Paperbacks, 2011.

—Lerner, Paul. *Hysterical Men: War, Psychiatry, and the Politics of Trauma in Germany, 1890–1930*. Ithaca: Cornell University Press, 2006.

—*Leo Baeck Institute Yearbook.* vol. 19, Oxford Journals. New York: Oxford University Press, 1974.

—Levine, Robert M. *Tropical Diaspora: The Jewish Experience in Cuba.* Gainesville: University of Florida Press, 1993.

—Levy, Richard S. vol. 1, *Antisemitism, A Historical Encyclopedia of Prejudice and Persecution.* Santa Barbara, CA: ABC–CLIO, 2005.

—Lewy, Guenter. *The Catholic Church and Nazi Germany.* Cambridge, MA: Da Capo Press, 2000.

—Ludwig, Carl. *"Die flüchtlingspolitik der schweiz seit 1933 bis zur gegenwart. Bericht an den Bundesrat."* In Yehuda Bauer, *My Brother's Keeper, A History of the American Jewish Joint Distribution Committee,* 1929–1939. Philadelphia: The Jewish Publication Society of America, 1974.

—Martini, W., *"Hebrisch unterm hakenkreuz."* In *Die Welt.* Hamburg, Germany: Springer Publishing Group, January 10, 1975.

—Manhattan, Arvo. *The Vatican in World Politics.* New York: Gaer Associates, 1949.

—Nagorski, Andrew. *Hitlerland: American Eyewitnesses to the Nazi Rise to Power.* New York: Simon & Schuster, 2012.

—Nicosia, Francis R. *The Third Reich & the Palestine Question.* Piscataway, NJ: Transaction Publishers, 2000.

—Niewyk, Donald L, ed. *The Holocaust.* Boston: Houghton Mifflin Company, 2003.

—Niewyk, Donald L. *The Jews in Weimar Germany.* Baton Rouge: LSU Press,1980.

—Oliner, Samuel P., and Pearl M. Oliner. *The Altruistic Personality: Rescuers of Jews in Nazi Europe.* New York: The Free Press, 1992.

—Oltmer, Jochen. *Kriegsgefangene im Europa des Ersten Weltkriegs.* Paderborn, Germany: Schöningh, 2006.

—Orwell, George. *Homage to Catalonia.* Online version. Reprinted 1953 edition. IndoEuropean Publishing.com, 2011. http://www. amazon.com/Homage—Catalonia—Library—Edition —George/ dp/1455121010. Accessed November 10, 2012.

—Payne, Stanley. *Franco and Hitler: Spain, Germany, and the World.* New Haven: Yale University Press, 2008.

—Phayer, John Michael. "The Silence of Pope Pius XII." In *The Holocaust,* edited by Donald L. Niewyk. Boston: Houghton Mifflin Company, 2003.

—Polken, C. "The Secret Contacts: Zionism and Nazi Germany, 1933–1941." *Journal of Palestine Studies.* Spring–Summer, 1976.

—Preston, Paul. *The Coming of the Spanish Civil War.* London: Routledge, 1994.

—Preston, Paul. *We Saw Spain Die*. London: Constable & Robinson, 2009.

—Rees, Laurence. *The Nazis: A Warning from History*. New York: MJF Books, 1997.

—Robinson, Douglas, and Harold Dick. *The Golden Age of the Great Passenger Airships*. Washington, DC: Smithsonian Books, 1992.

—Salazar, Max, and Al Angelero. *Mambo Kingdom: Latin Music in New York*. New York: Schirmer Trade Books, 2002.

—Segal, Sanford L. *Mathematicians under the Nazis*. Princeton: Princeton University Press, 2003.

—Shirer, William L. *The Rise And Fall of the Third Reich*. New York: Simon & Schuster, 1990.

—Sichon, G.E. "*Les volontaires juifs dans la guerre civile en Espagne: chiffres et enjeux.*" vol. 44, *Les Temps Modernes*. Paris, France: Gallimard, 1988.

—Snyder, Louis Leo. *National Socialist Germany: Twelve Years That Shook the World*. Melbourne, FL: Krieger Publishing, 1984.

—Sutton, Anthony C. *Wall Street and the Rise of Hitler*. Cutchogue, NY: Buccaneer Books, 2004. Accessed November 9, 2012. http://www.reformed-theology.org/html/books/wall_street/

—Syon, Gillaume de. *Zeppelin! Germany and the Airship, 1900–1939*. Baltimore: Johns Hopkins University Press, 2005.

—Toland, John. *Adolf Hitler*. New York: Doubleday,1976.

—Vincent, Mary. *Catholicism in the Second Republic*. London: Oxford University Press,1996.

—Zafra, Enrique, Rosalía Crego, and Carmen Heredia. *Los niños españoles evacuados a la URSS 1937*. Madrid: Ediciones de la Torre, 1989.

Made in the USA
Charleston, SC
07 August 2013